Dear Jen,

Lewis a great friend.
Hope you enjoy the
book. Best,

Rich

FELLING BIG TREES

a novel

Rich Garon

richgaron.com

Edited by Kiele Raymond

Print ISBN: 978-1-48358-323-5

eBook ISBN: 978-1-48358-324-2

To Karen

CHAPTER 1

Fran Stewart took duck steps and clenched his butt tightly. He opened the door to the congressional office building and tried not to walk funny, making sure he smiled and said hello as he always did to the Capitol Hill cop. As a member of congress, he didn't have to go through the metal detector. Those merciful seconds would possibly save him from a humiliation that would have all of Washington and his congressional district laughing for years.

He turned the corner from the entry foyer and looked down a brightly-lit corridor at the end of which, to the right, was his office. He thought he could make it. His twisted hands and arms began to pump as he walked faster. Then as the starter's gun cracked, he contorted down the hallway as fast as he could. The raging ghosts of the Somali restaurant had no intention of remaining put. His backside tightened. Hold on, he shouted out in his mind. That's an order; don't disobey a congressman.

He pulled out his key and slid it into the lock as he pushed the heavy oak door open. As he did every time he entered his office, he glanced at the plaque on the wall: *This Office Belongs to the People of the Tenth District of Tennessee.* At this point he cared little about to whom the office belonged.

He lunged for the bathroom and called to everyone on his body team to hang on for just a few seconds more. That's all, just a few seconds so he could get his pants down and land on the seat.

Ripping noises and foul animal smells attacked the tile walls and dust-caked vent. Then he felt only tranquility, resting in his chapel where his simple prayer had been answered.

Emerging weak and with what felt like a slight fever, Fran reached for the bottle of Evian on his desk. Drinking slowly, he finished half of it and picked up the blanket and plastic bag that contained his pillow. He took his tie off then draped it over his sport jacket and pants hanging on the back of his chair. Fran sat on the couch and gazed listlessly at the stacks of work on his desk: unsigned letters and birthday certificates for senior citizens, speeches for the week ahead, and remarks to review for tomorrow's hearing. Work was impossible now; his body tingled with exhaustion. But he couldn't tear his eyes away from a ten-year-old photo.

Carter Stewart would have been forty-three next week. Her dark hair hung in a shorter cut she had chosen impulsively. They both joked about it when the photo was taken. But it has become his favorite picture of her. Her noble cheekbones and perfectly contoured lips spoke of a true loveliness that could fend off the years. The necklace was a lucky guess on his part; she loved it and wore it on special occasions. Her eyes were a catalog of all the special times he'd shared with her. The neighboring photograph captured the same beauty. Fourteen-year old Becky Stewart was mostly her mother, although there was a hint of Fran's slight dimples.

Fran lay his head down and set his two alarm clocks. He was terrified that he would oversleep and have some of his earlier-arriving staff find him slacking in his office. It hadn't even been six months since he left the stately Capitol Hill brownstone he rented so that Carter and Becky would have a Washington home when they visited. He hadn't gotten into the routine of living in the office like most of his colleagues. It was horrible, but since Carter's death, he couldn't stay in anything resembling a home.

He struggled through the demands of a congressional day but at night shunned all receptions and dinners where he would have to make chitty-chatty small talk. Instead, he had sought small, obscure restaurants; places where official Washington was an outsider. But after tonight's surprise attack, he'd have to rethink that strategy.

His relationship with Feeney Craighill, Carter's mother, had soured during the first months following his wife's death. Yet Becky and her grandmother got along and Fran readily agreed when Feeney offered to have Becky live with her. He wanted his daughter with him but knew she needed a more stable environment than his congressional duties would permit. It was a temporary arrangement. His eyes stayed open long enough to glance at the photos of Yogi putting on his shin guards and The Mick resting a large piece of lumber on his shoulder. Yogi Berra and Mickey Mantle: two Yankee warriors from Fran's youth. Fran's life had become so complicated compared to those days when it seemed all he thought about was baseball. He'd work out something long-term.Fran was still woozy as he left his office and headed to the House gym. He passed bulging sacks of morning mail leaning like sandbags on heavy wooden doors. A golden circular seal, carrying the name and insignia of the representative's state, hung on most doors. In another couple of hours, these doors would open and reveal the people and machinery that kept democracy going.

Fran had a good staff. He and Carter had spent considerable time going through resumes and conducting interviews before assembling a solid mix of veterans and young kids who ate long hours and asked for seconds. They made him look good, and he respected them. Especially this past year, they had circled the wagons around him as he struggled to regain his footing.

These past months Fran would shower at the House gym, hoping to get in and out before his colleagues arrived for their workouts. He never used the gym when he lived off the Hill. He was an outside runner and ran eight, sometimes ten miles many days, rain or shine. His commitment to increasing his endurance had developed during his early years running track. Yet his first love was baseball. His quick reflexes as a shortstop in high school hinted at greater things to come. However, though several of his friends took full rides at Division I contenders, he was promised only walk-on opportunities with a possible chance for a scholarship. He decided instead to give up baseball and selected a school with a strong poli sci department. During his first term, Fran participated in the annual congressional baseball game between the two parties. He was one of the team's stars until he broke two fingers sliding head-first into second. It was a troublesome recovery and he didn't want to risk further damage to a pinky that never entirely straightened out.

He and Carter had long adjusted their lives around Fran's running schedule. In her favorite photo of him, snow clung to his long black hair hanging out from a red and blue knit hat. His lean 6'2" frame seemed even bigger in front of some children on their sleds.

It took all of Fran's energies to keep him focused; things he had done with instinctive polish now required thought, planning. He was slower asking questions at committee hearings. Before, officious witnesses could never find a place to hide, but now they always escaped as Fran's words meandered away from him.

Ten-years younger than his boss, Fran's chief-of-staff Neil Glider was skilled at running the office, knowing how to be a short-order cook or a master chef, depending upon what the political, legislative, or personal demands called for. He told anxious staffers to watch Fran in meetings; if he started to drift off course, they had to nudge him back on track.

Two staffers walked into Fran's office but he'd already picked up the phone.

"Dad, I'm on the way out but I have to fax you something. You'll notice the "A" followed by "fine work!" I got the only A in the class."

"That's great Becky, it really is. You okay?"

"Yes, Daddy, fine. I love you. Gotta go."

Fran hung up the phone and smiled at his two young legislative assistants. They smiled back. The whole office knew that Fran only smiled when he spoke to his daughter. Something in her voice provided tonic for a purposeless man. Carter always seemed to know where the finish line was. He wasn't sure he'd do as well, but for Becky he'd try. He flew home every weekend to see her. If the House were not in session on Friday, he could usually make a late Thursday-night flight.

After finishing at the gym each morning, Fran would stop at the carry-out before returning to his office and usually get coffee and a fried egg sandwich on white bread to eat at his desk. This morning he ordered plain toast and a small bottle of water. He looked on his desk at the stack of papers and began to go over his schedule. Five morning meetings, two lunches, three more meetings in the afternoon, and two speeches he'd have to deliver on the House floor. As his body reminded him of the fierce battle of the evening before, Fran's eyes raced to the end of his schedule to see when he could put another day to rest.

Maddy Ames, his scheduler, and Neil had become his vigilant caretakers and hadn't included any evening functions – receptions, dinners – on his schedule. Fran's instructions had been clear. But Maddy, both friend and employee, had still decided to try. At the bottom of his schedule card, he saw the following event: 7 p.m. Reception at the New Zealand Embassy, hosted by Ambassador John Blackman. Fran paused, clenching the schedule and looking up to see if Maddy was in yet. The New Zealand Embassy was a gorgeous building with one of the most beautiful gardens in Washington. On a May evening, the flowers would be in full bloom.

He had always liked Ambassador Blackman, who brought a man-of-the-common-people sincerity to the protocol-filled world of seasoned diplomats. He and Fran had a particular sense of humor that others often missed. Besides, the embassy always served lamb chops. Even his digestive plumbing could forget the previous night in the face of lamb chops. Fran would go; he'd take a cab, and if he didn't like the reception, he'd sneak out. He wouldn't say anything to Maddy or Neil, although he knew when they asked he'd tell them. That was the way things worked around there.

"Good morning congressman," Maddy said. She pulled back the door to Fran's office and flicked through a row of light switches for the reception area and two other offices in the suite. The overhead lights in his office were always off; instead several table lights sent out soft halos that caught the sunlight from behind his desk.

"Good morning Maddy," Fran said, wiping toast crumbs from his mouth. "You're here early. I haven't made much of a dent in the paperwork yet, I haven't even gotten beyond the front page of the newspaper."

"You all right Fran?"

"Yeah, I think I had a stomach bug, but I'm okay now."

"Are you sure? Did you take anything; do you have a temperature? What have you eaten?" she asked as she put down her bag and the folder of papers she had taken home the night before.

"I'm fine mom," Fran said. "Did you ever have Somalian squid in a green hot sauce?

She inhaled deeply and looked up. "Fran, I keep telling you, you have to stop eating in those restaurants. You're going to end up in the hospital."

"Yeah, I know. I wouldn't wish the revenge of the Somalian squid on anyone," he said, smiling. His office manager had long ago gotten used to his hit or miss deadpan humor. But he made up for it with the cookies he brought back to her from all the receptions. He had none of the pomposity or bursts of temper that the rumor mill always churned out about many other members of congress.

Maddy set up his office when he came to Washington; she was the master of order. She had walked Fran through her system several times and he now had a basic idea of who in his office was supposed to do what. Neil helped Fran decide where they were headed, but they wouldn't go anywhere if it weren't for Maddy.

Fran and Maddy had become good friends. She called him by his first name when they were alone or just Neil was there. In front of the staff or visitors, it was always "congressman." Maddy was in her late fifties, tall, with consistently perfect waves of light red hair. Her slightly lined ceramic face fluidly matched expressions to any occasion and her always tasteful fashions were cared for with military precision.

"Mornin, boss," said Neil. "You look a little funny. You feelin okay?"

"Yeah, I'm fine. I just need to work on the speech for this afternoon, and I need to review with you those items we discussed for the hearing." Fran separated his papers into piles then looked up to see if Neil had anything more for him.

"Just give a holler when you want me," Neil said maneuvering his bulging briefcase and accordion folder into his office. He was a problem-solver, rolling up his starched white cuffs first thing every morning and fixing his cobalt eyes on his daily-to-do list. He had eked out a B.A. from a small college in the south; but he was clever, always looking for and usually finding what he called "the angle." He had an inviting southern drawl and a slight lisp as he explained how he was going to get something done.

Fran walked to his closet, grabbed his suit jacket and headed out the door. "Be down at the trade council briefing," he called out, his work on the desk as unfinished as when he first looked at it. The bright hallway was starting to fill with congressmen, their aides, and TV camera crews pushing their gear to hearing rooms. A group of fast-moving lobbyists -- at least they looked like lobbyists – filled in the traffic. They're securing the beachhead already, he thought.

"Good morning, congressman. Nothing like getting an early start is there?" one said as Fran opened the door to the briefing room. Fran paused. "No, I guess you're right," he said and continued into the room.

Several smiling trade council officials welcomed Fran. "Thanks for coming," one said in a hushed voice so as not to disturb the speaker droning on about trade deficits and new markets. Fran sat down and began to pour some water from the pitcher. It's a good thing this guy is up in the morning, he thought. If this were a dinner, he'd have everyone asleep. He thumbed through the propaganda in the packet. He couldn't focus on what the guy was saying. I'll stay a few more minutes, then I've got to get out of here.

As he got up, he used the standard get-out-of-jail card: "I've got to go to another meeting," he whispered to his host. Everyone knew that members had a lot of meetings. Those wanting a few minutes with a congressman knew the rule even if they thought it rude.

Fran remained unfocused for the rest of the day, his thoughts lingering on the reception at the New Zealand Embassy. He had mixed thoughts. He had to break free of the Somalian restaurant cycle, yet he was frightened of the looming alternative: Washington receptions. He wasn't good at small talk. Things seemed to work only when Carter was there. Her engaging way with reception-goers kept him from going under.

He went to the committee hearing, stumbled through the statement that he never went over with Neil, and later read his speech without ever looking up. He barely pulled that presentation back from the dead by deciding to tell a quick joke that was so absurd that the audience broke up.

"Reminds me, he said, of my recent visit to a nursing home. I asked a patient in the hall if she knew who I was. She said 'Now don't you worry; it happens to all of us. Just go up to the nurse's desk and they'll tell you who you are.'" Don't know where that came from he thought. Then, like a tired dog walking the welcome trail back home, headed to his office.

In years past, Fran would enter his office at the end of the day with a full-voiced "Howdy, Howdy," to any staff he saw. "Howdy" they responded before presenting a long list of things for him to go over, and Fran spoke with each of his staff in turn. Transportation, taxes, foreign policy, education, post office: each staffer covered certain issues, and Fran had to have a handle on all of them. You couldn't be an expert on any of them, but if you listened carefully, there was usually a path you could follow from problem to proposed action. He would review with Maddy the schedule both for Washington and back home in the district and spend time with Neil going over the big-picture policy and campaign issues.

Until this past year, he would never leave the office until after his seven o'clock phone call to Becky, discussing her day or what homework she had. He'd be late to receptions, or to Maddy's dismay, just not show up, if Becky needed help with anything. That time was important to his daughter as well, so despite the distractions girls her age had, she was always there for her dad's call before passing the phone to her mom. Sometimes Fran would reach her on her mom's car phone and he would hear the local news station in the background. "Not saying anything bad about me, are they?" he would ask. "No, Daddy, but if they do, I know they don't know what they're talking about. You are the best congressman there is." What a campaigner his daughter proved to be. Handing out flyers, making calls, speaking with conviction. After all, she was talking about her Dad; how could there be anyone better?

Now, Fran's calls to his daughter were dictated by her grandmother's schedule, no longer at a fixed time. Feeney maintained it was impossible, what with her busy schedule and Becky's after-school activities, to wait at a precise time for a phone call. Fran had wanted to get Becky a cell phone, but her grandmother said that would be totally inappropriate. Besides, Feeney said, several of Becky's friends had gotten into trouble at school when they were caught making calls.

Fran hadn't anticipated Feeney exercising such control. Feeney changed markedly after Carter's death. Through some twisted logic, his mother-in-law had convinced herself that Fran's stressful career led to her daughter's failing health and eventual passing. A charge made by the same woman who had orchestrated his entry into congressional politics. Fran knew the claim was preposterous, but began in his grief to second guess himself. Feeney pounced on that as proof she was right. His thought had been for his daughter to remain temporarily in familiar surroundings. He needed to reclaim his daughter. Yet how, with a job that all but forbade time with one's family? He needed to come up with a plan.

He didn't say much these days when he came into the office; only a "Hey" or a nod. As he sat at his desk, he would go through piles of mail that had been prepared for him to sign. The pen that scratched out "Fran Stewart" above the words Member of Congress was often in motion before Fran read the "personalized" letter from him. He shuffled some other reports as if it would actually accomplish something.

"Did you get a chance to review your speech for the senior citizens meeting this weekend?" Neil asked. Fran hadn't. He doubted he would. Neil and Fran were doing this strange dance more and more frequently. Even if Fran hadn't read them, he knew his chief-of-staff knew what should be in the final version. Neil made that magic happen. Fran knew he wasn't going to review carefully, as he used to, any of the material his chief-of-staff gave him. Neil knew that as well. "Yes, I've started looking," Fran said. "It's over in this pile."

"Okay, just checking, I've put your folder on the table with tomorrow's statements as well the draft report you have to sign off on," Neil said.

"I'll take a look at it."

"Doing anything tonight?" Maddy asked as she brought in several forms for Fran to sign. Neil slowed on his way out, waiting for the response.

"Not sure."

"All right, just checking. Let me know if you need a ride anywhere." Maddy smiled and walked toward the door.

Fran looked at the clock. The reception started in one hour. Cab ride would probably take half that this time of day. He would arrive at about seven. The House was out of session and all the staff had left except Maddy and Neil, who looked far from finished with their work. Fran retreated to his bathroom, shaved and brushed black hair with slight lines of gray above each ear. His trips to the barbershop had become erratic. When his hair got this long and began to curl over his collar, Carter would ask if he were trying to look like a rock star. He brushed his teeth and stopped, then reached for the bottle of Agua Brava, a cologne he had purchased several years ago on a congressional fact-finding trip to Europe. He came back with one fact: he liked Agua Brava.

"I haven't smelled that in a while," Maddy said as he splashed it on then walked toward the front door. Fran said nothing as he stopped to sign several pieces of paperwork on top of her desk. "Are we going somewhere special tonight?"

"I don't know what you'd consider special. You have a copy of my schedule."

Maddy retreated. "I'm sorry, I didn't mean to pry."

"I'm going to the New Zealand reception. I'm sorry for being short." She remained silent. "Thanks for putting it on there. Maybe it's time to try."

She smiled.

CHAPTER 2

The traffic was predictably solid for thirty minutes. The fading spring sun flirted with an on-again-off-again early evening drizzle. As the cab turned on to the embassy drive the rain stopped. Fran walked up the front steps toward a stocky man, gesturing wildly as if in a theater production. Next to him was a wisp of a woman, who shook hands and pointed her guests toward the hallway. Seeing Fran, the man smiled and opened his arms before launching into a bear hug.

"Congressman, . . . Fran, I saw your name on the guest list and was delighted that you had accepted our invitation. How have you been? You know how sorry we were to hear about Mrs. Stewart."

"Mr. Ambassador, it's always good to see you. Your kind note meant a lot to me." Fran leaned over to receive a kiss from the Ambassador's wife. "I haven't gotten out much of late, but I've always felt very welcome here, and my wife and I were very grateful when you hosted us for dinner before we left for New Zealand."

Fran thought about that night, several days before Carter and he took an official trip to Wellington and Christ Church as part of a ten-day trip to Asia. Carter was most excited about New Zealand. The Blackmans gave them tips on shopping that could come only from an ambassador and his wife. Fran looked into the large dining room and saw the chair Carter had been sitting in that night, feeling for a moment as empty as the vacant room in front of him.

"How is your daughter doing?" asked Mrs. Blackman, motherly concern in her voice.

"Becky is a very resilient girl. She's in all kinds of activities at school and she's been staying with her grandmother during the week while I'm in Washington. We comfort each other a lot in our phone calls."

"Oh that's good that you two have each other. Let us know if there is anything we can do." She placed her hand on his wrist.

Fran nodded. "Please don't let me keep you from your other guests, I'm going to walk outside and take in your garden, which I'm sure is as beautiful as always."

"Oh do, absolutely, my dear, we'll be out soon."

Fran walked into the great room that led to the garden. There must have been over two hundred people caught up in a buzz of Washington chatter. Waiters struggled to hold trays as they were picked clean. The embassy's spring party was always one of Washington's top draws.

Fran felt a slight tug on his arm and turned into the embrace of a man who could make just about anyone smile.

"Fran, I haven't seen you out in a long time," said Tripp Lee. "C'mon boy smile up, it's good to see you here."

"It's good to see you, Tripp," Fran said. Tripp was from Alabama. He was five years younger but had been in congress two terms longer. He had divorced a couple of years back; the marriage couldn't withstand his congressional life. He had narrow lips and razor-cut hair, a good-looking guy who had developed a bit of a pot from long nights of drinking. Tripp had a drawl that even Carter had a tough time understanding at first. But she,

Fran, and Tripp had become friends. Fran hadn't seen him much over the past year. He hadn't seen much of anyone.

"Fran, we've got to spend some time together, you know, catch-up. Look, I need to get to four more receptions tonight, but we'll catch-up."

"Good-bye Tripp, yeah we'll talk."

Walking down the stairs, Fran recognized the people he used to see at receptions. He realized the room was serving more than the food on the trays. It was a lobbyists' feeding ground. These denizens were besieging administration officials, hoping for favors for them or their clients. He saw several of his colleagues from the Hill. As he got to the bottom of the stairs, Fran realized he was now in radar lock; some of the K Street boys began to approach.

"Congressman Stewart, Fred Sparser, with Barrons and Novar. We met last week at your committee's hearing on aid to Liberia."

"Oh yes, good to see you again, Fred," Fran said trying to shake him. But even if he had, there were more bogies coming in. Fran had never been good at this type of give and take. He would watch some of his more masterful colleagues. They nodded at just the right time and sounded as if they agreed with just about anything they were told. Of course it was said to them in such a pleasing, obsequious way, who wouldn't agree?

"We really thought your questions were right on target," Sparser said. "You know Liberia, which our firm has represented now for the last year, is not really understood by the American public. The government has launched a new economic plan that will -- and you can take this to the bank," said Sparser, pulling his collar down on his Hermes tie, "put the people of Liberia in a much better position in the next couple of years."

"That's encouraging, I hope you'll keep me up to date on what's going on there," Fran said. He had shaken Sparser, but another craft banked toward him. Fran had not been too badly hit, at least not yet, but he wondered if coming to the reception had been a bad idea.

"Congressman, Rocco De Gravias with Alpine Insurance. Haven't seen you for a while. When do you think they're going to get the budget resolution through?" Rocco asked, as sweat rolled down the two layers of pressed flesh beneath his chin. The top of his blue collar was soaked.

Fran didn't have the foggiest idea when they would get the budget resolution through, or even to the floor. Even the Speaker, whom Fran spoke to the day before, didn't have any idea. Time for more chaff as he moved toward the door. "Gee, that's a good question. I understand they're working real hard on it. Let me know what you hear." One more step and Rocco was left in the clouds.

The garden was as beautiful as he thought it would be: yellow and blue flowers with brown-fringed grasses, and orange-colored blossoms weaving through the rocks, a garden that was the pride of New Zealand. The finely-cut lawn, like a frozen tide, surrounded perfect bushes and trees. He began to smile, remembering how he had held his wife when they first saw the garden. She wrote down the names of several plants and had Fran try to replicate a bit of the embassy garden in front of their house. They had never gardened before and were thrilled when the plants flowered. They would make plans to visit some famous gardens, Monticello had been high on their list, but never found the time go.

The flashing light on his console told him they were coming in again. Then like a loud burst of machine gun fire coming from his wing man, he heard the Ambassador's voice. The lobbyists scattered.

"Congressman, can I get you something to drink?" he said, as he waved to one of the waiters. "And did you have any lamb chops yet? I know how much you care for them."

"No, I haven't, I was talking to some of your guests and just beginning to enjoy the best garden in Washington," Fran said as he ordered a club soda and took a small plate with three hefty lamb chops on it. "You have a good memory, Mr. Ambassador."

"That's an easy one," the Ambassador replied. "Everyone loves our lamb chops." Blackman paused, his big smile vanishing. "We were worried about you, Fran. You didn't come to any of our functions. People I spoke with hadn't seen you either."

Fran looked at the lines on the Ambassador's leathery face and remembered the stories this man, who many suspected might become the next prime minister, had told him about his beautiful country. John Blackman had been the subject of a recent documentary that chronicled his three-month journey through the mountains, sprawling meadows, and beach fronts of his two-island nation. Those chubby fingers and wrestler's girth belonged to one of the most accomplished members of the diplomatic community. He made you laugh and always made you feel at home. You knew he was bright, but no interrogation could get him to readily admit that he'd graduated first in his class, spoke five languages, and went on to advanced studies where his doctoral dissertation was hailed as one of the most brilliant pieces of research in university history. Fran admired him. Yet he wondered if the ambassador would hold it together if he lost Mrs. Blackman.

"Mr. Ambassador, I've always thought of you as a friend, and there aren't many to be found in these parts. I don't know, maybe it's me," Fran said, aware that he was beginning to open up to someone for the first time in a while. He noticed behind slightly smudged glasses that the Ambassador's eyes focused more intently on him. "I've got to start getting out more, and I feel very comfortable here. It refreshes me."

"That's the ticket, my boy," the Ambassador said as he put his arm around Fran's shoulder and gave him a light pat. They spoke for another twenty minutes, their conversation like a shield from hovering aircraft ready to strike. Nina Blackwood joined them as they ate their lamb chops and tiny pastry puffs with tangy cheese. Fran laughed, but didn't protest when the ambassador called for more lamb chops.

When Fran couldn't eat or drink anything further, he decided it was time to go. He said good-bye to the ambassador and agreed to come back for a private dinner in the near future. Mrs. Blackwood walked briskly with Fran toward the front hallway to check for late guests. Fran flew in her wake, so bogies could only wait for another try.

Mrs. Blackman hugged Fran. "You take care of yourself. I want you to call John or me if there's anything we can do. I mean that," she whispered into his ear. She handed him a small floral arrangement that had been sitting on a nearby table. "Take these for the office," she smiled.

The mist had become a strong drizzle, and the temperature had dropped dramatically. A cab approached, its headlights pointed to a muddy spot Fran hadn't seen. He side-stepped at the last minute, but was off balance. He felt two hands catch him before he landed sprawled on his back.

"Gotcha, pardner. You've got to learn to say no to those trays of free champagne."

Fran straightened up and looked at what remained of the flowers. Indignant yet embarrassed that someone thought him a mooching lush who had lost his balance, he looked at the smiling woman as she tossed back light honey-colored hair then placed one hand on her hip.

"Thanks, I guess I didn't see that puddle in the dark," he spoke clearly, to dispel the notion that he had too much to drink. The cab stopped and Fran opened the door. "Please take this; I'll get the next one." He knew he would be waiting a while, seeing no more cabs in the turn-around.

"Hey, you were here first."

"Please, you were kind enough to keep an old man from falling into the mud, it's the least I can do." He motioned for her to get in as the rain started to fall harder, dripping down their faces.

"We'll share the cab. Where are you going?"

"Capitol Hill."

"You get in first, I'm going to DuPont Circle. Hurry, we're getting all wet."

Accepting an order from someone who at least had a plan, Fran ducked into the back of the cab and slid over to the far end of the seat. She got in, slammed the door and shot out her address. Fran added his and looked again at his traveling companion as the fading lights from the embassy lit up the cab. She had on a sleeveless, cotton dress with a green flower print; now noticeably wrinkled. She started to put on a tan sweater. Fran reached over to help her free one of the sleeves that had become caught between her back and the seat. Raindrops trailed down the sharp curves leading from below her ears to a slightly jutting, almost challenging chin supported by a slender neck from which hung a thin gold chain. Her hair fell just short of her shoulders and her fingers brushed at the wet strands.

"Would you like this?" Fran offered her his handkerchief.

"Yes, that's probably a good idea. Glad you come prepared," she said as she dabbed at her face and the back of her neck. "There, how do I look?" she asked, handing him back his handkerchief.

"Great," he said, then blushed.

"Why, thank you," she said, her eyes sparkling. "It's been a long day, but I've been looking forward to that reception all week. Actually, the invitation didn't even come to me. A friend in the office couldn't go so he asked if I could go in his place. Isn't that ambassador a hoot? I mean he and his wife are just so nice. And that food. Did you have any of the lamb chops? And the white wine from New Zealand? I guess I had a couple of glasses.

That's the third embassy reception I've been to, aren't they great? Do you get to many? I'm sorry, I didn't even introduce myself. I'm Jo Ellen Driscoll. I have a three-month fellowship at the Environmental Defense Coalition. Our office works on several issues with the embassy. What type of work do you do?"

Fran looked at her as she sat forward with both hands on the back of the front seat. He wanted to stay behind the steel-strapped door he opened only for Becky.

"Do you work downtown?" she asked, not even realizing he hadn't spoken.

"Fran Stewart, I'm a congressman from Tennessee."

Jo Ellen sat up. "Oh my goodness, I'm so sorry. I just go on some times, brain and mouth not communicating. Why, you're the first congressman I've had any real opportunity to speak to. You know I have a meeting the day after next, well there are several of us going up to the Hill for a big meeting with a congressman. I'm putting together the background report. It's supposed to be a big deal; I'm not even supposed to say anything. Say I hope you don't mind listening to all my gabbing. And sorry about your flowers," she said, shifting gears with little regard for the clutch.

"No, no that's fine."

"The way you were talking with the ambassador and his wife, do you know them?

"Yes, we've met several times about issues he wanted to flag on the Hill. He also was very helpful in getting us prepared for our trip to New Zealand."

"You've been to New Zealand?" she said incredulously.

"Yes, there were several of us who went. We didn't get to stay all that long, but it's a beautiful country. I look forward to returning."

The cab stopped and the dome light came on as the engine idled, worn wipers scratching off the steady rain. She handed the driver several bills and opened the door. "Thanks again for letting me share the cab, Mr. Stewart."

"It was nice meeting you, Ms. Driscoll," Fran said. His smile met hers before the door slammed. He watched her walk away with a determined step, her hair and dress fluttering in a spring wind. He followed her closely as the driver accelerated away from the curb.

Back in his office, Fran turned on the light and saw the familiar stacks of paperwork on his desk. Farmers had cows that always had to be milked; Fran had paperwork. But farmers were diligent. Fran just convinced himself he was. He reached for his blanket and took the pillow out of its plastic case. How could his body be so at peace tonight after it was wracked and beaten the night before? He thought about his taxi companion. Their short conversation had refreshed him. He felt relaxed. Things change; the good is nothing if you haven't escaped from the bad. He settled into sleep, his thoughts scampering toward dreams.

CHAPTER 3

Fran finished off the last of his egg sandwich, pleased he had gotten through several piles of correspondence and statements he'd need for the morning's committee hearing. Then he looked at his packed schedule card. Maybe it wasn't so bad. His mind seemed clearer than it had in a while. He walked to his closet and pulled his jacket off the wire hanger, stopping at the sight of his running shoes. Undisturbed for almost a year now, they reminded him of that second wind that kicked in, when you actually sighed from the bounce going up your leg when your foot hit the ground. He hadn't gained much weight since he stopped running; but the discipline to run couldn't just be picked up like an old pair of sneakers. It had to be banged out by ready arms and a focused mind. With Carter gone, Fran had lost it. And it wasn't just running. Focus was important to Carter; she said so on their first date. She had been a superior student at a great school, while he had been a good student at a good school. There was a physical attraction, but they complemented each other in a number of areas. She saw in him a kind person who took quickly to new vistas. He saw in her someone who cared about the simpler things. The recipe for their fruitful relationship also contained a good measure of shared humor that kept the hard stuff from becoming overbearing.

"Good morning, Fran," Maddy said, the trace of her perfume trailing behind her. "How was the reception last night, are Ambassador and Mrs. Blackwood well?

Fran felt around in his pockets for his keys.

"Over on your shelf," Maddy said, reflexively.

"Thanks. The reception? I had a good time. The ambassador and his wife were as gracious as always. We're supposed to get together some time for dinner; he said he'd call. I'm glad I got out. Been in a little bit of a rut I guess. Thanks for putting it on my schedule, but no more just yet." He handed her the remains of two small broken flowers. "I had more but I slipped. It's a long story."

"That was very kind. I have a small vase I can put them in. They'll look very nice on my desk," she said, as she took the two wilted yellow flowers.

Fran walked into Neil's office. His assistant's desk looked like a recycling center, important papers mixed in with the debris of earlier congressional terms. It would be impossible for anyone who saw Neil, a Brooks Brothers' cover boy, to imagine that he would have a desk like this. Fran wondered how *anyone* could have a desk like that. Yet, if he asked for something, his chief-of-staff produced it in a flash. Fran smiled. He grabbed a notepad and drew out a traffic sign with the words "landslide danger" and taped the sheet to the top of the pile. The light came on as Neil walked in and glanced at the note.

"That's pretty funny, Fran," he said. "I think you missed your true calling." Neil placed his briefcase and accordion folder on his chair.

"Any rattlesnakes nesting in there?" Fran asked.

"I'll call you if I hear any rattles." Neil had work to prepare for Fran, but was struck by the smile on his boss's face; one on the verge of laughter. "You're going to need that creative energy to get you through this day. I hope you're hungry. Four lunches."

The laugh came. It had been gone for a long time. "I regret I have only one stomach to give for my country," Fran said as he headed for the hallway.

He eschewed the underground subway that ran from the House office buildings to the Capitol building and walked toward the large glass doors leading to Independence Avenue. Fran drew his first deep breath of sweet spring air. He was on his bicycle on the way to the little league field; he was warming up for the state track championships; he and Carter were playing with Becky on their rolling lawn in Tennessee. The sun caught the green sprouts starting to emerge on the branches of majestic trees that bordered the Capitol. He knew he had to go in, but he wished he could walk all day.

Fran entered the room in the basement of the Capitol where his party leaders were pointing to charts and visuals. "As you can see," one of them said, "we've made great progress since last year, and we're on course to do even better next year."

Fran counted only about ten of his colleagues. So much for mandatory meetings. Even the gourmet doughnuts didn't boost attendance. He knew others would show up eventually, even if only for a few minutes. "Did I miss much?" Fran asked a gray-haired man with black-rim glasses.

His colleague looked at him with a straight face. "Were you here last week?"

"Yeah," Fran said.

"Then you haven't missed anything," he said, his eyes melting behind the frames.

Fran listened, trying to get fired up by the presentation. He'd bring the hand-outs back to the office, maybe Neil could explain how they'd be of use. After fifteen minutes Fran headed for the wall phone in the back of the room. Nodding at some papers, he hoped it would seem clear to anyone watching that he had been called away to attend to some important matter.

He opened the door and slipped through the catering kitchen to a winding tunnel in the bowels of the Capitol.

He reached for his schedule and a pen, stroking through that first meeting. That schedule card was like a mountain he had to climb. He would hold it upside down after each scratched-out meeting and see himself getting closer to the summit, breathing harder at each level. It had been as tough for him lately. Fran's concentration lasted only minutes. The events on his schedule carried no substance; they were steps only to the end of the day when Fran would be able to get to his office and have an Almond Joy; his treat for making it through the day. Maybe he'd just resign and get it over with. Becky would understand. But how would she handle it? She was only now emerging from months of withdrawn grieving. He knew how much she loved her mother. There was a certain stability in his job, notwithstanding the need to seek re-election every two years. Becky had been so proud of him when he won his first election; proud that he could help people. That's what Carter told her Dad would do. That simple theme of trying to help people was one he tried not to forget. Helping people and serving honorably was something he was going to have to keep for Becky, Carter, and himself.

Maddy walked in with an iced bottle of water and placed it on his desk. "Do you want to look at this now or save it for later?" she asked as she handed him a list of phone calls that had come in for him during the day.

He ran through the list of about ten people. "I guess we should get back to our good party chairman in Davidson County," he said. The rest of the names he barely recognized, until he got to the one second to last on the list: "Jo Ellen Driscoll, Environmental Defense Coalition, regarding issues we discussed earlier."

"Do you want me to get the chairman on the line?" Maddy asked. There was no answer. "Congressman, the chairman?"

Fran put the list down. "Yes, I'm sorry Maddy, please get the chairman for me."

Chairman Calvert Dixon, a young party official, called often. He was the Energizer Bunny with a thick drawl, popping up everywhere in the county where he thought someone might be impressed by the fact that he was county chairman. A long-time supporter of Fran's, Dixon drew from that license to tell people what he and Congressman Stewart were going to do on a particular issue, or how he and Fran had brought sizeable amounts of federal dollars to fund projects in the district. Fran always felt tired after talking with him.

"Anything important?" Maddy asked.

"Chairman Dixon wanted to know if Henson Clark had agreed yet to address our annual county dinner."

They both smiled. Fran hadn't really been pushing the matter. He knew Henson Clark, the fiery up-and-coming Republican Leader in the House was buried with requests by party functionaries around the country.

"He never gives up, or maybe just never understands what can be done and what can't."

"You must admit," Fran said, "that people like Dixon get a lot, they're doggone unabashedly relentless."

"Any other calls?" Maddy asked. He knew he had already returned one more than she thought he would.

A feathery wave went through his stomach as he thought about the cab ride the night before. What did she mean, "issues we discussed earlier?" He remembered the damp waves of her hair and the tan sweater he had helped her into. Had he said something in the cab that he had forgotten?

"Yeah, let's see what this Driscoll woman wants."

"Are you sure? I can ask Neil or someone in the legislative office to give her a call."

"It shouldn't take long," he said, disappearing for a second behind the growing piles of paper work on his desk.

"Sure," she rolled her eyes as she walked out of his office.

His intercom buzzed. "Congressman," Maddy said, "I have Ms. Driscoll on the line."

Fran jerked forward in his chair and sat up straight. Clearing his throat, he became tangled in a cough and answered, "Hello Ms. Driscoll," in an unfortunate falsetto.

"Congressman, are you all right?" Jo Ellen asked.

"Yes," he replied after a little more throat-clearing. "Something must have gone down the wrong pipe."

"That can happen, you have to be careful." She hesitated then moved on to business. "First, thank you so much for returning my call. I won't keep you for more than a second. Remember, I told you that I'm working with the Environmental Defense Coalition, the EDC, and, well, we're having a reception on Thursday night. I saw you had RSVP'd no. It's going to be a nice reception. All of our board members will be in town, and we plan to introduce all the members of congress," Jo Ellen said as if an invitation to her event were as sought after as one to a White House dinner.

Gee, to think I came so close to missing this chance, Fran thought. "Ms. Driscoll, that sounds like a fine event. There must have been a conflict on my schedule, but I'll check into it, and have the office get back to you."

"I think you'd really enjoy the reception. You don't have to stay long. We sure hope you can make it. Bye-bye," she said, after giving him her direct number.

Fran put the phone down and stared at the TV across from him. He watched his colleagues debate some measure on the House floor. The sound was off. It was always off unless Maddy or Neil happened by and flipped the volume on as they passed, hoping that something would grab his interest. But as soon as he realized the volume was on, he'd grab for the remote and punch the mute button.

"Maddy, did they announce the schedule for Friday yet?"

"Yes, sir. They've scheduled votes for Friday, probably be done early afternoon. I booked you a flight home at three o'clock, so you'll have enough time to get to the Carpenters Annual Awards dinner."

"So I guess I'm here Thursday night." He put the key into the ignition. "Did you see an invitation from the Environmental Defense Coalition?" Maddy ducked out and came back with a folder. She picked out a tan sheet of paper and handed it to him. "Guess I have to eat somewhere along the line, please put this on Thursday's schedule."

"Okay," Maddy said, scratching out no and writing out yes in a red circle.

He could always turn around and not go. "We sure hope you can make it."

Maddy walked by Neil's desk and pointed to the invitation. He nodded approvingly. "Maybe this is the what everybody talks about when they say it takes time," she said.

"Fran is pulling through. He's been carrying a lot on his shoulders these past months. You know how much he loved her, Maddy." Neil tossed his pencil down and ran his fingers through his hair. "There were several times I thought he'd pull the plug and resign; even last week. Becky's the only thing that keeps him somewhat focused. He wants to keep all his options open for her."

"He loves his daughter very much," Maddy said as she walked back to her desk and scooped some walnuts into her mouth. You could tell the time of day by how many walnuts were left in Maddy's bag -- at least until six, when she often dipped into a reserve bag she kept in her desk.

CHAPTER 4

Feeney Craighill looked at her calendar as a general would survey battle maps. The size of a small coffee table book, it had a well-worn leather cover that contrasted with the bright white insert containing the days of the current year. Every year she ordered next year's insert on September 30, precisely as the insert's note instructed. Behind the louver doors of the closet to her right, sat a stack of twenty-five years of inserts listing every function she had attended and notes about allies, enemies and anyone in between. It was Feeney's hard drive, and she knew every file.

The late afternoon sun embraced the meadow-like backyard and hurled shafts of light between the green brocade curtains. The thick crown molding topped off green and yellow embossed wallpaper whose surface area had been reduced over the years by what seemed to be a constant stream of photographs, plaques, and awards. "Feeney Craighill, Tennessee Republican of the Year; Davidson County's Woman of the Year; American Red Cross Gala Dinner, Honoree; Presidential Appointment to the United States Military Academy's Board of Visitors; Republican National Committee, Eagle; In Honor of All Your Support in the Construction of the Craighill Medical Center in Port au Prince." Matted photographs showed a model-thin Feeney with presidents and state and local officials.

Other shots had her posing with Hollywood celebrities, sharing with them a natural poise. Such grace had been gained from modeling shoots for the magazine covers she adorned in her twenties. More recent photographs showed that Feeney had maintained that model's figure even with her latest sweep of gray hair.

These pictures also traced an aging Dr. Elias Craighill, her husband of forty-one years. Active in Tennessee politics from his teens, Elias Craighill took Feeney to her first rubber-chicken dinner to help the re-election campaign of a senator Elias had known from college. Feeney was hooked from the start and soon became even more active in political circles than her husband, especially after his heart attack limited Elias to his practice. He retired altogether only several months before a third and fatal heart attack. He missed by one month joining his wife, daughter, granddaughter, and congressman-elect son-in-law in the election night photo which hung alone on the wall behind Feeney's desk.

Aside from the times she donned gardening attire to tend to her curving rows of precious flowers and ornamental grasses, Feeney dressed for business. Pants were verboten; fashion to Feeney was Kennedy-era dresses with dainty antique gold bracelets and necklaces. If an occasion warranted, she wore white gloves, now less for formality than to hide the age spots and skin taut against the bones in her hands.

"*Windows for Dummies* is probably the best book to help you with the computer, Grandma," said Becky Stewart as she came into the room.

"What do you mean for dummies?" Feeney said, thinking that her playful tone bordered on impertinence.

"It just means it's for people who don't know anything about something. The library has a whole bunch of these books on all kinds of subjects. Do you remember what I taught you last week?" Becky asked as she looked at the dark monitor screen.

"Yes, I do, Miss Smarty Pants. I have the computer off because I don't want to waste electricity. You know, your grandfather and I did not get here by being wasteful."

"Grandma, our teacher said you probably use more electricity by turning the computer off and on."

Feeney was clearly not on solid ground. Dedication to her transcendent style stood as firm as the centuries-old trees outside the full-length window. But the computer? She wrestled with the idea, but realized she must be seen as keeping up in the computer age. Many young Turks in the party spoke in a gobbledygook about new fundraising projects or voter-outreach programs unknown four years ago. These same movers and shakers asked for her email address as though asking for her phone number.

"Becky, please put the book on my desk. I'll look at it when I finish with my paperwork. Candice is finishing cleaning the kitchen. Make sure she gets your snack for you. Piano lessons, candy stripers, then your Girl Scout meeting. You know Thursdays are busy, and you won't get dinner till eight-thirty at the earliest."

Becky sat down in the chair in front of the desk, her plaid school jumper and white blouse still as neat as they were when she left for school that morning. "I will, but first I wanted to try to get Dad. I thought I'd use your phone in case you wanted to talk with him."

"I don't need to talk with your father," Feeney said. "Why don't you use the phone in the hall?" Becky was already dialing her Dad's direct line, the one only her Dad or Maddy would answer.

"Hello," came the woman's voice.

"Maddy?"

"Hello, sweetheart," Maddy said, in a voice reserved for her favorite people. "What are you doing? No, it's Thursday, I know; piano lessons, candy stripers, then Girl Scouts."

Becky smiled. "You got it. Thursday is a winner, but it goes by quickly and I really like working at the hospital. How are you?"

"Busy. Your father's had a hectic schedule this week, and I know he's looking forward to getting home on Friday night. Let me see if I can find him. Hold just one minute sweetheart," Maddy said as she picked up one of her few remaining walnuts and headed for Fran's office. She knocked on his bathroom door as only she and Neil were permitted to do. "Congressman, Becky's on the phone." She turned quickly, walked toward her desk, and closed the door behind her. The light on her phone stopped blinking.

"Hi, princess. Thursday night, right, all set for everything?" Fran wiped traces of shaving cream with a hand towel.

"Yeah, ready as I'll ever be. Friday's going to be even worse starting next month. Remember you signed me up for gymnastics?"

"I'm glad you're starting that again; you were always very good."

"I asked grandma if I could drop piano, but she said it's more important than gymnastics."

Feeney listened impassively.

"Daddy, everything okay?"

"Yes, everything is fine, Becky. Everything okay with you?"

"Yes, I can't wait to see you tomorrow night. Want to talk to Grandma?" she said as she thrust the phone across the desk. Both Feeney and Becky heard the voice on the dangling phone say, "no, that's not necessary." Clearly, to both Fran and Feeney, Becky's request was like an incoming hand grenade, but she continued to hold the phone in front of her Grandmother.

"Hello, we have to go now. Becky has a lot of activities on Thursday. It's a lot of driving, and we've got the big county fundraiser coming up. Have you heard from Henson Clark yet? Is he coming?"

"We're still working on that Feeney, but you know how busy the Republican Leader is." They both rolled their eyes at the same time.

"Well, all right," Feeney said, handing the phone back to her granddaughter.

"I have to go Daddy. I'll see you tomorrow, bye."

"Make sure you have your snack. I love you."

Fran sat back in his chair. It'd take him a few minutes to get over that phone call. The newfound clarity he had brought to his job today turned fuzzy as he looked at his desk. Not fair, he thought, as he glanced at the paperwork already muscling its way into his weekend. He picked up a speech he was to deliver in the next two days, read through the first three paragraphs, and realized he didn't remember the people he was thanking or the initiatives he said he had taken. Neil has looked at this, and Maddy will check it too, he thought. He put the folder down and started signing form letters. He put his pen down after several dozen letters and threw back his shoulders as if he had actually accomplished something. That's why Neil put them there.

He didn't want to be among the first at the reception. He could leave the office in twenty minutes. Everything was ready; all he needed was to put on his suit jacket. He walked around the office, spoke with junior staffers in the back room, and watched the clock as if he were the mission-control chief of a NASA launch. He went into his bathroom one last time. One last comb, one last dab at the oil on his nose, and one quick toweling off of his moist palms. He was not sure why he was getting so ready. He carried a picture of her in his mind but tried not to concentrate on it. He felt as if he were going on a first date, but knew he was being foolish. It had been a short cab ride and his mind of late had not been able to sort and process as it should. He'd be back from the reception soon and start to pack up for the weekend.

Fran made small talk with some of his colleagues as he walked past the easel announcing that he was about to enter the Environmental Defense Coalition's Salute to Congress. An elderly lady behind the check-in table handed him his name tag.

"We're so happy you came tonight, Congressman Stewart. Jo Ellen was ecstatic after she spoke with you. I've been in our office for over twenty years and she's definitely one of the smartest summer staffers we've had. She loves Washington, said she may come back to stay one day."

"Yes, she is a fine young lady," he replied.

He must have come to at least fifty receptions in this room. The faces, reception set-up, and bar fare varied little. Most members stayed at these events for as little time as possible. During that time, they glad-handed with their hosts and attended to the buffet in direct proportion to whether they had dinner plans. Their profession had taught them to perfect the face that could convince someone so eager to go on about issue XYZ, that this was a member of congress that was genuinely interested in XYZ. That face was a work of art. Fran threw it on as some giant, rubber Halloween mask behind which he could hide as he was pummeled by requests. This past year, the mask rarely came off.

His eyes swept the room and found nothing out of the ordinary. His politician's intuition gauged there was no one to seek out or avoid. The second reconnaissance conducted a more penetrating probe, waiting till faces turned away, looked at him. There she was. He swallowed hard. She hadn't seen him yet, and his thoughts scrambled as he prepared for that moment. Prettier than he remembered, she wore a dark green dress and had her light brown hair pulled back in a gold clasp. She stood in a spot of fading sunlight, lingering by the tall doors that opened on to the patio and held what looked like a glass of cranberry juice in her small, expressive hands. She saw him. Several people were talking to Fran, but as Washington pros, they knew they were losing him and looked for other places to dock. Placing her glass down, she approached with the same determined gait he had seen the night before.

"Congressman Stewart, how wonderful that you're able to join us this evening," she said, her smile lingering.

"Ms. Driscoll. Yes, yes, your group has always done good work. I'm pleased to be here; looks like a very nice reception. I'm only sorry I won't be able to stay long," he said, as if he had pressed play on a tape recorder.

"Well if that's the case, let me quickly introduce you to Cecil Brown, the chairman of our board." She placed her hand behind his elbow and guided him across the room. "Tell you the truth, I just met him this morning. He's a little eccentric, but he's got more money than, well not more money than Bill Gates, but I've heard he's way up there. He just talks a little funny and well, you'll see. You don't mind, do you?"

"No, no, I'd enjoy that," Fran said. She flipped her bangs toward the side of her head as she looked up and smiled at the congressman who stood at least eight inches taller. The smile returned him to their first encounter.

Several people stood around Cecil Brown, leaving Fran and Jo Ellen in a brief holding pattern until the group recognized that a new member of congress had arrived and protocol called for him to be introduced immediately. Cecil Brown's blank look indicated that he didn't have the faintest idea who Fran Stewart was.

Fran thought he felt Jo Ellen's hand tremble slightly as she spoke. "Mr. Brown, this is Congressman Fran Stewart, he's been very interested in a lot of our issues."

Cecil Brown may have been one of the richest men in the world, but no one was as rich as the United States Congress. "Good evening, Congressman Stewart," Brown said in a high-pitched voice. Fran felt a slight reflexive jerk on his elbow. He wondered if Jo Ellen realized she was still holding it. "This occasion of fortuitous meeting brings me hope. Quite frankly, I'm gladdened by the many political aspirants I've seen during my visit that I believe have been willing to catch the lanyard I've thrown them."

Fran needed more than his rubber mask for that line, even as everyone around him nodded with conviction. He also began to recognize Jo Ellen's perfume, which had captivated him against his will in the cab the other night.

"It's a pleasure to meet you, Mr. Brown, I'm sure you're very proud of your organization. I've long been a supporter, and Ms. Driscoll here has been very helpful in updating me on the many projects EDC is involved in. I know she very much enjoys her fellowship here in Washington," Fran said, as Jo Ellen reflexively squeezed his elbow again. Fran looked down and smiled at her. She seemed to recognize for the first time that she had been holding his arm and dropped her hand as inconspicuously as possible.

"That's good, very good," Cecil Brown said in a voice that made the glassware shiver. "We must symmetrically prepare our new troops for the engagements that we old timers continue to carve on the battlefields." Those around Cecil Brown took their cue and nodded more determinedly than before.

"Of course," Fran said, straight-faced. "It's been a pleasure to meet you Mr. Brown, I'm sorry to have to leave so soon, but I've enjoyed the reception," Fran said. Cecil Brown nodded in a jerking motion as if to bless Fran's departure. Jo Ellen accompanied him as he headed across the room.

"See, I told you he talked funny," she said and flipped her hair again. "I mean, I know he's very important and has done a lot for the cause, but sometimes all I can concentrate on is his voice. Hey, I'm sorry I was holding your elbow, I didn't even realize it."

"That's fine. My elbow was tired today."

"I see a sense of humor in there somewhere, Congressman Fran Stewart," she said as he turned around near the door. "Say, I know you must have a lot of events to go to tonight, but some of the people in our office are getting together at *El Padrino* in about an hour or so to talk about some of the important legislative issues coming up. I know they'd love to hear your thoughts."

Jo Ellen tilted her head. Fran hesitated. Something was happening, and he needed to identify all available escape routes. He wasn't sure if he could see her again that night.

"That's very kind of you, Ms. Driscoll, but I have several functions on the other side of town." He hesitated. "Listen, I'm going back to my office to do a little paperwork. I'll check my schedule, and if it's possible, I'll try to stop by. But, please, don't you or your friends wait for me. Good to see you again, Ms. Driscoll," Fran said as if that were all it meant to him.

"Try to make it if you can. You know the environment, very important stuff."

"Bankers' hours again?" Fran said, smiling as he saw Neil coming out of the office with his two accordion folders." The clock chimed eight.

"Doggone, you caught me," Neil replied. "I thought if I got out now I could trick my body into thinking it had a regular job."

"This place will never be anything but a grinding wheel. If you can work up here, you can work anywhere." Fran paused. "I don't say it as often as I should but, you do a great job, Neil. You and Maddy have gotten me through some pretty tough times."

Eyes usually heavy with Capitol Hill grind opened wide at these words of gratitude. Neil smiled. "Thanks, boss. You're special to me and Maddy, and to a lot of other people. Never sell yourself short. Oh, by the way," Neil said with an impish grin. "If you get a chance, I know your constituents would feel so much better knowing you're hammering away at some of the paperwork on your desk."

"Pretty smooth, Neil. Did you ever think about running for office?"

"Maybe for a second, but, well, I like the thought that in my position, I could walk away if I had to. I think after you win your first election and find yourself a member, it's awfully hard to leave."

"Maybe you're right. I'll see you in the morning. There's nothing really on the schedule, so I should be able to get through a lot of that work. I want to get packed tonight."

Neil held up one his folders and waved as he walked down the fluorescent hall.

Fran knew it would only take him twenty minutes to pack for the weekend. Neil knew that too. He zipped up the garment bag hanging on the back of his door and could now do some work, watch television, go to sleep, or -- he had been thinking about it the whole time -- go to *El Padrino*. He had seen Jo Ellen Driscoll twice. He didn't know what she thought of him, and he wasn't sure what he was thinking about her. She brought life to things. The flowers in front of the building, invisible to him days earlier, were now deep red and bright yellow. What would he say to her if he went to the restaurant? What would she say to him? Had she really invited him simply to talk about the environment? She had held on to his elbow, he thought. She had a look in her eye as she flipped her hair. Carter would smile and say she recognized it when she saw other women looking at Fran. She thought her husband was completely oblivious to those looks. But Fran wasn't. He'd just never been interested in anyone but Carter.

Fran had fallen for her at the first political event he attended in Tennessee. A good friend, a political junkie of the first order, urged him to come along. It was a hot day and the only empty tables were near the barbeque pit. Fran and his pal sweltered as they ate messy portions of chicken and corn-on-the cob. Then a voice asked to take a seat at their table. Fran looked up not realizing his face was much in need of a napkin.

Carter pointed to her lower lip and smiled as Fran wiped his mouth. She was beautiful in that sundress. After his second phone call, she agreed to go out with him, thus beginning the love of his life.

But there was something about Jo Ellen. He dismissed the thought and watched TV for a while before acting on the decision he'd made much earlier that night.

Fran closed the cab door and walked toward the restaurant. He could still turn around, walk a couple of blocks and catch a taxi back to the office. Once he walked in and she saw him, it would be too late. She had that way, forward but not obnoxious, of making you feel you both knew each other better than you did. He consulted his watch, adjusted his jacket, and generally stalled as he considered going in. Suppose they weren't there? He could have a soda or just use the men's room and leave. It might be a relief to have more time to consider what the heck he was doing.

"How many?" the hostess asked as he peered around in the dark, searching out the corners of the front room and islands of tables in the room beyond.

"I had made tentative plans to meet some people. Mind if I take a quick look in the back?" Fran said.

"Be my guest," she said as she erased some numbers from a worn plastic sheet. He thanked her and started back through the aroma of pizza wafting around the ovens. He squinted to see those at the far tables but didn't recognize anyone. Turning toward a small area of three tables, all were empty, except one. Jo Ellen sat alone, head down, hair hanging forward over her face. He wasn't prepared for this; where was the group? He was three steps from the partition leading to the front room. If he moved now he could make it before she looked up, but he hesitated. She looked up and smiled, waving him over, as if she knew all along that he would come.

She stood and held her hand briefly on his shoulder as he paused behind the chair facing her.

"Well, guess I'm too late. I happened to be in the area after my last reception and remembered you folks were over here, so I thought I'd stop by. I was curious about several issues on your fact sheets. I'm sorry I missed the group," Fran said gripping the back of the chair tightly.

"Don't worry. It wasn't much of a discussion. They all left a little while ago. Since I invited you, I figured I should hang around for a bit. I'm really glad you've taken such an interest in the environment," she said, pulling his chair out while playfully prying his fingers loose.

"Oh, I really can't stay," Fran said. "The House is in session tomorrow morning and I'm leaving for my district in the afternoon."

"Boy, you think you have a lot to do. I mean, I know you work on all the big picture things, but listen to my schedule in the morning. I have to prepare a weekly round-up report for our ten o'clock staff meeting, then I have to fax a monthly progress report to my department chairman who's supervising my fellowship, and I have to finish an article for the EDC newsletter. But you know what, I'll get it all done. I always do, so why don't you sit for a while and then we can get going."

Fran sat down.

"Now what can I get for you?"

"What are you having?" he asked, pointing to her glass.

"Cranberry juice," she said, finishing the last of it. "Plain, but I'm going to get a refill with just a touch of vodka," she added, speaking to the waiter as both she and Fran waved away the menus he started to hand them.

"Just juice for me."

"Do you go back to your district every weekend?"

"Yes, though it all depends on the schedule. Sometimes we leave on Thursdays, sometimes Fridays. Your U.S. House of Representatives is not very family friendly."

"You have a family?" she asked, staring intently at him. Fran did not wear a wedding ring. He remembered placing it on Carter's finger as he stood alone with her in the funeral home. He suddenly felt like he shouldn't be where he was. The deep wound hadn't healed. He had never thought his lack of a wedding ring would make him a man without a family.

"Yes." He reached for his wallet. "This is my daughter Becky; she's fourteen, I think this picture is a year old; she had her new class picture taken last week. And this is my wife, Carter."

Jo Ellen reached for the wallet and moved it toward the candlelight. "They're both very beautiful," she said, smiling politely. "You must be very happy."

"I lost Carter last year. She and Becky were coming to pick me up at the airport. I was on an overseas trip and my schedule got all shifted so I had to get back early. Carter was the only one around to come get me. There's a narrow parkway near our house that doesn't allow any kind of trucks. But there was a pick-up, the guy had been drinking. He lost control, went sideways over the grass median and slammed into the driver's side. Carter was gone right away. Becky was knocked unconscious, ruptured spleen, broken arm. I feel very lucky that I didn't lose her too. She stays with her grandmother when I'm in Washington." Fran swallowed, looked down and wondered what had possessed him to speak so candidly to a total stranger.

Jo Ellen stared at him. "I am so, so sorry, I had no idea." She took in a deep breath and exhaled. "Want to order some calamari? This place has the best calamari."

"Calamari?" Fran asked. "Why not, I guess that makes about as much sense as anything else." He looked around, not recognizing anyone but wondering if anyone recognized him.

"This must have been a very difficult year for you. I can't imagine what it would be like to lose someone that you loved so much. My grandfather died about ten years ago, but other than that, it's me, mom and dad, and my little sister who's taking care of my cat Astrix. My apartment near the university isn't too far from their house. Astrix has a good deal, since I only have to teach two days I get to spend a lot of time with her the rest of the week. I feel so badly, I didn't mean to pry. I know what happened to you is very personal and it's none of my business."

"Ms. Driscoll, I . . ."

"If you want me to call you Congressman Stewart, I will, but can I ask you to call me Jo Ellen?

"Jo Ellen it is, and you can call me Congressman Fran Stewart." He smiled as he remembered what she had said to him as they were leaving the reception.

"How, about Fran?" she said, poking her finger into his hand.

"So, you're a professor; what do you teach?"

"American politics, but this is my first time in Washington. I should have come here a lot sooner, to get, you know, 'practical experience.' But my parents never had any extra money to set me up with an internship or volunteer position. Right after I got my Ph.D., a teaching position opened up at the university. With CSPAN and the internet, I stayed in touch enough with Washington. At least I thought I had, until I got this job and saw a little of what goes on behind the scenes. I get my travel paid for and a small stipend, enough to cover our calamari."

"Dr. Driscoll, let me take care of that. An official welcome to Washington."

When their food came, he held back. She was obviously hungry but made sure she dabbed the napkin to her lips after every fried piece she swirled in the saucer of marinara and ate. "You have to have some," she said as she pushed the food toward him.

He put two forkfuls on his plate and pushed the platter back toward her.

"Do you like being a congressman?"Fran looked at her. That was the kind of question Fran would get from a schoolgirl. Such a softball question could get him to open up more than he anticipated. Maybe Jo Ellen understood that.

"If you're asking whether I like my job, it would have been an unequivocal yes during my first term. I wouldn't have called it a job then, either, something more like a calling. When you first come here, I don't care what type of background you have, you come here with fire in your eyes, in your gut. Even as you see some of the old bulls who do little more than graze, you feel you're going to be different; you're going to get things done." He asked the waiter for the check.

Jo Ellen waited.

Fran scratched the back of his head then gave it a quick shake. But in answer to your question, it's okay."

"Please don't be impatient with me, I just wanted to know what you thought of your job, Fran," she said, her voice trailing off so that he barely heard his name. She rested her chin on her folded hands and scrunched her eyes. "I noticed that cologne the other night. It's pretty distinctive."

"You know a lot about men's colognes?" He wondered if she knew that her own sweet scent was something he'd had in his mind since he'd met her.

"I didn't say I did, just that it's interesting. It's zippy."

"Zippy?"

"Yes, zippy. What's it called?"

"Aqua Brava. It's a long story."

"Brave water, that's great."

Fran placed three tens on the bill. "Are you ready?"

"Sure," she said, then whispered, "Brave Water," before laughing.

"Do we share a cab again?" he asked. "I'm going back to the Hill."

"Yes, I'm on the way." She got in first and slid over to the middle. Fran noticed but didn't say anything. She gave the driver directions, but said nothing more. Fran stayed silent as well. When they got to her apartment, he opened the door, got out and reached for her hand. She looked at him, then the ground, then at him. "Would you like to come up?"

"Did you forget about all the work we both have tomorrow?" He walked her to the front door. He wasn't ready; he had climbed to the top of the wall but couldn't jump to the other side. "I enjoyed talking with you tonight. Don't forget to send me those materials you're working on. If you get a chance, drop them at my office. Let me know when, and I'll try to be there."

She smiled, then pressed the code into the keypad and waited for her door to open.

CHAPTER 5

The President, White House, Monday, 4:30 p.m. meeting to discuss the crisis in the Balkans. Fran looked at the rest of next week's Washington schedule. Once May started, it got packed. Wouldn't be so bad if Congress had been in session more in the early part of the year. But he learned long ago not to bring logic into congressional scheduling. He looked out the plane window. He was over his home, well childhood home, before his family moved to Virginia when Dad started his new job. Virginia was okay, but he loved Tennessee. His grandfather had been one of the driving forces in getting the Tennessee Valley Authority up and running, and his work could be seen in the dams and waterways visible as the plane started its descent. As a boy, Fran walked through the Great Smokies and over Fontana Dam, now part of the Appalachian Trail. There was no better guide than his grandfather. When Fran finished at the University of Virginia, there was never any doubt that he would return to the Volunteer State. He was able to find a job the next county over and that's where he met Carter Craighill.

"Flight attendants, please prepare for landing."

Gordon Stokes met him at the airport as always. It was easy to spot Fran's district manager: tall as his boss, his sunglasses perched atop yellow crayon hair and a bright bow tie that always jaunted to one side. Punctual, dependable, Gordon had worked for Fran since the beginning. He didn't mind the long hours, driving Fran around to functions in the mobile office; a modified Econoline van. But whenever Fran saw him, he thought about what would have happened if he'd only been available to pick him up that terrible night. Gordon had been on vacation in Canada hunting with some buddies. He had planned it around Fran's being out of the country. He tried not to, but Fran always thought during that brief instance when he entered the airport that if Gordon hadn't been on vacation all might have been different.

Gordon took Fran's carry-on. "Good to see ya, boss. Here's your new schedule, just a few changes. They wanted to start your advisory meeting earlier tonight, but you've got dinner reservations at seven with Becky. I told them you can't do it before eight-thirty. A little griping, but no big deal."

Fran smiled. "Good work, Gordo. Don't let them push you around." Fran sat back in the seat and began to dial as the van traveled down back roads to avoid traffic on Rte. 40. Signal dropped. "Damn," he muttered as he redialed. "They don't have all this new cell phone technology perfected."

"Daddy?" came Becky's voice.

"Be there in about twenty minutes, honey. Is your grandmother going to join us?" Fran said, taking a deep breath.

"She left about a half-hour ago to bring some materials to someone. She said maybe next time."

"See you soon, Honey." Seemed the only time he'd seen Feeney during the last year was when she didn't know he was coming to the house or at some political function they both had to attend. She was short with him in private, but plastered on a smile at events, making sure her son-in-law mingled with everyone.

Becky loved Fowler's. Ribs, chops, aged meat in glass refrigerated cases. Hush puppies, corn bread, stringy fries in baskets, and almond cake with vanilla ice cream. She always had almond cake with vanilla ice cream. They liked to sit in the back, although invariably Fran would see someone, or many someones and – this was part of his job – stop to talk. He would start grinding his teeth behind his smile, especially if it were a long story or problem. This was time off the clock he had with Becky. She was usually pretty good, but would start the hand squeeze when impatient. Fran tried to end the conversation without offending one of his good constituents. Sometimes it worked, sometimes it didn't. He found that he was beginning to care less how successful he was.

Becky was full of stories tonight. There was this new boy, and he knew a lot about her dad, and he wanted to know if he could ever meet the congressman. "One thing, I have to tell you," she said. "I think he likes me."

"Oh, is that so?"

"He's been asking my friends about me. The girls just think he's very cute. But I haven't spoken to him much, and when Candice and I went grocery shopping the other day, he was in the store. But I pretended not to see him."

"Well, you let me know if you want me to meet him. Maybe we could pick him up and go for a pizza."

Her eyes shot up. "Daddy, he has his own car. He's sixteen."

"Sixteen? Don't you think he's a little old for you, young lady?"

"Grandmother knows he likes me. She met his father, the new president of First Savings and Trust, and he said that Carl talks about me all the time. I think Grandmother plans to invite the family over for dinner one night to welcome them to town."

Just like Feeney, he thought, interfering.

At the end of the night, after dropping Becky off and meeting with his congressional advisory committee -- some good friends with good ideas, others that required the rubber mask – he walked up the sagging wooden steps of an old building in one of the seedier parts of town and placed his key in the deadbolt lock. It was a small room that he now called home. Most of his things were still in cardboard boxes. A formal living room lamp sat on a card table that he used as a desk. A wooden chair served as a night table and stood next to a box spring and mattress on the floor. The rent was cheap and the big rooms downstairs had been perfect for all the meetings, volunteer activities, and endless planning sessions of his first and subsequent congressional campaigns.

Feeney had offered him, at least in the slightest whisper he had ever heard, one of the rooms at her house. He couldn't see living there, even for short periods of time. Besides he recognized that with all the strange hours and late nights he kept at home, his being there would be disruptive. He kept telling Becky he was roughing it in the old storage room and that as soon as he got time, he'd look for a nice home for them. But he didn't know when that would be.

He hadn't realized much from the sale of their house; they hadn't put much down and he and Carter figured that while it would be tight getting in, their little mansion would build up equity for them quickly. Carter was making good money as a senior vice president of a telecommunications company that gobbled up new business as it brought a totally new dimension to the way people got their information and spoke to each other. His wife not only met the demands of her job, but took on assistant coaching duties for Becky's softball team. Fran was the one who had volunteered, thinking he could work it into his schedule. But congressional responsibilities proved too much and he ended up just giving Carter advice over the phone. Carter was also the go-to person concerning Fran's campaigns. She tried to stay in the background but the staff relied on her ability to grasp complex political matters. But in the end, there was little insurance money and the cost of Becky's private school and college fund, all managed on a congressman's salary; Fran just couldn't see how he was ever going to get a house, a house his daughter wouldn't be ashamed to live in. Carter had managed their finances. He was horrible with money. He would think about that at times when he voted on one multi-billion dollar program after another.

His answering machine kept flashing out "memory full" as he sat on the bed and listened to the distorted drone of messages. He was listening only for one voice; any others would eventually get to Neil or Gordon.

"Daddy, I just got home. I had a great time at the dance; wait till I tell you what I found out about Carl. I wish I could see you again this weekend, but I know you have to leave before I get home from the scout camporee on Sunday. Is there a later plane you could take? I love you Daddy." That was the last message of the night. He turned the machine off and realized he had erased all the messages.

He thought about Jo Ellen. There was no clear next step as he thought about the awkward way things had been left. Washington seemed so far away. He knew he still had a responsibility to those who had elected him, and he felt he could still stoke the dying embers in his gut if he had to. Becky was so proud of him. Could she be proud of him if he were any-thing else?

The weekend rushed by quickly. Gordon picked him up early on Saturday morning: pancake breakfast at the firehouse, breakfast at the 4H, breakfast at the rod and gun club, announcing the winners at the county science fair, three lunches with remarks at each, John and Katie's wedding and a brief stop at the reception, Knights of Columbus dinner/dance (ten dollars-worth of raffle tickets), teacher-of-the-year dinner, the town of Linton Republican man-of-the-year dinner with remarks, paperwork to sign in the campaign office. Back up the sagging stairs at one-thirty in the morning. Gordon would be picking him up in five hours; he had ten functions to attend before he left for the airport. It was an election year; one thing ran into another. He often felt like he was in a *Hard Day's Night*. Back in Washington, he took his pillow out of the plastic bag and knew that "working like a dog . . . he should be sleeping like a log."

May was a tough month; no holidays until Memorial Day and Congress actually had meaningful legislation to consider. In an election year, there were big chunks of time scheduled later in the year for recess. Members needed to be back in their districts to campaign. Fran would soon begin circulating his petitions to meet the end-of-June deadline so his name would be on the ballot. He sometimes feared a primary more than the general election in November, but so far no one in his party seemed disgruntled enough to challenge him for the nomination. Neil was on any rumor like a German Shepherd. Neil was not going to let anyone kick him out of his yard. Polls showed Fran comfortably ahead of anyone real or imagined. Unless he was caught robbing money from a poor box at a church, he was in.

Maybe now was the time to talk with Becky, explain that he'd done his best but that he didn't think congress was the best place for him now. He didn't want to be sleep-walking through an important job as did many of his colleagues who should have left long before.

But election year was a spinning kayak ride down a wild river. All efforts to get ashore, to talk about such an important matter, escaped him. The campaign brought a load of fundraisers, mailings, and even more events to shoehorn into his schedule at home. Then the debates, walks handing out literature, early mornings, late nights until mornings became nights and nights mornings. The light shining on the schedule in his mind went out, as if a circuit breaker in some basement had been thrown. He was okay as long as the breaker worked. Carter had known when to throw the breaker; he was still learning.

CHAPTER 6

His assignment to the Foreign Affairs Committee brought Fran to the White House more than he expected. Issues before the Energy and Commerce Committee were important to his district and he had worked hard to secure a place on that panel.

The Foreign Affairs Committee was his fourth choice. When the leadership asked him to also take a seat on that Committee, he figured why not. He had been interested in other countries ever since he and Carter on a whim early in their marriage decided to live in Portugal for four months. Even though he had several letters of introduction for international corporate positions, he couldn't land a job. Carter enrolled in a language course and Fran did most of the shopping until he came home with a five-liter container of olive oil. They did some local sightseeing on days she was free, but they saw the end coming. Returning almost broke and longing for football games and everything else he had taken for granted at home, he nonetheless recognized there was another way of looking at things out there.

He found he enjoyed going to the hearings, asking questions, visiting with foreign dignitaries when they came to the Hill. He knew Neil had at first thought this was a big waste of time, but he eventually saw the angle.

New groups of ethnic Americans were starting to play a more visible role in the political arena and making themselves known to the treasurer of Fran's Campaign Committee.

He knew others with him on the van ride to the White House had likewise not envisioned themselves as foreign-policy deliberators. Several read briefing books, some newspapers, one spoke on the phone, and two, the least visionary among them, slept.

Fran tried to study his briefing materials but his mind kept drifting to Jo Ellen. When would she call? Would she call? He thought about her a lot more when he was in Washington than back home. He had left rather abruptly the other night and wondered if that had been enough for her to write him off.

The White House's maps had wavy arrow patterns showing which way the Serbs were headed and where the Croats' positions were strongest. Bright colors showed the new configurations of territory in what was now a dismembered Yugoslavia. As the briefing began, a general shot at the map with a red laser pointer. He spoke about people and places whose names were tongue-tying jumbles of consonants. The presentation ended with no clear ending.

As the lights went on, Fran looked over at one of his colleagues who had nodded off about twenty minutes earlier. His eyes opened as the president said, "As you all can see, this Bosnia situation is not going to be easy."

The president continued on for another twenty minutes before taking questions from the twenty members who were seated around the big table. Fran had heard about these White House meetings. It was rambling all over the place, with the same questions asked in different ways, and the president and his assistants repeating the same non-committal and vacuous answers.

"Will the U.S. send in troops?" asked Fran's committee chairman.

"Don't know," the president responded.

"Can the UN troops there now stop the genocide?" The congressman next to him asked.

"We'll have to continue monitoring this issue," the president said.

"How much would it cost for us to launch a bombing campaign?"

The president turned to one of his aides. "Congressman, we'll have to see about funds from the next two fiscal years and determine how much is in the pipeline."

The meeting had run for almost three hours, and some members sat doodling, staring at the ceiling, or looking at their watches in disbelief. Fran realized he knew little more about Bosnia than when he first arrived at the White House. If that was the president's objective, he had achieved it. He could check the box that he'd consulted congress, but he certainly wasn't going to *involve* congress in running any war.

Yet, Fran to his surprise, still felt engaged and somewhat hopeful. Even though the President was discussing one of the biggest international disasters since World War II, he seemed relaxed. Did he have some secret plan, some card up his sleeve to win this geo-political poker game? Or did he realize he didn't have the foggiest idea and would have to feel his way in the dark, but was somehow not intimidated by that option? Fran didn't know. He hoped there was a plan. But he only saw everybody's limitations.

The rain they called for on Tuesday arrived in a downpour on Wednesday afternoon. Sheets of water pounded against the window in Fran's office. Looking down at Maddy's desk, Fran saw that all the walnuts were gone. He scanned the piles of paper until he found his call sheet. The name wasn't there.

"Anything, I can help you with?" Maddy asked.

"No, I'm fine. I'll get to those calls in the morning."

Maddy headed toward the back office. Fran started to close the door to the hallway when he saw a young woman bending at the shoulders and shaking her hair. The bottom of her dress was soaked, and she held a soggy newspaper that must have been used as a cover for both herself and the oversized white envelope she held in her other hand. She started to straighten out her dress, oblivious to Fran's presence.

"I have an umbrella you can borrow for next time," he said.

Jo Ellen turned with a start. He walked toward her and held out his folded handkerchief. "I didn't see you," she said, shaking her head. "I have no idea where that storm came from. It opened up pretty bad as I got off the Metro. I wasn't sure if I'd catch you this late, but I finished those background materials and thought you might want them."

End of the day. She shows up at the end of the day, Fran thought. "That was very nice of you. Come on in. Would you like some water, unless you've had enough?"

She smiled and walked into the office. As Fran went through the introductions, Maddy stared at the wet, unfurled handkerchief in the visitor's hand. She looked up at Jo Ellen. "My goodness, you're all wet. Let me get you a towel."

Neil walked out. "May I help you?" Now both his top advisers had become involved in a matter he wished to handle himself.

"No, the Congressman and I have things under control," Maddy replied as she returned. Neil nodded and walked back into his office.

"Thank you," Jo Ellen said as she handed Fran's handkerchief back to him.

Maddy's eyes rose above her glasses as she left the room. Fran and Jo Ellen stayed in the front office. He did not want to ask her into his personal office although he saw her look at it more than once through the doorway.

"Do you want to get something to eat?" she asked.

Fran hesitated. "Nothing on the schedule I can't put off till next year."

He wanted to leave quickly; if they stood around any longer Maddy would reappear and start her interrogation. It would be done very pleasantly; Maddy was an expert at getting things out of people. It was a knack that served Fran well as she passed on all sorts of gossip. But he didn't want her to find out more about Jo Ellen, not yet.

"Good," Jo Ellen said, smiling.

Fran detected a mission accomplished look in Jo Ellen's eyes as he grabbed the umbrella hanging on the back of his door. "See you guys in the morning," he called out to Maddy and Neil. "If you have anything for me, leave it on my desk." He and Jo Ellen hurried out the door before either Neil or Maddy could respond.

They were business-like walking into El Padrino, quite different than the cab ride over. Jo Ellen sat right next to Fran. Her hand was on his shoulder, then his hand, as if she were unsure that her words could convey to him how she felt, even though the conversation centered on only the traffic, the weather, her cat, and sometimes whatever was being advertised on the side of a passing bus. A rapt smile crossed his lips as he listened to her.

"Hungry?" he asked as they unfolded their napkins.

"Salad and pizza sound okay," she said. Maybe with a glass of Cabernet?"

"How did you know that's what I wanted?" Fran asked as his smile met hers. Her face shone in the reflected candlelight.

They had eaten their meal quickly and were now finishing a second glass of wine. They looked at each other.

"Congressman Fran, are you staring at me?" she asked.

Her tone was serious, and Fran felt himself stumbling, unsure of what to say. Maybe he had misread Jo Ellen.

"I'm sorry, I think I was daydreaming for a second."

"Well, if you were staring, I'm glad," she said as she placed her hand near his. He reached for her hand and held it.

Her head was on his shoulder during the cab ride to her apartment. There wasn't much heat coming into the passenger compartment and the car's poor suspension system put an exaggerated swerve into the car's turn.

"Please read the materials I brought over. I spent a lot of time preparing them. Quite frankly, it's the first thorough revision of the stuff they've been handing out. I worked on both the domestic issues, you know logging, emissions, etc., and also took a stab at tropical forests and coral reefs. I tried to keep the scientific stuff to a minimum. I want people to understand these issues, and I want them to feel that we need a national dialogue. Let's listen to all sides, but we need to be doing more while we still can. I hope you take the time to read what I've prepared."

Fran felt her keen interest in these issues. She seemed to know what she was talking about. "I'll read them. You know, I've always thought these issues were important."

"Good man, that Congressman Fran."

"Thank you, Dr. Driscoll."

The cab stopped, and the driver called out the fare. Fran handed him several bills and opened the door for Jo Ellen.

She looked at him. "I guess I'm going to ask you again. Would you like to come up?"

"Sure," he said. It was one of the simplest decisions Fran had made in a long time.

She lived in an old house that had been converted into three floors of apartments targeted to students. As they walked up the narrow stairs of worn linoleum, they entered a theater of faded spaghetti smells wrestling with the lingering aroma of what seemed like tacos. Eagles' guitar riffs dueled with some kind of rap music with a punching bass line.

She looked back at him. "Still with me, Congressman Fran?" she whispered.

"Absolutely," he said.

"Good," she kissed him on the cheek and continued up toward the top floor.

When the light came on, Fran found himself in a studio apartment that must have been home to an endless stream of transients. The fixtures were worn, but it was clean and all her things very neatly arranged. Books, what looked like journals, reports, and a pile of legal pads lay atop a card table serving as a desk not far from a small sink and mini refrigerator near the window. Two walls were bare, but the third one made his head snap back. There in front of him, neatly-spaced, hung three pictures: an oversized poster of Machu Picchu with a staring llama in the foreground; a similar-ly-sized poster of the Three Stooges playing football; and in the middle, a blown up photo of Jo Ellen in a white tank top, sun glasses, and a floppy hat, standing with a well-tanned man in sunglasses in front of Prometheus in Rockefeller Center.

She was silent, watching him the whole time. "Well?"

"Looks like a very creative mind has been at work."

She laughed. "I've always wanted to go to Machu Picchu."

"I've been there but wasn't brave enough though to climb that moun-tain there," said Fran as he pointed to dark green cliffs looming behind open spaces of grass.

"You've been everywhere," she said, somewhat annoyed.

"Yeah, I've been to New York City also, but I've never played football with the Three Stooges." Who's the gentleman in the photo with you?"

"That's Gardner Chase. Not much of a gentleman. He lives in New York. Haven't seen him since that picture was taken about two years ago. Hey, I have a small bottle of wine in the fridge, want some?"

"Just some water would be fine. I can't stay long. I've got five breakfasts tomorrow, one starting at seven."

"How long is long?"

"Maybe a half-hour." He put his hand on her shoulder. "Do you want to see my schedule for tomorrow?"

"No," she said, feigning sadness.

"You know it's not easy running this big government of ours. If they're going to get their money's worth out of Congressman Fran, he's got to get a good night's sleep."

She got them each a glass of water, and they sat on the tiny futon. Jo Ellen became withdrawn, talking about her work clinically. Fran couldn't follow a lot of what she was saying, but she didn't seem to notice. He took a final swallow of water and put the glass down. She seemed to love her work, bordering on obsessively.

He got up slowly and they walked toward the door. He turned and looked at her. She was very close. They reached for each other at the same time and kissed. He could feel the back of her dress pull tight as she reached up to pull him in. He wanted to stay and knew she could feel it. He eased his mouth to her ear, but she spoke first.

"I hope I didn't bore you with my ramblings. I just start thinking about these issues; there's been so much good research done. I just feel more and more that people here in Washington aren't taking these matters seriously enough."

"You may be right. Try to remember though there are lots of important things competing for people's attention."

"You're right. I had planned out in my mind what it would be like when you finally came up here and then I wasted time talking about my work. I'm sorry."

He smiled. "I do have to get going. Next time I'm here I'd like to hear what you had planned. I'll call you tomorrow." He opened the door. The lingering aromas – he thought the spaghetti was winning – and the Eagles and their rap competition –give the edge to the Eagles – accompanied him on his trip downstairs.

CHAPTER 7

"Not much white space on the schedule is there?" Neil said as he lay his files down. Maddy stood at the copier juggling an ugly pile of forms and short pieces of paper that had to be copied individually.

"Five breakfasts; that may be a new record," Fran said as he circled appointments and meetings. He looked at another piece of paper that Neil handed him containing a list of upcoming political events and fundraisers back home in the district. "Make sure I go over this with you today. Geez, I can't believe all this campaign stuff is upon us again. Right after the first vote, I'll call you so we can nail this down."

"Like the hair, boss," Neil said as he gave a thumbs up.

Fran touched his hair, which had grown out past his collar. "Yeah, starting to get the rock star look. Don't know, might stay with it."

"That's not the only thing different around here," Maddy added.

"It's tough to get anything by you and Neil, my watchdog committee." Fran knew whatever he said about Jo Ellen was locked away with his two top aides. "I met her at the New Zealand embassy, and we had dinner last night. She's a professor here for a few months on a fellowship with some environmental group. That's all there is, folks."

Meetings with his finance committee, media consultant, pollster, and the petitions for the fall election: he wondered if Jo Ellen would be as good as Carter at helping him with all this, then wondered why he was even asking himself that question. He headed to the House chamber as the cluster of bells announced a roll-call vote, figuring he had about another ten minutes to get there. It had warmed up so Fran took off his suit jacket and flung it over his shoulder. As he approached the Capitol, the strong midday sun hit the white stone of the building and spun out a glare. You did a lot of squinting in front of the Capitol on a sunny day. He was soon on the House floor and felt the slight drift of air conditioning circulating throughout the huge cavern. House Resolution 52, Commemorating the Contributions of the American Red Cross. He reached for his voting card and placed it into the electronic voting machine. He pushed the green button.

"I'm proud of you Fran, taking such a courageous position to support the Red Cross," said Sherm Levin, who had come to Congress the same year as Fran.

"You know me Sherm," Fran said.

"Well, I hope you show the same spine on these other bills. We have Commemorating Nurses Week, then one commending Sacagawea for helping Lewis and Clark, and another commending school-crossing guards," Sherm said, fidgeting with his rumpled suit then brushing at tufts of frizzy hair below a completely bald head.

"That's why the voters sent people like you and me to Washington; because they knew we could cast the tough votes," Fran said, matching his colleague's deadpan tone. "Now remember Sherm, there's an important resolution in that batch; the one honoring the Baseball Hall of Fame. I'm one of the original cosponsors I'm counting on you to get it passed. This is the *real* Hall of Fame."

They smiled at each other and Fran walked back to the cloakroom. There was one tucked away in each of the back corners of the House chamber; one for the Republicans, the other for the Democrats. As Fran walked into the former, he looked at the empty phone booths on either wall, relics of a past era. At the middle of the room was a miniature soda fountain where several members gathered at the counter, eating sandwiches and drinking coffee. Around the corner was a table and a line of oversized leather chairs facing the TVs broadcasting the House proceedings. Several of the members were hunched over, asleep. Young high school pages sat by the cloakroom manager's desk, watching as he spoke on the phone and monitored what measures the House was debating and when specific members had to be on the floor to speak. The cloakroom was a hideaway, a clubhouse.

Fran stepped into the booth, closed the wood and glass accordion panels, and sat down. The ceiling light and fan came on as he dialed Neil's direct number. He had all his folders in front of him. They had a lot to go through.

"We ready to roll?" Neil asked.

"As ready as I'll ever be."

"First thing," Neil said, "you guessed it, is our good local chairman Calvert Dixon. He's calling two, sometimes three times a day, wanting to know if we've gotten the speaker for his dinner. He's even gotten Creighton to start making calls." Creighton Tillman worked for Feeney. He was her muscle; a southern gentleman schooled in backroom politics and business. Feeney Craighill rarely lost her temper in public; only rarely did she give in to a wry smile. When she wanted something straightened out, people heard from Creighton. He never left any fingerprints.

"I'll handle Creighton," Fran said, a note of growing disdain in his voice. "Look, I'll try to talk with Henson Clark again. Who do we have as a backup?"

"Former state Senator Doris Brask. I've gotten rejections from everyone else," Neil said. "And even though Feeney is a friend of Doris, your mother-in-law will be just as mad as Calvert if that's the best we can do."

"All right, all right," Fran said as he leaned on the wooden platform below the phone. "What else?" For the next twenty minutes they went over various legislative proposals. "What's next?"

Your petitions have to start circulating next month; there's a package at the campaign office you have to review. I'll make a note and remind you to bring it back so I can look at it too. Hold just one second. Maddy's just handed me a note that Ms. Driscoll called earlier. Do you want her number?"

Fran copied down Jo Ellen's number. "So we about done, Neil?"

"There's quite a bit more that we really need to go over," said Neil, even as he realized that his foot couldn't stop this door from closing. "Your amendment's coming up this afternoon. Did you get a chance to look at your statement and the materials we prepared?"

"Not yet, but I will. I'm sure it's good. Anything else?"

Maddy could tell from Neil's end of the conversation what was happening. She touched at her hair, walked over to her desk and picked up the bag of walnuts.

"No, I guess not."

"Neil, we'll get to this just as soon as I get back to the office, I promise. Hey, maybe we'll even walk up the street and get one of those dirty-water dogs and a soda."

"Okay, boss," was all Fran heard as he hung up and proceeded to his next call.

"Jo Ellen Driscoll," came the voice at the other end of the phone.

"Dr. Driscoll, Congressman Fran Stewart returning your call. I'm out here on the front lines, taking care of your nation's business."

"Congressman Fran, that's just where I'd expect you to be. You're my hero, you know. You were going to call today, remember?"

"I know; I've just been snowed under. I have a monster schedule when I get back home tomorrow. I should be done around six. Want to get something to eat?"

"That's sweet, and any other time I'd say yes but not tonight," Jo Ellen paused.

Fran sat up quickly as the playful intimacy faded. He felt his palms begin to sweat and his stomach riddled with tiny comets crashing into each other. "You don't want to go out tonight?" he said plaintively.

She waited a little longer, testing him and herself. "I didn't say that. I'd like to go to a movie. *Forrest Gump* is supposed to be good; about this guy and this girl he loves and how he goes from one unbelievable situation to another. It's playing over in Rosslyn. Can you meet me at 6:30, the Metro entrance at Union Station? Get something to eat beforehand. We can have a big box of M&Ms for dessert."

Fran felt relief wash through him, along with clear recognition of his feelings for Jo Ellen. "Yeah, a movie sounds fine," he said, still searching for better footing. "I'll see you then."

"Good luck on your amendment. I saw it listed in the *Legislative Digest*. Wow them with your charm!"

There was a Metro stop about three blocks from Jo Ellen's apartment. They spoke about the movie as they held hands on the escalator to street level. She was over analyzing, but he loved listening to her and nodded whenever she said, "Don't you agree?"

His amendment had passed. She had watched it on CSPAN. "You're good Fran. I thought they had you a couple of times there. But you kept on message and you remained calm. As they got more agitated, that slight smile of yours showed a, well, good leadership quality. You showed real mastery of the issue. The smart alecks couldn't rattle you. Remember when you told that one fat guy that you received several letters from doctors in your district that food labeling could help fight obesity. You weren't mean, but you really zinged him."

"Oh, you liked that, did you?" The wind was picking up and Fran found himself pulling his hair back from his eyes more than usual.

"Yes, I did," she said with a straight face while squeezing his arm. "I like your hair longer," she said, absentmindedly flipping her own light brown hair.

"I'm not even going to ask this time," she said. "I'm going to open the door and walk upstairs."

He followed into her apartment as she turned on the light. It looked the same as it did the other night. Although he thought there were more books on her table. She took off her shoes and walked over to heat up some water, pulling two mugs from the cupboard and opening a bakery bag on the counter. "These were fresh last night," she said, pointing to two glazed doughnuts. "If we dip them into tea, they'll be fine."

"I eat day-old doughnuts all the time."

She placed the tea and doughnuts on the coffee table and sat next to him on the couch, folding her legs up under her dress. "Back home tomorrow?"

"Yup." Fran noticed that Jo Ellen was suddenly quiet. Usually she would have an array of follow-up questions about home, what was it like; what was Becky like? What was his house like – she was shocked at what sounded like a run-down room over the campaign office, just a step above him sleeping in his office in Washington. One night she asked him if he thought she would like it back home in Tennessee. He seemed startled, then smiled and said I guess you'd like it just fine. He couldn't picture her at home. All he could muster was a comment about all the great "environmental things" she could see: the mountains, the streams, the rolling hills of green.

She pulled him toward her and held his head in her hands as he took her waist. Looking straight into his eyes she said, "I like you a lot, Congressman Fran." She waited for him to answer and held him till he did.

Fran felt a smile twitch on his face. It hadn't happened this quickly with Carter, but he knew the feeling. He brought Jo Ellen closer to him.

"I like you a lot."

The words hung in the air as their lips met. "I want us to more than like each other. It's taken me a long time to begin to feel this way about someone again, but I really feel I can trust you. Fran, I might be a bit more complicated than you think. I had a rough time with someone. It almost destroyed me. Little by little I'm getting back. Please forgive me if I get harsh or impatient. I was in serious counseling. I don't know why I'm telling you all this. I know what a year it has been for you. But since I met you, I've dreamed about the two of us. Pretty far-fetched, right? I mean you a congressman and me; well I'm not much of a player am I?"

Fran took it all in. Maybe she needed him as much as he believed he needed her. She lay now in his arms. "I've thought about you since the embassy."

"Love at first sight, Congressman Fran?"

"You can change moods quickly."

"If I'm going to keep up with you I have to be quick on my feet," she said, shooting him a playful look. "Was it?" she asked.

"You might be on to something."

"Oh let's make it something more than liking each other."

"Yes, let's see. But you know I need to go now."

"Will you call me this weekend?"

"Yes."

CHAPTER 8

There were fewer people than usual on the plane and Fran made it quickly to his rendezvous spot with Gordon. "Nice pants," Fran said, pulling on his own blue seersucker pants and pointing to Gordon's brown pair.

"What can I say? Guess seersucker's breaking out all over." He didn't particularly like matching his boss, but Gordon loved seersucker too much to give it up.

Fran flipped through the four-page schedule and stopped when he came to Saturday morning. "When was this added?" He pointed to the 10 a.m. appointment with Creighton Tillman.

"Creighton called about an hour before I left to pick you up. He said it was 'quite important' that he meet with you and that you would want to meet with him as soon as possible. You know that way he talks to people at the office as if we're a bunch of lab monkeys."

"I've often wondered if Creighton tapes our conversations, then plays them for Feeney."

"That Creighton, I've learned never to underestimate him. I hated to put it on the schedule, but I didn't want you to get hit by an angry call from Feeney."

"You're right, Gordo. Maybe I can call Creighton early in the morning and ask him to stop at Ruth's Bakery and get some doughnuts."

"I'd love to see that."

"So, I'm meeting Becky at Fowler's?"

"Yeah, she said she was getting a ride with one her friends."

Fran wondered if it was Carl, the sixteen-year old. Fran removed his sunglasses as he got out of the van. His fingers, like a resolute sheep dog, worked to bring the errant hair tufts back in place. His eyes adjusted slowly to the restaurant's subdued lighting and several constituents greeted him as he approached the hostess station.

"Your daughter is back around to the right, congressman," said the smiling girl who didn't look much older than Becky.

As he turned the corner, he saw Becky, her face aglow as she spoke between bites of bread to a curly-haired boy in a tan jacket, blue oxford and striped tie. Fran paused, even as people began to recognize him. She looked so much like her mother, and the curly-haired boy reminded him of how he might have looked in Carter's eyes. He had that same hesitant, awkward presence that Fran recognized from his first dates with Carter. And Becky had all the ebullience and confidence that attracted him to her mother.

A powerful thought grabbed him. It might not be this boy now, but sometime she'd be staring into the eyes of the one who would carry his daughter away. Fran would be alone.

"Daddy, hi," Becky said as she jumped up and hugged her father.

There was still plenty left in that hug, Fran thought, as he leaned over to kiss his daughter on the top of her head.

"This is Carl Mahon. He moved into town a little while ago." The young man sprang up quickly, knocking over his half-full water glass.

"I'm so sorry," Carl said as he reached for the glass. "I'm very pleased to meet you, sir."

Becky giggled then caught herself, returning to the introduction she had practiced so carefully. "Carl is real interested in politics, and knows a lot about what's going on in Washington. You watch C-SPAN too, don't you Carl?"

"Yes sir, I do. I saw you when you had your amendment before the House. You did a real good job, sir."

"Well, thank you, Carl. I sometimes wonder how many people watch what we're doing in Washington." Fran knew Becky was watching him closely. She didn't see any red flags, and continued forward.

"Carl's Dad is president of First Savings and Trust, and was at the White House once for a meeting."

"I hope he got some of those White House pads and some cuff links or something," Fran said.

"Oh, he did sir, yes sir," Carl said eager to respond. "He even let me wear the cufflinks once."

"I had a pair, but I think I lost them," Fran added as the three looked down at their menus.

"Daddy, I told Carl you'd tell him all about how you got started in politics. He wants to run for office one day."

Fran brought his napkin to his lips and placed it back into his lap. He eyed his daughter to let her know he knew very well that he was in the middle of one of her hard sells. He had to admit, she was pretty good.

"Well, Carl, I admire anyone who is willing to work long, hard hours to be a public servant. If you do it right, it's a tough business, not glamourous like a lot of people think. People can say some pretty mean things about you, even your family. You can't lose sight of why you're elected: to help people, to help the country. It's easy after you're in office for a while to start to get a big head. It's happened to me at times."

Carl's mouth hung open. Becky narrowed her eyes. He was rambling.

"Dad, why don't you just tell Carl how you got started in politics, just the basics." Carl fidgeted.

"Yes, yes, I can do that. Well, Carl, you're starting at a much younger age than I did. Quite frankly, I wasn't very interested in politics. My folks would talk a little about elections and the economy when I was young, they voted, but that was about it. When I graduated from college in Virginia, I came back home and met Becky's mom. Her family was a different story. Her parents were very active: going to dinners, organizing campaigns, running the county committee. They lived for politics. Mrs. Stewart didn't have much choice in the matter. She started helping at a young age. Stuffing envelopes, answering phones, handing out campaign literature, going to parties. But she was never interested in running for anything, even though she was very popular and very smart. Her mother tried to get her to run for class president in high school and she refused. They got into a big fight about it."

"I never heard about that," Becky said.

"Oh yes." As they finished their salads Fran continued. "Anyways, I got involved through her. Mrs. Craighill always had Mrs. Stewart and I going to one function or another, and we met a lot of the political big shots when we helped out on their campaigns. Then something happened. Chester Randolph, who had represented this congressional district for twenty-five years, announced he had advanced stomach cancer and would be resigning his office immediately. It was a bombshell. They called a special election. Mrs. Craighill came to our house and looked me straight in the eye to ask me if I wanted to run. She said she could keep other Republicans from running, but she told me she would have to know then and there. Becky's mom said it was up to me, but I think she wanted me to run; that was the feeling I got. I told Mrs. Craighill yes. She put on the biggest smile I'd ever seen on her face, and told me she would have a press release prepared for the morning. The next two months of campaigning were a blur. But somehow, I turned out to be pretty good at it, mainly because Mrs. Stewart had such a sharp insight into how we should play issues and how I should package myself for different groups. I won by eight percentage points and the next thing you know, Becky, her mom, and I were heading to Washington."

"Wow, that's amazing," Carl said. "I mean, you really knew how to take advantage of a great situation."

Becky watched her crush continue to ask questions of his new hero. Fran had no events to go to that night; he could wow Carl for as long as Becky wanted. But as dessert came, she told her father that they had to get to a party. She assured her dad that yes, Carl would bring her home by eleven. He was a very good driver, she said. Fran finished signing for the bill. The way Carl looked at him assured Fran that his daughter would return home safely. Becky kissed her father and walked out with Carl. Fran asked the hostess to call him a cab and went back to his room. He picked up the phone.

"Hello."

"Is this Dr. Driscoll?"

"Congressman Fran, how nice of you to call from so far away in Tennessee. In so early; no meetings to go to?"

"Amazing isn't it? I just had dinner with Becky and her new boyfriend."

What's his name?"

"Carl Mahon."

"Carl Mahon. Carl Mahon. What does he look like?"

"He's short, a little on the heavy side, his nose was always running, has a flatulence problem. Well, it was a little embarrassing."

"Very funny. What does he look like?"

"Oh he's a nice-looking boy, about five-ten, blond curly hair, nicely dressed. Seems to be fairly intelligent."

"As smart as Becky?"

"Yeah, probably, but Becky has that extra something, just like her mother. People open up around her. I'm not sure Carl realizes that yet."

"Do you miss me?"

"Yeah, I do."

"Do you wish I were there with you now?"

"Yeah."

"Me too. I want to come to Tennessee and meet everyone."

"Okay."

"Call me tomorrow."

Fran smiled as he heard the slightest smacking of lips. "I will."

On Saturday morning, Gordon sat at his desk in the outer office, listening to his phone messages. The storefront in a strip mall was easily accessible to constituents, had plenty of free parking, and affordable rent. Yet, tacky was the word that popped into Fran's head when he pushed the dust-streaked front door.

"Are they going to clean this? Or do they just want us to have a place to play tic-tac-toe?"

"I called," Gordon said. "They said they'd be here Monday."

Fran walked over to the Mr. Coffee, poured himself a cup, and opened up the Ruth's Bakery box Gordon had picked up on his way in. Glazed, sugar, old-fashioned. He took the old-fashioned. He didn't want his mouth or hands to be messy when Creighton came in, though he could make you feel as if you had crumbs on you when you didn't. Fran saw a big, black, late-model Cadillac pull up in front of the store.

"Darn, he's early," the congressman said as he chewed quickly. He grabbed a few napkins and hurried into his office.

The front door opened smoothly and an impeccably dressed man with perfectly groomed gray hair stepped in. His steady gait exuded authority.

"Good morning, Gordon. Is the Congressman in?" Creighton Tillman asked in a pleasant yet icy tone.

"Good morning, let me tell the congressman you're here," Gordon said.

"Creighton, can I get you a doughnut?" Fran asked. Creighton replied with a slight, involuntary scowl.

"No, thank you. I appreciate your meeting me on such short notice; I won't take much of your time. As you know, the big county dinner is three weeks from today. We are faced with a particularly troubling problem: as yet, we do not have a speaker. Our good county chairman, Calvert Dixon, is particularly upset. Feeney has assured Calvert that you will get him someone of national stature. You know he has asked for the Republican Leader. Feeney would like to be able to tell Calvert that you have resolved this problem," Creighton said, adjusting his already perfect Windsor knot.

Fran thought he was getting better at handling Creighton. No longer was he intimidated by the older man who spoke four languages, graduated first in his class from Yale Law School, and had developed and patented several medical devices that had made him tens of millions of dollars.

"Look Creighton, Henson Clark is a very busy man. He told me that he's sorry he hasn't been able to commit yet. He has several obligations, and he is exploring, as a favor to me, if he can somehow juggle his schedule and make our dinner. He will let me know as soon as possible." To Creighton's look of disgust, Fran shot back, "Look, I know this is a big headache for everyone, I'll speak with Calvert and I'll speak with Feeney."

"I'll pass on your comments to Feeney," Creighton got up from the rather worn chair provided by U.S. taxpayers.

Fran noted how out of place Creighton looked and thought hard as the older man left the room. Were Feeney and Calvert deliberately testing Fran to see if he had sufficient clout to get the Republican Leader to come to their dinner? The situation was taking on far more importance than it deserved. Yet clout was an important currency in politics. Fran wondered the cost to him if he failed. How would the vindictive Feeney play it? What was in it for the ambitious Calvert? How serious a wound would it be for his congressional career?

As Gordon drove him to the Elks' pancake breakfast, Fran took another look at his schedule. He figured he could grab an hour for himself if he arrived late at his only lunch and left early from his final breakfast. He wasn't going to call Feeney. He would take a chance that he'd catch her at home. He hoped that Becky would be there too.

The van drove up the pebble driveway bordered by azalea bushes whose white flowers seemed as large as linen napkins. The huge magnolia tree in the center of the turnaround towered higher than the roof. Candice, the Craighills' housekeeper of more than thirty years, stood on the front porch and waved as the van approached.

"Candice, haven't seen you for a while, have you lost weight?" asked Fran, even though he knew she hadn't.

"Maybe a little, Mr. Stewart, maybe just a little. It's good to see you, but Becky isn't here. She left about an hour ago to go shopping."

"Was she with Carl?"

"How did you know?"

"Just a lucky guess," Fran said realizing his little girl had her first steady. "Candice, what do you think of Carl?"

"I like him, Mr. Stewart. He's very polite, just like you and Mrs. Stewart taught Becky, and considerate. He makes her happy. She's always telling me, 'Carl this and Carl that.'"

"I'm glad to hear that. Please tell Becky I'll try to get in touch with her before I go back to Washington. Is Mrs. Craighill here?"

"Yes, I am," said Feeney, opening the front door.

"Good morning, Feeney," Fran said in a greeting that to an outsider would reflect none of the subtle animosity that Feeney and her son-in-law had directed toward each other in recent times.

"What can I help you with?" she said as Candice went inside. "I'm about ready to leave for a luncheon."

"May I come in for a minute?"

She exhaled deeply. "You may."

Gordon remained in the van sorting papers as Fran walked into the house. Feeney had stopped several feet from the door. The sheer curtains in the hall window puffed forward, caught by the light breeze cooling the house. She looked at Fran but said nothing.

"Feeney, I'm sure Creighton told you about our conversation this morning. I'll handle Calvert. We'll have a speaker for the dinner."

Feeney hesitated. She was not prepared for her son-in-law's direct approach. She tugged on the narrow belt of her dress and moved her head slowly to face him, like a destroyer readying one of its big guns. "Getting a speaker is the not the issue. Getting *Henson Clark* is the issue. We were led to believe that you would be able to get him. You have a lot of people counting on you." The big gun recoiled and Fran realized he had been hit. "Look, I'm sorry, it hasn't gone as smoothly as planned. I'll stay on it. But

Feeney, can't you cut me any slack? I've been doing the best I can this year. I know this has been rough for you, very rough. And I don't know what I'd do if you hadn't so graciously taken in Becky."

Feeney's glare intensified. "I don't know if you'll ever know how I feel. It was all senseless, so avoidable. And it isn't easy with Becky. Her mother had such plans for her and now it falls on me." Her eyebrows rose and her nostrils flared. Then, looking toward the mirror, she smiled and reached for her purse and her white gloves. "I must go. I will tell Becky you were here."

"We both had plans for her. Her mother wanted her daughter to be happy above all else. She knew her daughter," Fran protested, then paused. "I give up Feeney, I won't keep you any longer from your lunch."

"Good-bye."

She never called her son-in-law by name any more. Fran knew what she thought. She had been wrong all those years ago when she thought he was an up-and-comer. He didn't have it after all -- that drive to get to the top. Because of him her daughter had learned to settle. Then what he did to her that night. How dare he make her daughter come out. It was all so unnecessary. His driver should have been there. She didn't care what Fran said. He should have been there.

"I'm sorry I missed you Daddy," Becky said.

"I called yesterday afternoon and then again this morning," Fran said as the signal on the cell phone started to fade.

"Daddy, I can't hear you, where are you?"

"I've got meetings most of the day. I've got to get you a cell phone."

"Daddy, I still can't hear you very well."

"Then I've got to race back to the airport for a six-thirty flight." Gordon held his finger to his ear as Fran shouted into the phone. "I'll call you when I get to Washington."

"Daddy, I'm sorry. I still can't hear you very well," Becky said. The call dropped.

CHAPTER 9

"I guess this means we don't get to see each other tonight," an annoyed Jo Ellen said into the phone.

"The plane got in late. I've been up since five-thirty this morning driving all over Tennessee. I promised Becky I'd call her when I landed and now it's too late. It was not a great weekend," Fran said, stretching the phone cord to its limit as he walked from his desk to his bookcase.

"Okay, start at the beginning. What happened?"

Fran explained the speaker fiasco and recounted his fight with Feeney, about feeling like he was letting Becky down. He swigged some water and realized he had been talking a lot. It had been a long time since he had opened up like that to anyone. "I think I just need some sleep."

"You're tired, Fran. I've been looking at your schedule for tomorrow. You have too much. You need your sleep tonight. Skip some of those events tomorrow night, and come over here, say about seven. I'll get a movie. Call me in the morning."

"Okay."

Fran called Henson Clark's office first thing in the morning.

"Congressman, he won't be in today. He has several functions on the West Coast," the receptionist said.

"Is there a way to get through to him?"

"Congressman, we will certainly try to let him know you called if we hear from him, but we've been told he's going to be very hard to reach today."

This whole thing is nuts, Fran told himself. "Fine, if that's the best we can do."

Fran hung up and buzzed Neil. "What about your friend in the Leader's office? Heard back from him?"

"He said they would try to get a definite early this week," Neil replied. "But he said the same thing last week. We may have to nail down one of our standbys."

"No standbys, we need Clark," Fran snapped back. I'm going to have to go over there first thing in the morning."

Neil was quiet as he placed the phone down. He rarely saw his boss this angry.

Maddy opened Fran's door. "Congressman, the Frost Elementary School group is outside for their appointment, about twenty of them. You said you wanted to talk with them then have a photo on the House steps. Do you want me to bring them in now?"

"No, I'll buzz you when I can," Fran said.

"Okay," Maddy said as she retreated to the front office.

Neil walked in. "Boss, I know you have a lot today, but we have that list of things I gave you to discuss. There are some conflicts with your upcoming election events, and we've got to get the mailings out."

Fran needed a second. He walked to the door, his mask on. "Hi kids, come on in, thanks for coming to see me this morning."

Fran closed the phone booth door in the cloakroom and dialed Jo Ellen. He left a message then went into the House chamber and took a seat in one of the back rows. He waited half an hour and called again, hanging up as her voicemail came on. Call me in the morning was what she had said.

The afternoon was long. He still hadn't heard back from Jo Ellen. On his way to a briefing on the situation in Rwanda, where a genocide had killed over 800,000 people in less than a month, he passed one of the main reception rooms. Outside, stood an easel with a poster and a table with brochures and newsletters. "Stand up Tall to Be Heard," sponsored by the Association to Prevent Discrimination Against Dwarf-Americans," the poster read. Fran looked in the door.

"Congressman, we're so glad you came. Here's your name tag," said a girl who rocked slightly and stretched out an arm about half the size of Fran's.

"Oh, thank you very much," he said, his mask only half on. "I'm already late for a briefing, but who is that in there speaking?"

The young girl got up and opened the door a little wider. "Oh, that's Carson Handle. He's a great singer. His presentation has been about discrimination in the music business. You should hear his CD."

"Well, I'd like to stay, but I'm already late for an important briefing."

"Please take this, I'm sure you'll enjoy it," the girl said, as she handed a CD to Fran.

Fran looked at the title: "Moments Meant for Dawg Lovers," and the name Carson Handle. Can I take this under the new gift rules? Fran wondered. I guess I can always return it. I can't be mean to *this* girl and refuse to take it. "Thank you very much. I look forward to listening," he said.

"Bye, Congressman."

Fran walked into the briefing and sat down at the rectangular table as several colleagues, staff and even the briefers noticed his CD. He put it in his lap.

The briefers didn't paint a pretty picture. They pointed at maps showing the location of refugee camps and arrows identifying routes that emerging guerilla bands used to launch their attacks. "There are still major health problems in the camps. While the UN is nominally in charge, thugs and former military really run these camps, terrorizing anyone who causes them trouble. Sanitation is a real problem. While some have returned home, others are petrified at what might await them if they leave. These camps were set up as a temporary measure. Plastic sheeting only lasts so long."

"How are they doing on tracking down those who participated in the genocide?" one of the members asked.

"The new government has caught quite a few. They've got several thousand holed up at the soccer stadium. It's not the best situation, but its taking a while to set up the judicial machinery to try these characters."

The genocide was over, but as Fran listened, he wondered if the killing would ever end. The Tutsis and the Hutus still hated each other. When peacekeepers and aid missions pulled out, festering grievances would explode, and the machete would once again be king of the night.

Fran looked over at Burl Stephens, a member of the Committee for the past thirty years. How many of these briefings had old Burl been to? How many problems had he heard had been resolved only to hear later that fighting had broken out again? Burl nodded off.

When the briefing ended, Larry Bowling, a government consultant and former aid worker for Children's Relief International, walked over to Fran. Larry had been one of the first on the ground after the killings, before the big cholera wave hit the camps. Fran had known and admired Larry for several years, valuing his first-hand, unvarnished accounts of what was going on in the field. Larry looked down at the Carson Handle CD then looked at Fran.

"Fran, looks grim I know, but we've got to keep trying. I wanted you to know I left CRI several weeks ago. We were just going different ways. I got an offer from the State Department, so I'm doing some consulting for them. As always, any questions, give me a ring; here's my new card. And I have something else I wanted to give you. I've shared it with several people. A month or so after the killings, I visited a church school in Kigali. It had become a refuge for the new orphans. There were so many kids. Anyway, I took a shot at putting some of my thoughts down on paper. I've seen a lot of suffering in my time, Fran, but that day at the orphanage was something else."

Fran looked at the piece of paper Larry handed him. "Tears at St. Paul's: The Children of Rwanda." It was a poem. "Thanks for sharing this, Larry, thank you." Fran folded the paper and put it on top of the CD.

"Fran you must have had your beeper off. I tried to get in touch with you. Jo Ellen has called several times," Maddy said.

"I'll call her now." Fran looked at what remained in the bag of walnuts, he figured it was about five o'clock. He looked up: 4:50.

"I've been looking for you," Jo Ellen said, her voice hanging on the "you" for extra measure.

"I did exactly as you told me, Dr. Driscoll, but you weren't there."

"Well, now isn't that exactly like you, to call me when I'm not there. I've been in meetings all day. I'm gonna have to pull an all-nighter tonight. Our beloved chairman, your old friend, Cecil Brown, is testifying in the Senate tomorrow afternoon and I've got to put together testimony based on his notes. You know how he talks as if he's from another planet. I've got to put it into something that won't have the Committee scratching their heads. It's the first time he's ever testified. I'm afraid he's gonna go off on some tangent."

"So I guess I won't be seeing you tonight."

"Do you miss me?" she asked.

"Yes, I do."

"Be brave, Congressman Fran, we'll have a real nice time tomorrow night. Can't wait to see you." The last part was whispered, as though someone had come into her office.

"Can't wait to see you," he said, as he looked up to see Maddy walking in the door.

"Do you want me to come back?" his secretary asked.

"No, no come in."

"I like her Fran, I wasn't sure at first, but I've really gotten to like her."

He looked up, knowing by her expression that she wondered if she'd gone over the line again.

Fran smiled and nodded. "So have I, Maddy." He'd told someone how he felt about Jo Ellen. It felt good.

When Fran looked back, the two weeks following that discussion with Maddy was a series of steadily larger brush fires. In the end, he thought he had them contained, but the worst was to come. He had spent most of the week-long Memorial Day recess in his congressional district. His relationship with Feeney had deteriorated to maybe a two, with zero being the worst. Calvert Dixon managed only a curt hello, and Fran noticed a chill as he greeted some of the party regulars at the big county dinner. The Republican Leader was sorry, he tried to make it work, but couldn't do it. Fran, you let me know next time, and we'll try to put it together. That's what Fran, after not being able to get through to Feeney, told Creighton

Tillman. That's what Fran told Calvert Dixon, who was shocked. Calvert will get over it, Fran thought. What's he going to do, not support me? Does he think he could ever find a candidate that could beat me?

Nevertheless, it was embarrassing to listen to Feeney's old friend, state Senator Doris Brask deliver an after-dinner speech taken out of moth balls. It contained every cliché you could think of, and contained no specific references to anything. Fran hadn't seen her in a while. Doris was in failing health and Feeney was clearly uncomfortable watching her long-time friend stumble. Great job, Fran, Mr. Big Time Congressman, this is the best speaker you can get for the big dinner? Fran looked over at Becky and Carl. They sat expressionless as they watched Doris. Becky rolled her eyes over at him.

The whole episode rattled Fran for several days as he traveled around meeting his constituents at one food trough after another. The local paper, which seemed lately to take more shots at Fran after a moratorium following Carter's death, had a nasty piece about how Henson Clark hadn't shown up and several hundred party faithful had been treated to a real snoozer by Doris Brask. The malicious reporter confirmed that he recognized the speech as one he had heard twenty years ago. He could never forget a speech that bad, he said.

The dinner thing would pass. He wouldn't let something like that happen again. He'd get some big name into the district soon. He'd schedule some event. He'd get Neil and Gordon working on something right away. This whole thing would blow over.

He was more concerned about something else. He'd had his first fight with Jo Ellen. It was a fight that as he reflected, sought to define their relationship. She had bought him his own shaving cream, toothbrush, and other toiletries so he would have them at her apartment when he would spend the night there. She checked his next day's schedule every evening and would tell him he was spreading himself too thin. That's politics he would say. How can you do all this well, shouldn't you try to focus a little more? He smiled. You're going to wear yourself out, get old before your time, Congressman Fran. A photo of them, taken when Jo Ellen was holding his elbow at the EDC reception, now hung where the Rockefeller Plaza photo had been, right between Machu Picchu and the Three Stooges playing football.

Jo Ellen adjusted the photo. "That's an important place for our photo to hang," she said.

"Definitely, between two cultural icons."

"Congressman Fran, let me tell you something and do not let this go to your head. I think about you all the time. You're my hero; unflappable, and I know you care about things I think are important too. You're kind to me and I think you want to be with me." She gave him a coquettish smile. "Also, I think you're handsome."

"Also? I'd list handsome first."

"Well, what do you like about me?"

"You're very attractive, I want to be with you; you put me at ease, you're smart, and you seem to be a person who wants to do her best in anything she does."

"That's a good start, Congressman Fran. Do you love me?"

"I guess I do. We've both had tough times recently and we seem to make each other happy."

"So you love me?"

"I said I did, I mean I do."

She stood on her toes and whispered, "I love you."

Two days before recess, she told him her plan. As soon as he heard it, he knew it must have been in the works for a while.

"I found a cheap round-trip flight to Tennessee. I thought it might be fun if I went back to your district with you," she said. "I even ran it by Maddy and she just said to tell you right away. As a matter of fact, she sounded kind of excited about the idea; she was a little breathless."

Fran was immediately disoriented. What was she talking about? Go home, to the district? What would he tell Becky? What would his constituents say? Or the paper? Or Feeney? He loved her and had, he admitted, thought about bringing her back home. But he shuddered about all the obstacles he'd first have to overcome and never came up with a plan. Jo Ellen was just part of his Washington life now. Going home with her was out of the question, especially with this dinner fiasco. Fran at this point could only half-listen as she enumerated her plans, then he jumped in. "Jo Ellen, you can't come home with me now."

"What? I don't understand."

"It's a long story. I just need to go over all this in person."

"Is there someone else?"

"No, look I'll be over tonight."

"You don't want people back home to know about us, do you?"

"That is not the point."

"Maybe it's better that you don't come over," she said, choking back a sob.

"Jo Ellen this is not the right way to handle this."

"I've got to go."

She didn't answer the downstairs door buzzer at her apartment that night or the next two nights and his calls to her went to voicemail. On the night before he left for Tennessee, he followed someone through the front door and walked up the stairs to her door. There was no answer. He left a note asking her to call him.

CHAPTER 10

Washington drew this evening from its swamp heritage, reserving for all arriving passengers a merciless humidity. Halogen lights in front of the airport fizzed in the damp mist and spread a translucent glaze over everyone and everything. Standing about tenth in line for cabs, Fran looked down at the sweat lines emerging at the knees of his pants, which by now had all the crispness of flannel pajama bottoms. There was nothing he could do to stop the streams of sweat that had broken through his shirt and now his jacket.

His plan was to go straight to Jo Ellen's but he hadn't planned on looking so disheveled. He hoped he'd dry off enough during the cab ride, but the old clunker was struggling to pump out the AC. He didn't have another plan, so he went to her apartment. It dawned on him that he didn't have a key. Why had she never given him one? Maybe he was making too much of it. If she weren't home, he'd walk into the building with someone and wait in the hall. He'd withstand the spaghetti mist. Maybe the Eagles would be on again. He liked the Eagles.

He pushed the button on her intercom.

"Yes," she said.

"Jo Ellen, it's Fran." She didn't say anything. Then the buzzer sounded and he opened the door. Walking up the steps he wondered why she hadn't spoken. He smiled at two college-age guys coming down the stairs who looked at his bags. They knew where he was going and smiled back. Fran felt like a rumpled, middle-aged man. It's not how he wanted Jo Ellen to see him. But maybe that's what he was, maybe this relationship was foolish. There must be some place entirely new he could run to. She knew how long it would take him to get up the stairs and opened the door just as he let go of his bags.

Her eyes completed a full inspection. They both knew she had home field advantage. He wondered how forlorn he looked. The woman before him, someone he'd known for about a month now, would soon issue her verdict. Her words would carry more weight than those of anyone now in Fran's life.

"Need an iron?" she said as she opened her door wider.

He knew that she meant for him to come in. "It's a little humid out there. I thought I might catch you at home before I went to the office." He hadn't planned to go to the office; at least he didn't think he did. "I've been trying to get in touch with you all week. You never returned my calls." He had to find out right now what she was thinking.

"Sorry, I wasn't expecting company. I think there's a little iced tea left. I saw that you called. And just what were you going to say to me if you had reached me? Here, let me hang up that wet coat. Sit down."

Fran sat, using the time to think how he was going to respond. His wet backside stuck to the chair as he tried to get comfortable. "I was going to tell you that I was sorry that we left things as we did. I mean, I said some things, probably without thinking. There are parts of our relationship that I haven't thought out too well, or completely."

She sat across from him, wearing an oversized, red T-shirt with the word Georgia across the front. It came to just above her knees. "Doesn't tell me a lot so far," she said.

"Well what would you have wanted me to say?"

"Nothing you didn't want to," she shot back. "But I think you might have taken a little bit more time to think about my feelings. I mean, I know you're the congressman and I'm just, well sometimes I don't know what you think I am, but I thought we had a little something going there, Congressman Fran. I thought my feelings counted for something. Maybe I read you wrong. Maybe you don't love me at all. If that's the case, I can see why you don't want me to go to Tennessee."

"Not taking you home doesn't mean I don't love you. But there are a thousand eyes on me. If they see me do something they think is wrong, stupid, inappropriate, they get offended and feel betrayed. I'd like to say I don't care about any of it, but I can't be that careless, not if I want to keep my job."

She looked at him and swallowed her iced tea. How frazzled was he tonight? "So let me see if I understand, see if I can stop your thought train, or at least slow it down. Do you care more about your job than you do about me?"

He looked at her. She was dead serious. It was a simple question that she felt had a simple answer: yes or no. Her hair hung just over the top of her shirt. Simple answers were precious commodities in politics. They were thinking in two separate worlds. "I can't bring you home now. I didn't say I don't want to bring you home." He told her about, Feeney, and Calvert Dixon, and Creighton, and the dinner fiasco, and Doris's horrible speech, and the paper taking pot shots at him. "I've got some repair work to do."

"Okay, you avoided one simple answer. Let's try another one. Are you going to bring me to Tennessee?"

"Yes."

"When?

"July Fourth recess."

"Good. Not so hard is it?" She walked over to him, put her arms around him and placed her chin against his shoulder. He was glad it was over. He would take her home.

Maddy was on the phone when Jo Ellen came into the office carrying two robins-egg colored gift bags. She pushed her bag of walnuts farther behind her computer monitor and cut her phone call short.

"Jo Ellen," Maddy said in her official-warm-welcome-to-our-office tone, a tone that was becoming less official and more genuinely cordial. "He's not here right now."

"Policy Committee meeting, HC-5 Capitol Building," Jo Ellen said.

"You know his schedule pretty well. That's where he's supposed to be. But we know that our favorite congressman sometimes strays from his schedule."

"But that's where he's supposed to be."

Maddy smiled. "That's where he's supposed to be."

"Maddy, I think you'll like these. I have one bag for you and the office and one for Fran. He was talking about these peanut butter cookies he got at some bakery at home. I think he said Ruth's. Well, I found this bakery not far from where I live and there they were: peanut butter cookies. See the little fork marks on the tops?" she said as she lifted the package of plastic wrapped cookies out of one of the bags.

"Dear, they look delicious. That was so thoughtful of you to think of us. Would you like to put Fran's bag on his couch?"

Jo Ellen smiled. "Yes Maddy, I'll just place them on the couch." With a broad smile she stepped into her Fran's office and put the bag on the couch. "If you hear from Fran, could you tell him I'll look for him at his committee hearing at two o'clock? If he's running late, I'll try to catch up with him later."

"I will," Maddy said. "And thank you again for the cookies. I'm sure everyone will enjoy them very much."

"Jo Ellen," Neil said as he approached Maddy with a huge stack of papers.

"Good morning, Neil. How are you?" Jo Ellen asked as she glanced at them. What did the the papers say? Neil knew. Maddy knew. Fran knew, probably.

"I'm just fine, what's this I hear about cookies?"

"From Jo Ellen, peanut butter cookies fresh from the bakery," said Maddy, holding the bag for Neil to see.

"Great." Neil said. "How's the fellowship going?"

"It's going very well. Though sometimes I feel like I've been in Washington forever and other times it still seems totally confusing. Still, I've gotten a lot out of it in the short time I have. I'll be done at the end of next month, right before the big August recess."

Neil looked at her. She had certainly gotten a lot out of it. But what would happen when she left Washington? Where did she fit in after that? He realized it could have an enormous impact on the election. He had thought about it before but was still looking for the angle. He knew he'd find it if he had to.

"Yeah, Washington confuses me as well, more often than I'd like. Well, back to work, good seeing you again, Jo Ellen." Neil said.

"Bye Neil, Maddy," Jo Ellen said as she shifted her notebooks and picked up her well-worn "I Love New York" canvas bag.

"Good bye, dear. Thank you again."

Fran called right after Jo Ellen left. "She's going to meet you before the hearing. She also left you a little gift, one for the office as well," Maddy told him.

"What is it?" Fran asked.

"Oh, I think you'll like it better if it's a surprise."

"I'll be right up."

Walking down the hall, Fran rushed through the materials in his folder for a hearing entitled: "Environmental Threats on the Border: Prospects for U.S.-Mexico Cooperation." He was eating a peanut butter cookie. Jo Ellen was by the door, wearing the same green dress she wore to the reception at the New Zealand Embassy. She smiled at him, though more demurely than she would if they were at her apartment. She was catching on, too many eyes around.

"Looks like a good cookie, Congressman," she said as he swallowed a mouthful.

"These are better than Ruth's. Did you have one?" He was letting down his guard, darting glances at the huddle of people waiting in front of the committee door.

She smiled. "I'll take your word for it." People looked over. "I know you must have to get inside. It was nice seeing you again."

Fran wiped a crumb or two from his lips. "Same," he said before walking into the room.

There were only five committee members on the dais. Fran saw two, maybe three reporters at the press table. As he looked at the audience, he saw Washington enviro-types, groups of State Department and Environmental Protection Agency lawyers with notebooks open in case the Administration witnesses were asked "tough" questions. He saw very few tourists or student groups. But the Peace Lady was there. She was always there, with her big homemade "Peace" button on her white blouse. And she could talk your ear off if she snagged you in the hall. When Fran first came to Congress, he stopped on a couple of occasions to speak with her when she approached. He tried to be patient and kind at first, but she spoke mostly gibberish about her belief that we could have peace one day. Now if he saw her in the hall, he would start speaking to anyone nearby.

Fran had a clear sight line of Jo Ellen as she sat in the middle of the audience taking notes. Their eyes would meet on occasion, and she would lower her head and smile while she continued writing.

These were tough times on the border. Hundreds of millions of gallons of raw sewage flowing into Texas, leading to all kinds of damage to rivers, streams, agricultural and tourist areas. Uncontrolled emissions pumped out of hastily-built factories in northern Mexico. On some days, several of the witnesses said, there were perpetual black clouds hanging stubbornly in the steamy air. Asthma rates among children on both sides of the border had risen at alarming rates. Fran listened to his more senior colleagues question the witnesses. We're making progress, they said dismissively. They knew there was a problem but they didn't need any useless recommendations. Likewise, representatives of the business community said they were developing a good working relationship with their Mexican counterparts. They had their own study showing their progress.

"Congressman Stewart," said the chairman, recognizing Fran for questions.

"Thank you, Mr. Chairman. I have been listening carefully to our good witnesses, and I have two questions. Who is responsible for this mess and who is going to clean it up?"

All the witnesses stared at Fran. As they began to talk, they morphed right before his eyes into the Thomas Nast cartoon of Boss Tweed and his cronies standing in a circle, each pointing to another as the bad guy. Not me, Boss Tweed said. Not me, said each of his cronies.

"Thank you, gentleman. I have no further questions, Mr. Chairman. I would request, however, that our witnesses expand upon their testimony and submit it in writing to our Committee."

"Gentlemen, can you accommodate Mr. Stewart and his request?" the chairman asked.

They all nodded reluctantly.

"So ordered," the chairman said.

The environmental groups were next to testify. They were all smiles after hearing the bumbled answers to Fran's questions. Jo Ellen nodded gratefully at Fran.

He stayed for most of the enviro-testimony, but left through the side door on the dais before the questioning. Jo Ellen, sitting now with other EDC staffers behind their witness, watched Fran stop and look at her before leaving. Outside, he stopped and wrote out a short note and folded the paper. A committee staffer was entering the room.

"Would you give this to the woman in the green dress in the front row?" Fran asked.

Jo Ellen opened the note and, recognizing Fran's writing, held it close. "Proud of me? C.F."

Tripp Lee was at the small counter and called out to Fran as he walked into the cloak room. "Fran, want to split a tuna sandwich?"

"Who's buying?" Fran asked.

"Don't I always take care of you?" Tripp handed the woman two dollars and told her to keep the change. "Ever known her to cut a sandwich straight down the middle? Here you take the big one. I'll take the weeny one. Like old times, Fran, sharing tuna fish sandwiches. Tuna is good for you. It's got your protein and got your mayonnaise, and I think there are some of the important food groups in there too. When's the last time you had a tuna fish sandwich?"

"I can't remember, Tripp."

"I've seen you, you know. Living it up at that fancy restaurant. I had a few the other night, and as I was walking out from the bar, there you were. And you were looking into that young lady's eyes pretty good. I didn't want to come over and say something I shouldn't so I just kept on going."

Fran moved his tongue around to get the tuna fish out of his teeth. "You should have come over."

"Well, you know what, next time I will. But what do you want me to say? Are you going to tell me about your new lady friend? Here, take the pickle," Tripp said, making smacking sounds as he chewed.

Fran sat back in his chair. "Why do you think she's my lady friend?"

"Why, you old rascal. Who's the quickest, sharpest mind in Alabama, even when he's workin on a snootful? The same guy that just finished that weeny tuna fish sandwich right in front of you boy. Tell me she ain't your lady friend."

Fran told Tripp about Jo Ellen. Carter said you could trust Tripp and Fran agreed.

"People know about you and Jo Ellen?"

"A couple of trusted people in my office. But you know, we've been around a bit lately, so I'm sure the wheels are turning in some heads. I haven't told Becky yet, not sure when I will. I'm going to ask you to tell Feeney," Fran said with a straight face.

Tripp nodded seriously. "Yeah, you just give me the word. You know old Feeney and me are buddies. She still got that slippery henchman working for her? Crawford? What's his name?"

"Creighton, yeah. I've really had to watch my back this past year. I've promised Jo Ellen I'm going to bring her home over July Fourth. Not sure how I'm going to work it. Not sure at all."

"Well you just do it boy. If you think it's right. I'm happy for you. I haven't found my second-time-around woman yet. Who knows? But I'm happy for you. Look I've got to go. I've got to meet this tap dance club from my district for a photo on the House steps. They're here to thank me for my vote to get some funds to build that Tap Dancing Hall of Fame. Shit, do you believe that, the damn Tap Dancing Hall of Fame?"

CHAPTER 11

"Yes, I was very proud of you today, Congressman Fran, Mr. 'C.F.'" Jo Ellen said as she leaned against Fran's shoulder. She got up to turn off the light above her stove and came back to the narrow couch turned bed. "You know I saw a package and card on the table."

"Yeah, that's for tomorrow. I'm out early in the morning, before you're up. I didn't want to forget."

"I can't believe it. Twenty-nine, I'll be twenty-nine tomorrow. I'm getting to be an old woman."

"You don't look twenty-nine."

"That's because I'm not twenty-nine yet. And anyhow how do you know what I'm supposed to look like at twenty-nine?"

"Come here," he said bringing her close to her.

He tried to be quiet the next morning as he got ready to leave, but she was up and walked toward him

"Happy Birthday," Fran said as he kissed her on the forehead.

"Let's see what's in the box," she said as she picked up her gift.

"Read the card first."

"Okay, Okay," she said as she opened the envelope. Two bears, drawn sitting on a crescent moon, were looking at each other. One bear wore a red bow tie, the other a red hair ribbon. The printed message inside said, "I'm on top of the world when I'm with you. Happy Birthday." He had written, "To Jo Ellen, love, Fran. p.s. This will give you what you need for an upcoming trip."

Inside the box was an oversized paperback, *The Big Illustrated Guidebook to Tennessee.*

"It's the best. Let me know if you have any questions as you read it."

"I'm really going aren't I?"

"You're really going. You let me know what you want to see after reading the book." He was happy, working on what he would say to Becky.

He pointed to a piece of red paper in the front of the book. "What's this?" she asked. "One coupon," the paper said in Fran's handwriting, "for two tickets to the Grand Old Opry."

"And don't forget our plans tonight. A special birthday dinner."

She looked at him. "Fran you make me very happy. I'm so glad I have you."

"Last vote tonight is seven. See you at seven-thirty."

Neil was already in the office, accordion folders all over the place. "Everything okay?" Fran asked.

"Yeah, I guess. I'm a little concerned about the petitions. They have to be filed in a month and we're just having a rough time getting them organized. We've got to get more volunteers and get this together. I'm going to have to fly back to the district and get this straightened out. Some of our good party leaders, including Calvert, don't seem to have been paying attention to us on some things. Don't worry boss, I'll get it squared away."

Fran didn't want to worry. He wanted Neil to fix it. "Okay, let me know when you're going and if you need me to do anything. Maddy here yet?"

"Inside," Neil said, as he got back to his paperwork.

"Mornin, Maddy. I can't remember, did we talk yesterday about the reservations for tonight?"

"We did, twice. I know you'll have a good time. The Willard Room has a nice secluded corner all ready for you and they will bring out a little cake with candles after dinner. I told them this evening was very special and Humberto, the maitre d', assured me that you will get the very special treatment you deserve."

"You do good work Maddy." He stopped and looked at her. "I don't know what I'd do without you, I'm serious."

"My pleasure."

"Gone, I'm off to breakfasts one through three. It's a beautiful day outside, just feels like a very special day."

Fran spent most of the day on or near the House floor. He had a large legal-size folder with him and sifted through old papers. He looked at the poem about Rwanda that Larry had given him and started to read it. Unbelievable, the horror, the killings, the helpless children, the broken promises.

Fran picked up his yellow legal pad and began to write an introduction to the poem, and a few things about Larry. He was going to put it into the *Congressional Record*. Larry deserved it; the lost children of Rwanda deserved it. Fran signed the top of the sheet and gave it and the poem to one of the pages. What are we doing here when we can't stop the brutal slaughter of eight-hundred thousand innocent people?

"C'mon down from those clouds there, boy. You look like you got the fate of the whole world on your shoulders," Tripp said as he plopped himself down in the chair next to Fran. "I've been watching you the whole time I've been walking over here, just staring into space."

"Just reflecting a bit, about Rwanda."

"You can reflect all you want. They hate each other to death over there, the killings won't stop. And not a damn thing we can do about it. Not a damn thing. What are we gonna do, send our boys over there to die? Lot of us will never have anything to do with something like that. I can tell you that."

"What you say makes sense, Tripp, but there must be another way."

"Maybe. But we're already barely hanging on with most things, and maybe that's the best we can do. Keep one step ahead of this whole world collapsing. It's got too many moving parts. You fix one problem, and it screws up something else. I used to fiddle around and like fixing my car. But now -- they got so many computers and modules, and space-age bull-shit. I can't fiddle around with my car any more. Did this winter, and it cost me three hundred dollars to repair the damage. Things just get more complicated all the time. Get your head out the clouds, boy, I'm telling you. Fix what you can fix. That's all you can do."

"Where you going, Tripp?"

"Got to meet with an important group in my district: Grandmothers for Safer Playgrounds. They're all riled up about unsafe playgrounds. Damn, when I was young, I had a tire swinging over the creek. Everybody said I was pretty good at missing the rocks when I jumped into the water."

Fran waved as his colleague headed out. A page handed Fran a note that said he had a phone call in booth three. Fran closed the door. "Hello."

"Fran."

"Well, it's the birthday girl."

"Thank you for my gift. Tennessee looks so beautiful. I just wanted you to know how much I loved it and" her voice lowered, "how much I love you. See you at seven-thirty."

Votes for the day ended a little before seven. Fran went back to the office for a quick shave. Maddy was gone for the day and Neil was on the phone, probably solving some big, important problem. Fran didn't know what he'd do without him. Fran stopped and pointed to his chest. "Need me for anything?" he whispered.

Neil shook his head and waved goodbye.

Fran was convinced that the Willard Room was the most elegant restaurant in Washington.

"It's beautiful here," Jo Ellen said as her eyes took in the marble columns and mahogany-framed glass panels. The groaning chandeliers of crystal recalled the hotel's prior grandeur as did the brocade drapes and ornate moldings. The elegant, oversized menu spoke first of spring appetizers.

"Fran," she said as if she'd found the hidden treasure, "I'm getting this one: Blanched Salinas Green Asparagus, Topped Salmon Roe and Osetra Caviar Crème Fraiche."

He lowered his menu and smiled. "Fish eggs?"

"I had it once. I don't know why but I liked it."

"I'm going to have this," Fran said letting her read it.

"Sautéed Tiger Prawns Marinated with Fresh Herbs and Saffron Braised Fennel Finished with a Lemon Sauce."

Fran ordered her a Tanqueray and tonic and for himself, a Gentleman Jack with a splash of water. They were both clueless about wines. The waiter suggested a bottle of Chardonnay to go with their Charred Filet Mignon of Tuna Complimented with a Slice of Foie Gras and Sweet Potato Galette.

"I can't believe the prices," she said. "Did you come here often?"

He shook his head. "A couple of times," he replied, remembering the evenings he had shared with Carter.

"I've never had a birthday dinner like this. This is very special for me."

"For me too," he said, as he raised his glass to toast her birthday.

The conversation turned quickly to their trip to Tennessee. She would tell him about something she read in her new book and he would expand on it. It was all she wanted to talk about. All, that is, until he handed her a formal parchment envelope with the names in calligraphy of Representative Fran Stewart and Guest. She pulled the invitation from the envelope and read about a formal dinner week after next hosted by the Secretary of State.

"Will you be my guest?" he asked in a mock formal tone.

They had finished their second round of drinks and the wine had been presented. "Yes, of course." It was her best birthday ever. The man she had grown quickly to love was taking her home and to a formal dinner in Washington. Everyone would know about them.

The waiter came back to pour more wine and they both probably said more often than they might have, how delicious the food was. "You think this is good, wait till we get back home and I take you to Duke's. The best meatloaf sandwiches in the world. You won't believe it."

She giggled. "I didn't see anything about Duke's in the book."

"That's fine by me. I don't want too many people knowing about Duke's; it'll get too crowded."

Jo Ellen got up and headed to the rest room. Passing by her, a man stopped for a second, then walked into the room.

"May I help you, sir?" the head waiter asked.

"No, no, that won't be necessary, thank you. A friend of mine is supposed to be here," he said wandering a little farther into the room. "And there he is, thank you."

"Fran -- thought you might be in here." Tripp Lee had on one of his smiles, the one that said Tripp Lee loves everybody and everybody loves Tripp Lee. Well, almost everybody. And it got even more mischievous after he had a few of his doubles.

"Tripp?" Fran asked, somewhat startled.

"Saw your lady friend in the hall. Mighty pretty. I want you to know now, Fran, she had a big smile on her face. She must be happy with you."

Jo Ellen walked back into the room, her gait just slightly unsteady. She saw Tripp and went to shake his hand. "Hello, I'm Jo Ellen Driscoll."

"Mighty pleased to meet you, Ms. Driscoll. Tripp Lee, I'm a friend of Fran's."

"Tripp is one of my colleagues, from the great state of Alabama," Fran said, standing with a half-smile. He hoped Tripp would leave.

"It's so nice to meet you Congressman," she said politely, with that familiar trace of awe. "We're celebrating my birthday."

"Your birthday. My, this is a special occasion. Happy birthday."

"Please, won't you join us?" she said.

Fran cringed imperceptibly.

"Oh I couldn't. Look at me, I just barged in here. Just wanted to say a quick hello to my old friend, Fran, I should be going right now."

"No, please, I insist, even if you can only stay for a bit."

"Well, that's very kind of you, ma'am, but you're gonna have to let me treat you folks to an after dinner birthday toast. Drambuie? Waiter, three Drambuies!"

Fran sighed, trying to see the interruption as a blessing in disguise. After all, he was taking her to a formal dinner at the state department soon. Having Tripp here now would be like a dry run. And he and Jo Ellen seemed to be getting on very well. They were all getting on very well. Amazing what two Drambuie birthday toasts can do. Jo Ellen's hand reached for Fran's. Tripp had made it a real party.

"Fran here's a good man; one of the best in Washington. Heck, one of the best anywhere," Tripp said. "I can vouch for that. And let me tell you both now that I've had an opportunity to meet Jo Ellen, well, I'm betting you two are going to be real good for each other." They both squeezed each other's hand. "Now I've got to get back to the office. My staff said I've got some material I've got to go over for some meeting or other. I'm gonna square with the waiter on the way out for our birthday toasts."

There was more chance the moon would fall on the Willard than Tripp going back to his office and going over that material. He was a bit unsteady as he left the room. Fran and Jo Ellen were also a bit wobbly, though it didn't seem to bother them as they swung their hands ever so slightly.

"Where to birthday girl? It's still your birthday for another hour and a half," Fran said as they walked through the elegantly-appointed lobby where one hundred and twenty-five years ago President Ulysses Grant roamed with his brandy and cigar. They always found him, those guys in the lobby. They always wanted something. Those damn lobbyists, Grant would say.

"Congressman Fran, have you been drinking?"

"I don't know if I should be the one to tell you," he said somewhat clumsily into her ear, "but we've both been drinking, a lot. But it's okay, it's your birthday."

She closed her eyes and lifted her head. "Let's go to the Lincoln Memorial. We'll sit on the steps and look up the mall and see if we can find where you work. You do want me to come home with you don't you, Fran?"

"Yes," he reassured her. "Why do you always ask me that? You know I do, I said I do."

"Fran, please don't be short with me."

"I'm not being short with you, not on your birthday at least." He said as he held her waist and pulled her closer. His eyes followed her hair down to her pearl earring, toward the top of her mid-cut halter top dress, down to the flip of her hem which broke at her knee. It was a new dress, at least he had never seen it before; a light purple chiffon that clung to her. "Lincoln Memorial it is. The birthday girl would like to go to the Lincoln Memorial."

"Yes sir, right away, sir," said the doorman as he waved furiously at a cabbie.

They sat on the marble steps that by then had relinquished most of the heat from the hot June afternoon. A dozen or so tourists mingled, some taking photographs, some reading guidebooks, some staring at the reflecting pool. No one seemed to notice Fran and Jo Ellen.

"There it is, that's where you work!" she said pointing at the Capitol building. Her voice shook and she smiled as she leaned her head to her shoulder.

He lifted her arm and pointed her finger toward the Capitol. "You see that little glass door on the House side?" he wasn't even sure that he saw it as their fingers swayed back and forth across the entire building.

"Yes," she answered.

"Good eyes," he said semi-sarcastically.

"Well, there's a terrace that opens from one of the leadership offices on to the west front of the Capitol. There were about six of us, and you have to swear, Dr. Driscoll, that you won't tell anyone, okay? Good, okay. Well, we had this competition, if the House were in late at night, we'd go into the room and we'd each have an orange. We could tell them apart by the color of the markers we'd use on them. And then we'd open that door, go out on to the terrace, make sure no one was looking, and then fire away in the direction of the pool at the bottom of the hill. After the last vote, we'd go down and see whose orange had gone the farthest. I usually did pretty well."

"Congressman Fran, you know, you're a little more daring than I thought."

He touched his forehead to hers. "Yeah, it was a lot of fun until one night, the Speaker happened to walk in and saw us tossing oranges out of the Capitol Building. Geez, he was none too happy and he read us the riot act."

Still mesmerized by the twinkling waters of the reflecting pool, they listened as one of the tourists called out to the others. "Hey, they're filming a movie down there, c'mon."

Fran and Jo Ellen followed the tourists to the base of the Lincoln Memorial and walked past several maintenance trailers. Sure enough, bright lights – like walking into a baseball stadium for a night game -- revealed cameras, technicians, tangled cables, reflecting devices, humming generators. But nothing was happening.

"I've been here for an hour watching these guys. Somebody mumbled something, then I heard 'cut' and they've just been moving things around since then," said a man, turning to all the puzzled looks.

"Is this a movie?" Jo Ellen asked.

"What's that?" The man asked.

"She wants to know if this is a movie," Fran said, trying to speak more clearly.

"Some new cop show."

"Let's go," she said.

"Thanks," Fran said to the man.

They walked over to the reflecting pool. A young guy in a tank top and baggie shorts was tossing a Frisbee to his dog. The mix, must be some shepherd, hard to tell what else, rose as if captured by high-speed photography, and with precision timing, clamped down on the saucer. She did a little victory run before returning the Frisbee to her master.

"Gosh, that's amazing. You think he'd let me throw it once?" she asked.

"Let's see," said Fran as he walked over to the guy in the tank top.

"Evening, Fran Stewart. That's my girlfriend over there and we've been admiring your dog. He's fantastic. Well, I was wondering, see it's her birthday and she wanted to know if she could toss the Frisbee once to your dog."

"Sure, no problem,'" he said, figuring that Fran, while a little tipsy, was nonetheless, on the up and up. "Flixie, see that lady over there by the water, she's going to throw the Frisbee to you. And it's her birthday, so try extra hard to catch it."

He gave the Frisbee to Fran who walked back to Jo Ellen. Flixie sat where she was, appearing to know that while there seemed to be a change in the routine, someone would throw the Frisbee to her.

Fran handed the Frisbee to Jo Ellen. "Ever throw one of these before?" he asked as he watched the way she held it.

"Sure, I have."

Fran didn't think she looked very coordinated. "Just bring it back and bring it forward, snap your wrist and let it fly."

Jo Ellen wound up several times, then with a throw that had crash landing written all over it, turned her whole body around, and hit the Frisbee into her leg. The Frisbee flipped a couple of times on a trajectory that sent it into the water. Jo Ellen, losing her balance, followed. She heard the sound of muffled air bubbles as her head went under water.

Fran jumped in after her as did the dog's owner. Flixie dove in to rescue her Frisbee and locked her jaws on it. She jumped out of the water just as Fran was pulling Jo Ellen from the shallow pool. The dog crashed into Jo

Ellen and she fell back dragging Fran with her. They sat in the pool looking at each other, their clothes suctioned to their bodies. One of Jo Ellen's dress straps had slipped down her shoulder and as she pulled it up, she convulsed in hysteric laughter. Fran got up and sloshed over to her, his progress measured by his own fits of laughter.

"I'm so sorry," Flixie's owner said. "What can I do to help?"

"Not your fault, not your fault," Fran said, lifting Jo Ellen to her feet before they both rippled together in cackles of laughter. "Guess it's really my fault for not teaching my lady friend here how to throw the Frisbee the right way. My apologies Flixie."

Fran and Jo Ellen walked to the street and grabbed a cab. "No air-conditioning, please!" she screamed at the cab driver.

"Sorry, Fran said. "Had a little accident, windows open would be great."

She was shivering, but still chuckling as they walked up her stairs. "Flixie. What kind of name is that for a dog?"

They entered her apartment and got dry. They celebrated her birthday into the next morning.

CHAPTER 12

Fran picked up a *Congressional Record* from the pile near the back door of the House chamber. He sat down and turned to the page that had his tribute to Larry Bowling. He had written about Larry's selfless career; his long record of getting his hands dirty helping the poor in forgotten corners of the globe. "We need many more people like Larry Bowling if we're to stand a chance of ending the suffering of the impoverished, the sick, those who can't help themselves if we don't give them that initial boost. Accordingly," Fran concluded, "I am pleased to include at this point in the *Record*, a moving poem of Larry's which I'm sure my colleagues will agree poignantly captures the tragedy facing us:

Tears at St. Paul's; the Children of Rwanda

A deserted place, potsherd buildings and broken souls cradled by verdant hills. Far away for many, yet we are all there and if we stop to think, to feel, we might rescue that place and ourselves.

Some come to help those still moving; those who clung to the edge while others were swallowed by the crevasse. The slaughter, but we shook our finger, our indignation like a cannon at those devil hands.

The dread smoke of those camps – a fog, clouding our thoughts and suspending the inhabitants for now as we searched for a plan – there must be a plan!

Why do we struggle to assemble the pieces and glue the splinters of yet another vase – consider not a deeper shelf, it's so simple, or are we glorified by yet another reconstruction?

The numbers, the numbers, the numbers. Which is the intolerable one? Which one cuts as if it cuts us? A machete cut so deep the flesh can never be repaired.

But the numbers have faces, each number a different face; you can't hide from the face of a single number once it captures your eyes.

And the door to the schoolyard opened; the vacuum broken, they came to us slowly. Who were we and would we change their lives, would we wake them from the sleep that stole the touch and senses that only families share?

Three hundred, four hundred – we never found out how many children there were; their lives as make do as the clothes clinging to their forms.

They breathed a happiness from the smiles and pats that came their way, it was easy for us to do; bring to them an instant of hope that some magic could bring them home..

But even so, I saw him as my eyes began to sweep the courtyard. Eleven or twelve years old; they're not as strong as we think – he rested, stooped against a tree, a line of tears, a badge upon his face.

A sorrow so horrible had gripped him, unrelenting; his thoughts of loved ones lost in a death campaign crafted in Hell? All the children, at some time that day, would wear that badge.

Never again, never again – how true to our word? The children, fragile as our own nascent wandering, shattered as a pane of glass. Always some excuse, always children's tears.

Need to be more like Larry, Fran thought. I'm actually in a position to do something. If I'm as smart as I think I am at times, I should be able to get some of the other folks in this building to recognize we've got to put our heads together and do something that works. Fran looked up at the grand expanse of white ceiling under which many great men and great women had the determination and courage to change things.

"Congressman Stewart," said the page.

Fran walked to booth #4. "Hello," he said into the receiver.

"Boss, Peter. I think we have a situation." Peter Goodman's voice was uneasy. Very unusual. One of the reasons Fran had hired the twenty-five-year old several summers ago to be his press secretary was because of his poise and unflappability.

How bad could it be, Fran thought. Someone didn't get the flag they requested? No, got to be something with Feeney. "What's our situation Peter?"

"Kevin Fairchild, you know the guy who writes the Living and Style Section. Well, he called about ten minutes ago. Neil wants you to come back to the office right away. He's on the phone with the editor."

"Peter, you're not telling me what our situation is," Fran said somewhat impatiently.

"Fairchild has pictures of you, quote, frolicking, unquote, in the reflecting pool in front of the Lincoln Memorial with a young lady. He says he's going to run them in his column and wants to know if you have any comment. As I said, Neil's on the phone with Fairchild's editor to see what the heck they're talking about. Boss, were you there?"

Fran closed the door to the booth and the fan started to stir the musty air inside. He took a deep breath. "Yes, Jo Ellen and I were there last night, after dinner. It was her birthday," Fran said in a nervous tone Peter had not heard before. There was a sudden ringing in Fran's ears and a slight twitch in his hand. This wasn't anyone's business, but he wanted Peter to know what and how things happened. He knew his press assistant needed the whole story if he was going to be on the frontlines and counterattack to their best advantage.

"Boss, you there? Were you in the water? Is it possible someone has photos of you in the water?"

Fran told Peter about the guy in the tank top and Flixie the dog and how Jo Ellen fell in the water trying to throw the Frisbee and how he jumped in to rescue her.

Neil got on the line.

"Fran, here's the deal. They've got a sequence of about four shots. One of Jo Ellen falling into the pool, next one has you pulling her up, then you both falling in, last one has you both sitting in the water laughing, with the lady's dress top hanging down in a quote, rather suggestive way, unquote."

Fran was still trying to hold on, but he felt disoriented and helpless. "Neil, where, how, did they get these pictures?"

"I've worked with this guy. Sometimes he's reasonable, but he thinks this is fair game. He wouldn't tell me who the photographer was, I guess we'll see who gets the credit when this story runs. Seems he was covering this new TV show they were shooting last night, saw you, and started snapping away. After you left he approached the guy with a Frisbee and asked him if he knew you. He said you introduced yourself as Fran Stewart. Photographer digs around and finds out you're a congressman."

"All right, I'm on my way over; let's figure out how we're going to fix this."

Neil and Peter looked at each other. They both knew there was no way to fix this. Should they go for full disclosure: don't you expect him to jump in and save someone who's fallen into the pool? Yeah, but this wasn't some grandmother or a small boy who looked admiringly at Fran their hero. No, this was a babe. Neil and Peter knew that was the story. Who's the babe, Congressman? Looks like you folks were having a great time. Just wanted everyone to see what a great time you were having. Fairchild would be vicious. People ate it up.

"Okay," Fran said as he, Neil, and Peter walked into his office and closed the door. "What do we do?"

"We give him a 'no comment' otherwise that bastard is going to twist whatever we say for more material," Neil said.

"I agree," Peter said.

"Wait a minute, that's the best you guys have to offer? Just let these photos run and be at the mercy of this guy? We need some better thinking than that. This is going to be a disaster. Is that the best you guys can do?"

"Fran, it's far enough out from the election that we'll be able to manage it. You're not married. We can develop a story about how you've been seeing Jo Ellen. You guys weren't doing anything wrong. You weren't caught robbing a bank. Someone fell into the pool, someone tried to help that person, and they both were laughing a little. Could have happened to anyone. We've got to make this a one-day story," Neil said. Peter looked at him, knowing that was impossible; the good ship Stewart had taken on too much water.

"I'm not ready to go that route yet," Fran said.

"Fairchild's deadline is six," Peter said.

"Congressman, Jo Ellen on line four," Maddy called out.

"Yes," Fran answered.

"Fran, thank you so much again for yesterday," Jo Ellen said.

"Jo Ellen, I'm in my office with Neil and Peter. We have a bit of a problem."

Jo Ellen began to lose her footing. "Oh?" she said.

Fran explained what he knew so far. Jo Ellen had never heard him sound so troubled, so unsure. "Can't you just tell this guy it was my birthday, and I slipped and you came in to help me? I don't understand what the problem is."

Neil and Peter looked at Fran and waited.

"Jo Ellen, this guy doesn't want to hear it was just this or it was just that. If you're in his column, the harder he can slam you, the happier he is – and the happier his readers. For me, this will get in the papers back home, Feeney will explode; she'll try to take me down. And Becky is smart enough to see through a lot of this, but she'll be hurt I didn't tell her about you. And what about you? What will the people running your program say? What will your school say? We've got to work through the judgment as this thing plays itself out. It will play itself out. Are you okay?"

She was quiet. What would people say about her? Would she lose her job here? Would she lose her job at the university? What would her parents say? She had told them about Fran – not everything. Now they would be known at home as the parents of the babe who was frolicking in the reflecting pool with some congressman. Didn't she hear Fran say he didn't care what people said, he loved her and the hell with everyone else?

"I have to go now, I . . . I, call me later," she said.

Neil and Peter prevailed. There would be "no comment" for Fairchild. They would prepare a statement for the onslaught tomorrow morning. Fran canceled all his meetings for the next day. He spoke to Jo Ellen several times that night. She just wanted to be at home to prepare. She just wanted to sleep. They hadn't done anything wrong, she told Fran. We didn't, he said, don't worry, we'll get through it. I love you. I love you too, she said softly into the phone. He had told her what she wanted to hear. She could deal with tomorrow. At least she thought she could.

Fran looked at the clock. It was too late to make the call he dreaded. He had started to dial Becky several times during the afternoon but, never finding the right words, hung up each time. That call would have to wait until tomorrow

He pulled out his blanket and pillow from the plastic case. He climbed back on his couch and turned on his television. His life rolled through his head as he watched some nature show about hundreds of millions of Monarch butterflies flying back from Mexico to the United States.

CHAPTER 13

Fran jogged up to the row of newspaper machines by the Metro. There was only a trace of morning in the sky. He let the two coins fall in, opened the door and grabbed the innocent-looking paper. He took the first punch pretty well, but they kept coming until he felt short of breath. The story and pictures took up most of the space above the crease. It was all exactly as Neil had described. Fairchild had used all four photos.

WHO SAID THE POOL'S CLOSED? Congressman and Swimming Buddy Say "Come on in, the Water's Fine!" Visitors to the mall late last night were treated to a rare aquatic performance at the reflecting pool in front of the Lincoln Memorial. Practice for the water ballet? Hard to tell. Congressman Fran Stewart (R-TN), pictured here with an unidentified woman – a trace of dishabille – had no comment when this reporter contacted his office yesterday. Judges give them a "3" -- not enough arc as they fell into the water.

Son-of-a-bitch, sick bastard. What does he out get out of doing something like this? Fran read the story again, this time stopping at the end of each word, measuring how when taken together they could have such a devastating impact. He walked back to the office. He and Jo Ellen had nurtured something special. She showed him how he could care for someone, love someone again. Now, this fragile blossom entrusted to him was trampled by the snickers of everyone who would see this story in the days to come. Wouldn't take Fairchild long to figure out who Jo Ellen was. Probably be another story tomorrow. She would take a big hit.

Neil, Peter, and Maddy were in the office when Fran returned.

"Looks like that slime ball got us pretty good," Fran said as Maddy poured him a cup of coffee and patted him on the shoulder. "I've got to call Feeney, but I want to get to Becky before she goes to school."

"Shame I didn't keep that photo I had of Fairchild. That gross slob could be Moby Dick's brother," Neil said as he stared again at the photos. He returned quickly to the battlefield. "Look it could have been worse. I'll help Peter with the phones. We've got our statement to start faxing out. Let's just stay calm and not get flustered. We'll ride this out, we just can't give him any more story."

"Do we tell them about Jo Ellen, if they ask?" Peter said.

"No, absolutely, not," Fran fired back. "I'm going to call her now."

"What do I do now?" Jo Ellen asked after Fran read her the story. It was easy to pick up the tremble in her voice.

"Listen, don't get upset. If someone asks you point blank if that's you, it's hard to deny. But just tell them you slipped. Better yet. Can you come over to the office, let's say around noon? We'll sit down with Neil and Peter and see where we're going with this."

"Why is this happening to us?"

"We'll get through this. I love you, see you at noon."

"Candice? Good morning, it's Fran."

"Good morning Mr. Stewart. You doing okay?"

"To be honest with you, I've had better mornings. I need to talk with Becky. It's important. Did I catch her before she left for school?"

"Oh my, yes sir you did, Mr. Stewart, let me run and get her right now." The phone knocked as it was placed on the table. "Becky, Becky, your father is on the phone. He says it's important. You hear me? Becky!"

"Daddy, is something the matter?"

"Becky, I never tried to beat around the bush with you. You're too smart. So please try to listen to what I have to say with your head as well as your heart."

"Daddy, what are you saying, what's the matter?"

"Becky, Daddy has met someone. I wanted to make sure, before I spoke to you, but I know now that I have strong feelings for her. Her name is Jo Ellen Driscoll. She's working temporarily in Washington. Maybe I should have told you before."

Becky's fist tightened around the phone cord. She looked up at the portrait of her mother on the wall. "You found someone to replace Mommy?"

"No, honey. No one could ever replace your mother. I've found someone that is coming into a new phase of my life," Fran scrambled for the words that he thought would have come to him by now. It was dawning on him that this was the hardest thing that he had ever tried to explain, and the bombshell was still yet to come.

"Do you love her, Daddy?"

"Yes, Becky I do. And I've got to tell you all about this in person. But I had to let you know about it now, because, well remember when I said sometimes they'll say things about me that are untrue or try to make a story about something just to make me look bad? Well, that's happening now. Some reporter came across the makings of something he thinks he can turn into a sleazy story that will sell papers." Fran described what had happened.

Becky pulled the curls out of the phone cord, starting to cry. "Daddy, I have to go to school, now."

"Becky, I'm going to be with you soon and explain everything. Everything will be okay, do you believe me Becky? Becky?"

"I've got to go to school." He heard her start to sob as the phone traveled to the cradle.

Ten minutes passed. "Fran, Feeney is on the phone," Maddy said.

"Hello," Fran said.

"What are you doing telling this girl about some affair you're carrying on with some Washington floozy? How could you do something like this? Doesn't the memory of my daughter mean anything to you? How dare you," said Feeney, her words like piercing arrows.

"Feeney, I know this is upsetting to Becky, and I . . . "

"Upsetting? Oh, you think it's upsetting? My granddaughter is balling her head off upstairs. You betrayed her trust. We worked so hard to get elected, but you've let everybody down. And this isn't the first time. You, you . . . but this will be the last time, this abominable, reprehensible behavior, this is the last time. Don't call this house again!"

"Feeney, I'm Becky's father. Don't you forget that!"

"Well, we'll see about that," she said as her phone slammed down.

Fran paced his office. "Damn that woman, she's wanted nothing more than to see me in this position."

"Easy, Fran," Neil said, "we're going to have a lot coming in today so we have got to pace ourselves. We'll take care of Feeney, we'll take care of them all, just got to keep focused, keep that indignation in check."

The phone lines lit up. Neil instructed the staff carefully. Bottom line, all calls were to go to him or to Peter. Several reporters hovered in the outer office and a camera was being readied for a shot into the middle of the camp.

"Do not come over to the office," Fran told Jo Ellen. "Meet me at Union Station instead, at noon, inside the front entrance to the right."

Fran opened the door and prepared for the gauntlet of reporters.

"Congressman Stewart, quick comment please on the story in today's paper. We've been told the woman in the photos with you is Jo Ellen Driscoll, a summer employee at the Environmental Defense Coalition, is that true?"

"You guys are reporters aren't you? Don't ask me to do your job; you find out!"

"Congressman do you deny that the woman with you in those photos is Jo Ellen Driscoll?" came an annoying whine from somewhere inside the cloud of gnats.

"Slow news day, hey? Yes, I admit it, the woman in the photos is the woman in the photos, hope that clears things up."

"Congressman, look. Fairchild already has confirmation and is rushing it into his next column. We just need to know what your relationship is to her?"

Fran continued walking and grabbed a cab to Union Station where Jo Ellen waited inside. She had been crying; tears had etched trails of makeup below her sunglasses. "They know Fran. Everyone knows; they all saw it. You wouldn't believe what it was like for me in the office this morning. I laughed it off at first, but the jokes came too fast for me. And my supervisor called me into the office. He was not happy. He said that EDC had given me an opportunity, and this was how they were repaid? And that most of our board members aren't the type to tolerate this indiscretion. Fran, I can usually handle these characters, but I was overwhelmed. I didn't think it was a big deal. I mean it's usually just you and me and now we are out there in front of everyone."

"Jo Ellen, I'm sorry this is happening," Fran said as they walked to one of the tables and ordered coffee.

He told her about Feeney and Becky and she started to cry. Heads began to turn. He realized he had unloaded too much on her all at once. She was taking this hard. One camera, one misanthropic reporter, the humming presses of one of the most powerful papers in the world – then it hit the street, the wires, some TV and radio looking for a cheap shot. What had he and Jo Ellen done?

"Fran, I don't know if I can go back to the office, I feel like I'm going to throw up. I've got to finish this testimony for the Senate tomorrow, but I don't know how I can write anything. What should I do?"

He hesitated, then told her to go back to the office, finish up what she could, and then go home. He would meet her there and they would get everything figured out.

Peter leaned over Fran's desk and gave his boss a pile of phone messages requesting a comment on the story. Most were from the press, but there was one from Calvert Dixon and one from Creighton Tillman.

"Well which ones do I have to get back to?" Fran asked.

"None, if we have their fax number we can send them our release and let it go at that," Neil said. Peter nodded in agreement.

"Done," Fran said.

"We've had some calls from the leadership offices; not happy, but I think they're okay so far with what I've told them," Neil said.

Jo Ellen looked out her window and then around her small apartment. She thought about how she had planned to go home with Fran. She stared at the photo of her and Fran. Maybe now she wouldn't be able to go.

Fran sat at his desk, staring into space. He'd always envisioned what it would be like at ground zero, Washington, D.C., if the Soviets attacked. Not likely now, and besides they were Russians these days. He was tired. Things were falling apart. The air seemed heavy, he was having a hard time breathing. Maybe it was a heart attack. The article on his desk seemed to be taking all the life out of him. Becky, Jo Ellen, what had he done to them? His job – his damn fiduciary trust – all his hard work, the good he had tried to do. He would never get past those pictures of him in the water. And they were coming after him: Feeney, Creighton, more stories in the paper. It would get worse, he knew it. He didn't care what anyone said, Feeney would get to the party leadership. Those guys never liked him anyway. There was no fight left in him. He looked at Carter's photo. A year without her, and he had screwed up so badly. The white light of the firestorm flashed through his window. His Washington had taken a nuclear hit.

CHAPTER 14

Fran sat at his desk, where he had spent most of his time over the past several months. Maddy had gotten him a small foam pillow that he placed behind his lower back. She was busy packing, and boxes littered the office. The following Thursday was Thanksgiving and the votes planned for the next couple of days would be Fran's last. That is if they let him on the floor. He had gotten into several altercations with the Sergeant-at-Arms. Fran had forgotten his tie. They overlooked it the first time. But they finally confronted him on the day he wore jeans, the day the decorum of the House said enough to his long, stringy hair and bird's nest of a beard. Maddy scolded him, pleaded with him, as if he were her own son. He tried for her to be more mindful of his appearance. He started to bathe more frequently and got his hair trimmed, though it still hung to his shoulders.

"Neil did good, didn't he, Maddy?"

"Yes, he did Fran," she said, as she had patiently every time he asked her that question.

Fran looked at the accordion folders Maddy had made for him. Press clippings, letters, notes, everything about the past several months was in those folders. Fran went through them every day. He even had a little ledger book that he had purchased at the House stationery store. The first page began a section about Becky. He had other entries on Jo Ellen, another on Neil, one about Feeney and a section about himself. The material in the folders was keyed to the entries in the ledgers so when he read about something he had jotted down, he located an article or letter to which he had referred. He would spend hours wrapped up in his ledger book and folders. He looked up to watch the TV only on rare occasions.

His ledger book had red markings, underlining, stars, and asterisks. He had read through the pages so often that some had fallen out and he had to tape them back in. Fran had a special inbox where Maddy placed anything she thought he wanted for his folders. Fran picked up the new article from a paper back home: *"Congressman-elect Glider Reports on Orientation Meetings for Incoming Congressmen."* He liked reading about Neil. When Fran announced he wouldn't run again, Neil decided he would make a run for the seat in a primary that filled quickly with candidates. Fran did whatever he could to help out, which on some days wasn't much, and tried also to stay way out of the spotlight –- for Neil's sake. Still, they never thought there was a chance in hell. Feeney's candidate, with whom Creighton worked closely, quickly built up an imposing war chest. Seven other candidates, some millionaires with unlimited resources entered the special election. Neil had to scramble for money and endorsements. He had to scramble also to stay out of Feeney's rifle sight.

Fran had never seen anyone campaign harder than Neil. He worked his angles: quietly picking up endorsements from local committees, working with many of the groups and businesses he'd come to know while in Washington, speaking very convincingly at candidate forums, and focusing his limited resources on key media buys and targeted mailings. While other candidates worked the big picture and spoke in the abstract, spending millions in all the wrong ways, Neil continued to make progress. But no one saw him beating Feeney's candidate, state Senator Rodney Herman.

The tide started to turn when Neil emerged as the clear winner of several key debates. Herman, many long-time observers agreed, turned in some of his worst performances ever. Neil's carefully-timed ads began to play just as the local newspapers announced their endorsements. One by one they were coming out in favor of Neil. Feeney, word had it, was now personally managing Herman's campaign. She had ousted Creighton.

The polls right before election-day still had Herman and Neil pretty close. With eight candidates and no run-off, who knew how much it was going to take to win? But the results came in quickly and Neil won with a 27% plurality. He wanted Fran to join him on election night but Fran thought it best to pass. He celebrated with pizza and beer in his Washington office. Neil went on nailing the angles and beat his opponent in the general election by 6%. Feeney lost. Fran never thought he would see the day. But while Feeney had lost the election, she had beaten Fran, helping to turn Becky against him.

Fran turned to the ledger section labeled Becky. It by far had more notations than any other section. He had only one additional conversation with Becky after the photos with Jo Ellen appeared in the paper. He had kept notes of everything his daughter said. Fran's daughter told him she didn't want to speak to him ever again. She had retreated from that position. Her anger had much more to say. You were my hero, she said, the one I could always look up to and count on, and now you've betrayed me. It hurts so much, she told him. Maybe she was better off without him.

It had been too much for Fran; he couldn't handle losing in one year both his wife and daughter. He had always tried for Becky, he thought that even though he was away a lot, that their bond, their love was strong.

He knew Feeney had been working on her. Still, Becky was her own person. She had hit him hard with her questions. Do you think if you died that Mom would be running around with someone else? I always had one father and one mother, in my mind we were a family, even now. *We are still!!* Fran had written in red pen, underlined twice. And you didn't even tell me. How could you not tell me?

Fran had a section on Feeney. It cross-referenced some legal documents supporting her efforts to secure custody of Becky. Her characterizations of Fran were venomous: someone who had caused significant suffering; a self-ish father who cared little for his daughter, even as he brought shame to his office and to his family, to say nothing about the memory of his widely-ad-mired, and devoted late wife. Several quotes of Fenney had slithered into the paper. *You old battle axe!! None of this is true and you know it. I loved your daughter with all my heart, and I don't care what you say or what legal papers you and that cretin Creighton file, I'm going to get my daughter back!* Fran added some more underlining, this time with a blue pen.

He turned to the section on Jo Ellen and paused, absorbing the mosaic of notes, scribbles, big and small hearts and the Jo Ellens written in the margins.

Fairchild had done several follow-up blurbs in his column once he had confirmed that the woman in the pool was Jo Ellen Driscoll. *I hope you're happy, you asshole! Happy that your damn articles brought Jo Ellen's life and our relationship crashing down?* The EDC board asked for Jo Ellen's imme-diate resignation; she had become an embarrassment to the office. They even sent a scathing letter to the university and amidst the media distor-tions, Jo Ellen was called before an administrative review committee.

Fran turned to the next page in the Jo Ellen section. Fran had made notes of the first phone conversation he had with Mr. Driscoll, Jo Ellen's father. Jo Ellen would tell us all about you, she was her happiest when she spoke about you to her mother and me. She told me how difficult it was your last couple of times together before she came home. It was all too much for her. She's been staying at our house and won't be teaching until this administrative review is over. Fran, you see, Jo Ellen's had some emotional problems in her life, she's been to a lot of counseling, and her mom and I thought she was making some good progress. She worked so hard to get her Ph.D. and she was always a perfectionist in her teaching. Yet, she still needed a little, sometimes more than a little, support in the background. Jo Ellen has been staying at our house, she needs some time to get herself better. Her mother and I think it's better that you not see her for a while. We don't blame you, she just needs some time, we've seen in the past that it takes her awhile to get better. *But I need to see her. I love her. She knows I love her.* Fran had written ten times in two rows of five. The last entry in the section on Jo Ellen noted the dates Fran had left unreturned phone messages at the Driscolls. *Please call me back!*

Fran put his accordion folder and ledger back in their corner of his desk next to half-filled boxes, the photo of Carter; the photo of Becky, and a photo of Jo Ellen he had taken as she stood, sunglasses resting on top of her head, in front of one of the big trees on the Capitol lawn.

Maddy was on the phone. She and two other women were all that remained of the original staff. And when the packing was done, there wouldn't be anything more to do. They had to vacate the office the Monday before Thanksgiving. Another member was moving in and his staff had already begun to bring in some boxes. Maddy was going to work for Neil; for a short time, she said, help him get set up, then who knew? She had put in enough years in to retire.

"Are you going again tonight?" Maddy asked.

"Yeah," Fran said, as he looked out the window at the cars stopped waiting for the light. The exhaust weaved a smoky wreath as it rose from the tailpipes and hung over the intersection. "Another cold one Maddy."

"And how many more nights are you going to be out?" she asked, her brow rising.

"Looks like they've scheduled the final vote on the big appropriations bill in two days, so I guess tonight and tomorrow night. I'll be all right, Maddy, we all huddle pretty tightly and the grate puts out a good amount of heat."

"I don't care what you say, that photo of you and your two colleagues with those homeless people, I'm sorry, you all looked like you were freezing to death," she said.

"The main thing, Maddy, is that they keep writing about it, they keep taking photos. People are calling, they're writing, I think the members up here are starting to feel the pressure. I know we only have two days, but I think we're going to get that $10 million for the new shelter. It's like camping, Maddy, I have a big bowl of Dinty Moore Beef Stew before I go out there, and I'm pretty good to go."

Maddy walked away; she stopped and shuffled through some papers and then went for the bag of walnuts. He'd noticed during the past week that she was replenishing the bag as early as four o'clock. All the change was getting to her.

Fran did get through those next two nights, but now he was struggling to get his tie on. His fingers were numb, they were like mechanical claws, and he fumbled as he made the worst knot of his life. His striped tie didn't fit well under the collar of his green plaid, flannel shirt. The shirt maker had never anticipated that a lumberjack would wear a tie. He put on his sport coat that also wasn't prepared for that shirt. The coat looked two sizes too small. Fran had slept outside in front of the old shelter for four nights. He hadn't showered, the men he had been with those nights hadn't either, and he pulled, at times, tugged, his comb through his hair and beard.

"They've given me one minute, Maddy, one minute in support of an amendment that has our $10 million in it," Fran said as he looked at two yellow pieces of paper ripped unevenly from a legal pad. There were crazy scribbles across translucent grease spots and coffee stains. "Wish me luck."

Maddy, her hair coiffed, her pants suit perfectly pressed, hugged the homeless man as he left his office. A tear came to her eye as she watched him shuffle down the hall oblivious to that trace smell of burning garbage and damp basements. She watched the TV, waiting for him to appear.

"The gentleman from Tennessee is recognized for one minute," said the gray-haired man in the dark blue suit at the podium. He laughed behind his hand as he spoke to one of his assistants crouched nearby.

"Thank you, Mr. Chairman," Fran said.

Maddy looked at the screen. She had never in all her years on the Hill, seen anyone that looked like that speak in the House chamber. The TV lights glared off Fran's oily twists of hair.

"Mr. Chairman, I understand that this amendment has been worked out and will be approved. I've been asked not to speak so we can speed things up. I can't do that. I'm going to use these last sixty seconds in what will be my last speech on this floor. I'm sure many of you must think this time has come none too soon.

I don't have the foggiest idea what else is in this amendment, and I'm sure many of my colleagues are in the same position. But I do know that there's $10 million to fund a new homeless shelter less than a fifth of a mile from here. We sure wouldn't want it any closer would we?

Now, I know we need a strong military; lots of bad guys in the world. And I've voted accordingly. Our free enterprise system? The best there is, helped to make this country what it is today, lot of people have good jobs and security for their families because of it. But if this card, this little voting card, is to stand for what we all come down here and preach about as good, American, holy, whatever, then all of us in this chamber, we're all only as good as the good we do to stoop down and help those clinging with beaten hands to that last piece of humanity. You know where those people are, though you try to avoid them, or tell yourself they can wait a little longer for help. . ."

"The gentleman's time has expired," said the impatient voice at the podium.

"I request unanimous consent for an additional fifteen seconds."

The man behind the podium grew more impatient, but he didn't hear any one object. "Without objection," he snarled.

"Thank you," Fran said. "Look, I don't want to detain my colleagues any longer. I just ask them to think about this. Think who needs this card the most; give them a chance. If you can't, well . . . this is about the only thing this card is good for," and with a back-handed flip he launched his plastic voting card into a glide path that took it right in front of the Speaker's podium.

The impatient man now found that it was hard to control his voice. "The chair advises the gentleman that that type of behavior is against House rules; it is an affront to the decorum of the House; it, it," he whacked the gavel. "The chair will not permit the throwing of any objects."

Fran walked out of the chamber. He knew the huge bill which few if any members had read would pass. It was the only way they would get home for Thanksgiving.

Maddy had fallen backward on to Fran's couch when her boss tossed his card. She got up quickly, reaching for her reserve can of walnuts, and returned to the TV. It was all over.

CHAPTER 15

The hall was quiet. It always was on Saturday. Maddy put her key in the door and found it unlocked. Music was coming from Fran's office and she looked in to see someone who looked quite different from the man on the TV yesterday challenging the man with the gavel. The man with the gavel would be back and so would all the rules and so would all the procedures which when necessary broke all the rules so that the people's business could be conducted by those who knew how to conduct the people's business. The trees inside the Capitol had long stood as strong as the well-rooted sentinels whose linked branches hung above the lawn just outside. The man in Fran's office, however, would be gone.

"Morning, Maddy," Fran said as he lifted two duffel bags on to his couch. "Yeah, decided to get cleaned up a bit, lose the beard, did a little trim job on the hair. I'm almost ready to head out."

In his jeans and dark green T-shirt, Fran showed he still had that Mick Jagger muscle tone, if not the swagger, to do a *Jumping Jack Flash* on stage. The rounds he had fought with Washington had left a few more lines on his face and a trace of gray in the hair by his temples. It was the whipping he'd sustained inside that led him to wonder at times why the ref hadn't stopped the fight. He would try to recover. Another fight was out of the question.

Maddy's stare changed to a smile. "I'm happy to see you this way Fran. You didn't take care of yourself these past few months." She paused, thinking she might cry, then looked at the folders on her desk. "I've got everything you need right here and I called the hotel last night just to confirm again. It's a nice upgrade and they said that if you wanted to extend your stay past two nights, there wouldn't be any problem at all."

Fran looked at the things she had placed into one of her folders. As with anything Maddy did, everything was organized with parade-drill precision; with paper clips and little post-its, and underlining so it would be virtually impossible for Fran to screw up whatever she was giving him to do. A typed sheet contained crystal-clear directions: approximately 400 miles, 6 ½ hours driving time to Cooperstown. Next was a brochure on the Carillon Hotel with a photo showing the lake at sunset as seen from the sweeping porch. Confirmation numbers, names of the people she had spoken with and when were typed on a small white note clipped to the brochures. Finally, a brochure on the Baseball Hall of Fame and one from the Cooperstown Chamber of Commerce about sights to see and places to eat.

Fran looked at the material. His face could have belonged to a nine-year old looking at flyers from some theme park he had always wanted to visit. "Should get there between four and five I figure. This stuff's great, Maddy. Remember two weeks ago when I said I was going to take this trip? You stared at me as if I were crazier than I looked." He paused. "I went by the car this morning; the garage guys really did a great job. Tell you the truth, I wasn't sure it would make it up here, but good old Gordo did it. I don't know why I hung on to it; guess I thought Becky might want it. Hey, a Pontiac Sunbird, stick shift, rally wheels, moderate mileage, decent stereo. Well, I like it, it's going do me just fine." Fran looked around to make sure he wasn't forgetting anything. "Guess it's time for me to go Maddy. I'll stay in touch in case there's some great crisis, but you're going to be congressman till the end of the year," he said as he looked into her eyes. He reached out and hugged her.

She ignored Fran's passing of the torch. "Be careful, try to relax, and call so we know you got there safely. I packed you some snacks and water so you don't get dehydrated in the car. Fran, remember there are still a lot of people that care about you very much. You know how Neil feels about you, and you know how I feel about you. Give Becky some time, she'll come around. She hurts because she loves you so much."

Fran half-smiled and shrugged his shoulders. "Maddy you know I never would have made it without you." The door closed behind him.

It was a cold day and he turned his back to the breeze as he stopped after several hours to get some gas. It was refreshing, but he was glad to get back inside his car and turn up the heater. Some Thanksgiving travelers, he thought as he looked at people coming out of the service area. The winter had claimed the sky early this year; he was almost sure those were snow clouds floating above fields whose harvest had long since passed. He wondered where Yogi Berra was having Thanksgiving dinner. Fran knew Yogi had sons; so probably with their families. Yogi, who could ever forget number 8 running out and jumping on Don Larsen after Larsen pitched that perfect game in the 1956 World Series? Maybe Larsen was dead now. Fran wasn't sure.

The stereo was loud. Stations faded in and out. He got mostly classic rock, some good songs, but mostly the ones that were still as bad as when he first heard them years ago. He hadn't been keeping up with music. As his fingers fumbled around under his seat, he found two cassettes: Byrds, *Greatest Hits*, and Harry Chapin, *Greatest Stories*. They both brought back memories. He and Carter didn't see the Byrds in their prime. The Byrds had only their leader, Roger McGuinn, when Fran took Carter on an early date to see the group. The music, however, was still fantastic and only intensified the feelings the budding young lovers had for each other. They hadn't seen Harry Chapin, but what a storyteller. As Fran began listening to *30,000 Pounds of Bananas* he thought what a great song for a long car ride.

The rest of the trip through the overcast afternoon went quickly once Fran hit the exit for I-88 at Binghamton. He thought back to that Saturday-afternoon game against the Indians before they renovated Yankee Stadium. After his grandfather got that new job with an engineering company, his grandparents moved to a suburb just north of New York City. For several years, before his grandmother got sick and couldn't take care of him any-more, Fran would spend part of his summer vacations as a kid in New York. He was sitting there right now, in the reserved seats behind the first base line keeping score in the program just as his grandfather had taught him. When Fran got home, his friends didn't want to hear about the Yankees. They hated the Yankees. He didn't hate people because they were Orioles' fans or Cubs' fans or even Reds' fans. But his friends just hated the Yankees; they won too much. Wasn't that what a baseball team was supposed to do? It was a simple answer, or so he thought. But he didn't convert any new fans.

Off the interstate now, maybe only a half-hour to Cooperstown, Fran entered a hall-of-fame of rural America. Splintering, clapboard barns aban-doning the vertical and horizontal rules of construction stood next to silos overgrown with vines that had turned a wintry gray. Lonesome cows stood by a gate at the far end of a muddy field, eager for that one someone to let them in before nightfall. At some sites, new equipment or an addition sug-gested that the farm had some life in it yet. There were some newer spreads along the route, but the old timers defined the road. We had our good times too, the faded, smiling faces seemed to say on one rotting billboard as they drank from what remained of those old-fashioned Coke bottles.

He was half way to Cooperstown when he recognized the road. He had seen it before in Tennessee, and he thought he had remembered it from

Virginia as well. A couple of convenience stores, a small used car lot with lines of waving aluminum pennants strung from a trailer, feed stores, and a farm implement dealer greeting Fran.

Fran got to the hotel after dark and relied on the flood lights to define the towering portico and white columns. After checking in, he stood in the lobby and took in the families with little boys who were as excited as Fran about seeing the Hall of Fame. He mushed his feet in the soft carpets, sat briefly in an over-sized chair that swallowed him up, and felt the warmth of a fireplace that seemed to know people were counting on it more now that the sun had gone down. He hadn't been this happy in months; an almost-former congressman in Cooperstown soon to see the Baseball Hall of Fame.

His plan was to get something to eat at the grille, go back to his room and go over the material on the museum and his two books on the Yankees so he would be well prepped for the morning. He didn't feel well at dinner. He was tired, had the chills – he tried not to think about the biting cold from those nights outside the shelter – and eschewed the beer he had ordered, drinking instead the water the waiter kept refilling. He remembered Maddy's warning; maybe he had gotten dehydrated. He had to leave a great steak sandwich half-finished and when he got back to his room he didn't have the energy to read anything. He pulled up the comforter and sheets with their starchy hotel smell as far as he could and held himself in a tight curl as he fell off to sleep.

He awoke at six and showered and dressed, feeling much better. It had been the night's sleep he knew he needed. He might even go jogging when he got back.

"Right down there and turn left," said the bell man as he pointed to the room with the breakfast buffet.

Fran finished a glass of orange juice, a bowl of Wheaties, scrambled eggs and bacon, some kind of blueberry pound cake and two cups of coffee. These were the kinds of breakfasts that he, Carter and Becky would have on vacation. He thought about the numerous trips Becky would make to the buffet bar and how at the table they would plan their day. He was the only one now.

He went back to his room and started reading. There was material about the founder of baseball, Abner Doubleday who had lived in Cooperstown at one time. The glossy brochure highlighted the Hall of Fame's treasures. Fran then turned to his books on the Yankees.

He remembered the summer his grandfather bought him a whole box of Topps Baseball Cards: twenty packs at a nickel a pack. He had never gotten a gift like that and there were few since that he thought as good. It was the tenth pack that he opened, that, as he shuffled through the cards, produced the orange-bordered Mickey Mantle card. Three packs earlier had a Bill Skowron card showing the Moose stretching off the bag to beat the runner at first. The last package opened had hurler Bob Turley. The rest of the Yankees were doubles, or triples of cards he already had. He would spend hours those first days on his bed going through those cards and one time put three pieces of bubble gum in his mouth until he realized he had to do a better job of saving his stash. He wondered how many of those cards ended up in a landfill. A few people were smarter, or maybe they had more storage space, or didn't move as much. Fran was most people; he had no idea where his Mickey Mantle card was. Bob Turley would surely be worth something today. Even utility infielder Jerry Lumpe would be worth something. Fran looked at the copy of the Hall of Fame Resolution that had his name on it as one of the key cosponsors. He remembered how proud he was that the measure passed. He packed it to show someone at the Hall, but now thought that was all too complicated. All he wanted to do now was to concentrate on the museum, not be grilled about a past congressional career.

Fran got out of the car, walked toward the brick building and then under the stone archway. The Hall of Fame Gallery greeted him with a nod of its regal head in much the same way as famous cathedrals welcomed their worshippers. There, mounted on a wall of polished tan wood, set off by black marble columns supporting the sanctuary, were the plaques of this religion's saints. The memory from his childhood sent him looking for his patrons. And there they were. He walked up to Mickey's first and drank in the accomplishments. Fran was most impressed with Mickey's having been named to 20 All- Star Teams and his .365 batting average in 1957.

Those and other staggering numbers had been Mickey's key to getting into the Hall of Fame. But there was so much more to Mickey than the numbers. Fran's little-boy-mind hadn't known about Mickey's drinking and carrying-on, but he did know that smile spoke confidence more than anything; and that swagger when he went to the plate, either side; and The Mick's dogged determination to continually play through pain to help his team, his buddies: Yogi, Whitey Ford, Billy Martin and the rest. Mickey was dead now, but the little boy in Fran remembered #7.

Fran walked to find his other hero. There was Yogi's mug; no-nonsense, steely, as if the camera had nailed his profile right after the second game of a doubleheader Yogi had caught. He too was a powerhouse hitter and also had caught 148 consecutive games without an error.

Yogi behind the plate. Could you imagine how glad the Yankee pitchers must have been to have Yogi behind the plate? Everyone, Fran thought, needed a Yogi behind the plate.

The almost-former congressman walked among the game's greats. He walked through the various exhibits of recreated locker rooms and stands from actual stadiums. He stared at displays of balls, bats, uniforms, and other paraphernalia. As he did, the doors to his own baseball hall of fame opened, releasing the smells, sights, and sounds of each distinct part of the major league season: spring, summer, and even the beginning of fall when the Yankees would be in the World Series. Newly-emerging grass, grass recently-cut, grass fresh with the smell of rain starting drop by drop to turn the infield a darker brown. Baseball glove oil, leather cleats, balls hitting bats that produced the sound only wood could make, the dust you would eat when someone slid into your base. And then the trips to the baseball stadium on which everyone on the small field Fran played on hoped to play. The House that Ruth built with its facades, perfect field – there was nothing in the world more perfect than that field –the monuments in center field, Bob Shepherd's authoritative announcer's voice with its double echo blending with vendors' cries as they hawked hot dogs – those beautiful dirty water dogs – beer, and Crackerjacks.

Fran took in so much. He began to realize, that even in this shrine with all these things that helped him resurrect the innocent pleasures of his youth he was like a water-logged sponge. He couldn't take in any more. No more, he thought, until he saw it: Yogi's catcher's mitt from Don Larsen's perfect game in the 1956 World Series. He was so far away from that glove that October afternoon so many years ago, and now, Yogi's mitt was right in front of him.

CHAPTER 16

Fran sat at the small desk in his room thinking about what to have for dinner. He knew this moment would come, but he wasn't afraid. The planned part of his life after Congress was over. He had some nice souvenirs from the Hall of Fame gift shop, a book, a pennant – he had pictured it in Becky's room – and five sets of baseball coasters that he could give as gifts. Christmas was coming up. He watched a little television, thought about writing some postcards but didn't know what to say or to whom he would send them.

He opened his wallet and counted out $500 in cash. He opened a plastic sandwich bag he carried in his pocket and thumbed through ten one hundred-dollar traveler checks. He had a gas card, and a Visa card with a $15,000 credit limit; he figured he owed about a thousand. He wrote down balances of $2,000 in a checking account and $3,000 in a savings account. He had two more paychecks coming – those were going into the trust account he had set up for Becky—and a small pension. After that, he needed to come up with $ 600 per month; those were the terms of the agreement Feeney had come up with. Fran knew it was more to hurt him financially. Feeney didn't need the money. "Any attempt to contact and cause further emotional upset to Becky" the letter continued, "would trigger a vigorous legal effort demonstrating to the appropriate authorities that Francis Stewart was an unfit father and accordingly, should be denied custody of his daughter." Fran was far from up to the ferocious legal battle to which Creighton alluded. Becky would come around on her own. Feeney's inculcations notwithstanding, he knew his daughter loved him. It might take some time but he would think of something.

He would have to get some type of job. He thought about the guards at the Hall of Fame. He could guard baseballs and gloves, and also keep an eye on the bats and smile at the kids. He could work weekends too; he didn't have anything else to do. He remembered the convenience stores he passed on the way up. When the time comes, he thought, there would be plenty of opportunities.

He considered going someplace else, maybe farther north or even east. But there was something about this area he liked; it didn't seem to ask too much of him. He remembered about twenty miles south, not too far from a river, there was a Best Western. He thought that might be a good place to stay, at least temporarily. He was sure they would have some weekly, maybe even, monthly rate.

After breakfast, he checked out and lay his duffel bag down on the veranda of the venerable hotel. He headed for a dirt path. His work boots crept softy like the moccasins of ancient Indians who also walked the shore and gazed at the lake as a curtain of steam rose above it. As he sipped coffee, he thought that in work boots and dungarees, a long-sleeved, three-button pullover, and flannel shirt, he could survive in the woods. Didn't have to worry about having a neat crease in your pants, or shine on your shoes.

He walked toward his car and loaded his things. He looked at the buildings and shops as he drove through town, imagining Norman Rockwell at his easel. Fran remembered the fifties and the sixties, at least the early sixties before things really started to change. There was a book store, a gift shop, and a restaurant. More opportunities, he thought; I can sell books and gifts, and I can wait tables. He doubted he would see a help-wanted sign looking for a former congressman. Then he remembered he still was a congressman, and there was a rule about outside-earnings, and that he'd probably like to wait until after the first of the year to look for work anyway, and the more he thought about it, he didn't think there was anything wrong with that.

Cooperstown was behind him, at least for now. He wondered if there would ever be a Congressional Hall of Fame and what would be the criteria for getting elected? What would take the place of batting averages, home runs, and pitchers' winning percentages? How would you measure which congressmen really deserved such an honor? Were there those so selfless and driven by a compassion to help those truly in need while at the same time somehow possessing the strength to keep the country great? How would you define Selflessness? Compassion? Vision? Strong? Positive? Great? These, somebody would say are abstract terms, and we have to come up with meaningful definitions. Fran thought the primary criterion, whether anyone wanted to admit it or not, would be making sure that an equal number of Republicans and Democrats got in each year. And where would you put the Congressional Hall of Fame? Now there's a fight to the finish, all those construction jobs, new business for the town selected. Would this hall of fame ever have over 350,000 visitors a year? Fran didn't think so. He knew he wouldn't go.

His ride south was very similar to his ride north. Same overcast sky hanging over everything. He'd found a new station on the radio though. The DJ was funny and had more of a smooth, big city voice than the others Fran thought seemed more suited to reading farm reports. Several good songs so far; Fran pulled one of the radio buttons to program in WCSA.

"Don't forget, starting tonight at Pearsall's, it's Dawg Feat. I saw them last summer and I'm sure our listeners will agree they're one of the best bands in the valley. Don't miss it, starts tonight at Pearsall's, great food -- the lasagna brings people flying over from Italy -- and always great music and plenty of room to dance. I'll see you at Pearsall's. Stay with us now for more of Raintree Country, with your humble host, John Raintree."

He sounds pretty friendly, Fran thought. That Pearsall's seems like a good place to go, might go there tonight. I like lasagna. Fran pulled into the Best Western and carried his duffel bag into the lobby.

"Help ya?" the desk clerk asked.

"I'd like a room," Fran said. "And do you have weekly rates?"

"We sure do, lemme see," the clerk said as he put on his glasses and looked at a smudged note card. "Save you $35 if you do it that way."

"Good, I'll take it." Fran filled out the registration card. Nice and cozy in here, I could do this. He handed the card back to the man whose twitch was becoming more noticeable. Nice fella, but he needs to use a mirror when he shaves, look at that big area he missed. And that white shirt, he must have washed it in a dark load. Gotta be forty pounds overweight, not good for a man his age, Fran thought.

"All set, Mr. Stewart. Here's your key, room's right around to the back. Continental breakfast goes from six to ten. My name's Casey, let me know if there's anything I can do for you."

"Gotta a lot of brochures over there."

"You betcha, a lot of things to do in the valley. You gotcher Hall of Fame. The college up on the hill has a big Indian museum with a lot of arrow heads and stuff like that. If you're interested in farmers, there's a farmers' museum about five miles up the road. Has all kinds of farm equipment from the pioneer days and some cows and goats you can feed. Like hiking? Here's a brochure on all the trails, and the lake, and tells you about all the animals out there."

By now, Fran had a half-dozen brochures in his hand. "These will do fine," he said. "What about getting some food? I heard about a place called Pearsall's, any good?"

"You betcha. I go there for the lasagna. Oh boy, can't beat that lasagna. But I try to get in and out before that music starts. I can't stand it. Another place, Duke's, nothing but an old diner, but I go there for the hot meat loaf sandwich; always get it with gravy and French fries. Ask 'em for extra gravy, they give it to you no extra charge."

"They have a Duke's up here? That's amazing, they have a Duke's at home, and they've got the best hot meat loaf sandwich too," Fran said happily.

"Where's home?"

"Tennessee. Though that was a while ago," Fran said catching himself.

"Nice place, I've heard, that Tennessee."

"Yeah nice place," Fran said as he walked out of the lobby.

Not quite the Carillon, but warm and smells clean, Fran noted as he looked around his room. He lay down on his bed. It was early afternoon, but he wasn't hungry. He had two new friends: John Raintree the DJ and Casey the desk clerk. Maybe he'd meet some more people tonight. He was going to Pearsall's for lasagna and Dog Feet. He should really call Maddy. He'd try her later. Just going to take a little nap and then maybe drive around for a bit.

CHAPTER 17

The room was dark except for the last light of afternoon that snuck in under the sides of the window shades. The clock radio said 4:45, at least that's what it looked like. One of the lines on the LED display seemed to be missing. Fran sat upright on the bed, stared at the wall and remained motionless. His mouth was parched from the room's dry heat and he went to the bathroom and filled a glass of water to the top.

He lifted a small notebook from his duffel bag, got an outside line, dialed in his phone card numbers then Maddy's home number. After a few rings, she finally answered.

"Maddy, things going okay?"

"Fran where are you?"

"Just a ways from Cooperstown." He gave her the motel's phone number.

"Well, we're out of the office, though we still have our phone number and an answering machine till January. It was tough leaving for the last time. Gordon has two more weeks before he's got to get out of the office back home. He still hasn't found work yet, and he told me you said he could stay in the room above the campaign office till the building sells. I'm not sure if Neil will keep him."

"Thanks for taking care of all this Maddy, I know it's been a lot to do. I'll talk to Neil about Gordon. He's a good man, but I know there was always a little friction there between him and Neil." Fran saw the rub: Neil was the boss, but Gordon thought at times he should have been the boss.

"Have you thought any more about what you're going to do?"

"No, still trying to get the old head together."

"Right, right." Maddy thought about telling him but decided against it. Hearing that Fairchild had taken some cheap shots at Fran for his behavior on the house floor, wasn't something he needed right now. *From Frisbee to Voting Card, Rep. Stewart Demonstrates He Likes to Flip Things Around. From the looks of him, Fairchild wrote, he could really use a dip in the pool right now.*

"Did we hear from anyone on anything?" was Fran's way of asking if Becky or Jo Ellen had called or written.

Maddy understood the code. "No, no just routine. I'm going in during the week to pick up the mail, and I'll be checking the answering machine. I won't bother you unless it's necessary, but please call every once in awhile, and let me know when you leave there. Please take care of yourself."

"I will. Good-bye Maddy. Thank you again for everything."

Fran lay back on the bed. He thought of Becky; there'd be a break-through. He knew it. She'd have to speak to him during the holidays. Jo Ellen; she might be gone for good. He didn't dare call after hearing from Mr. Driscoll. But he always thought if she didn't call, then at least she'd write. Maybe over the holidays. And Maddy, she was older but attractive, looked younger than she was and dressed so tastefully, kept her figure. Fran had more than once thought about Maddy in those first few months after Carter died. He was confused he remembered telling himself. But he thought about Maddy now and how much she cared for him.

Fran turned on the TV then shaved and showered to get ready for Pearsall's. He was going to get there by seven, eat, walk around town for a while, then go back by nine to listen to Dog Feet.

Pearsall's was in the middle of town on one of the winding roads that eventually led to the railroad tracks. From the parking lot you could see trains rush by the flashing lights on the gates in front of the track. A white-one story building housed about a half-dozen businesses, with the restaurant at the very end. Its name was captured in blue lettering on a plywood sign above the door.

The wind had picked up again and Fran looked forward to being some place warm with good food and a couple of beers. A poster right inside the door announced that DAWG FEAT would be there for a week, starting tonight. Clever, Fran thought, Dawg Feat. There was your standard band publicity shot pasted to the middle of the poster. It was a dark photo, but Fran thought one of the band members looked familiar.

There was a bar running down the left side of the room, a few tables, and a pin ball machine. Several neon beer signs littered the walls. It could have been a movie set depicting the late 1960s, early 1970s. He stood for a while and then saw a hostess coming from what appeared to be the dining room.

"How many tonight?"

"Just me," Fran answered.

Most of the dozen or so tables were occupied. It was just a little after seven. Maybe they were concerned, like Casey, about getting out before the music started. Looked like a lot of people had ordered the lasagna, it was a huge portion, with meatballs on the side covered with Mozzarella cheese.

"Something to drink?" asked the slender waitress her hair pulled back in a twist and a pencil resting on her ear.

"I'll have a draft Genny," Fran said referring to the local beer he had in Cooperstown. She handed him a menu. He opened it and there it was, in the middle of the page, bordered by little black spades: Pearsall's World Famous Lasagna, with bread and fresh green salad. He closed the menu and wondered what the waitress' reaction would be when he ordered the lasagna. How many orders of lasagna had she taken?

"It's very hot, please don't touch the plate," the waitress said as she placed the lasagna in front of Fran. She didn't look at his face as she turned and headed back toward the kitchen. It should be world-famous, Fran thought as his teeth kneaded the olive-oil drenched mozzarella. He continued to eat and looked around, smiling at the other diners who occasionally looked his way. He never planned to be in Dranesville, but here he was, not thinking about anyone or anything except how happy he was to be in a warm place, with people who smiled at him, and with some of the most delicious food he ever had. He wasn't down tonight about being by himself.

With a half-hour to kill before the band started he decided to see what else Dranesville had to offer. A town built on railroad traffic at the turn of the century had tried and failed to hang on to its former glory. Abandoned buildings seemed to outnumber functioning businesses. In many of those, rusted signs with sputtering neon or missing light bulbs spoke of tenants that probably were just hanging on. One shop looked to be newly remodeled and seemed to be doing a brisk business selling subs and pizza. As he rounded the corner on his way back to Pearsall's, he noted what also seemed to be a good business: he must have passed a dozen bars.

A white van stood by the building and several people carried guitar cases and mike stands through a side door into the restaurant. Fran was surprised that the empty bar had gotten so crowded so quickly. He made his way towards the back and into a side room, not much bigger than the dining area, where the band was setting up. Guys younger than he, they looked rock and roll: long hair, some beards, tight jeans, boots, some colored T-shirts, one guy wore a fedora with what looked like a crow's feather in the hat band.

They were set up for four people on a raised floor that had earlier held dining tables. In that spot now, were a drummer, bass player next to two piggy-backed keyboards, another guitar player, and another mike stand that obviously hadn't been unscrewed up to its normal height. Just then Fran saw one of the roadies bring over a stool with two steps and a rounded steel bar around the top. The tuning now done, the guitar player, the one with the fedora, stepped up to his mike.

"Evenin everbody, thanks for coming tonight, we're Dawg Feat." The lights dimmed as the group began a throbbing instrumental lead into "I'll be There" by the Four Tops. Fran saw people upfront stepping back and looking down as the bass line pounded. He realized soon that the mike stand wasn't supposed to be raised. When the dwarf emerged from the crowd and stood on the top step of the stool, the mike was precisely where it was supposed to be. He had a great voice, good back-up vocals from the group too. Then Fran realized he recognized him. It was the same guy he saw in Washington, the same face that was on the CD that woman gave him in Washington. Carson Handle, that's incredible, Fran thought, it's got to be the same guy. The song ended. The woman was right. Handle had a great voice. The group shot into "Cripple Creek" and did some Beatles, Allman Brothers, Bee Gees, and another song by The Band.

"They're good aren't they," said a guy with a beer bottle almost tipped into Fran's ear. "Carson's so damn good, I just worry about him falling off that step stool."

When the half-hour set ended, Fran looked around and found himself in the hoopla of people drinking beer and shaking the buzz out of their ears from the amplifiers that had made the entire room vibrate. The band and several ladies were camped at a table in the corner. Should he go over and introduce himself? Fran had been so conditioned to do that. Why not? Someone you want to meet? Go over tell them you're a congressman. Everybody's impressed. Well, not everyone. Fran remembered someone pushed his way backstage at a Grateful Dead concert. He said he was a congressman. The Dead security people didn't understand the password. They threw him out, just as if he were a regular guy.

Fran didn't know what he would say if he walked over. He was a congressman for another five weeks or so. But his story was too complicated. They didn't look as if they'd be interested, and it was too noisy to say more than "Hi" or "you guys are good."

Suddenly Fran felt alone. He saw his waitress walk by, but even though she looked at him, she didn't say anything. Fran remembered John Raintree, the DJ, and wondered if he had come to Pearsall's as he said he would. He sounded friendly, maybe if Fran found him they could talk. At least there was Casey back at the motel. Fran could talk to him in the morning about the lasagna. The band began its second set and dancers headed to the floor. Fran wondered what Yogi would do if he found himself in the middle of a crowded room in Pearsall's listening to Dawg Feat.

As the band started its final set, Fran walked toward the bar. He was on his third, well if you counted the one he had with his lasagna, fourth bottle of Genny. The place was still packed and a group huddled over some space invaders video game that had its back to a Bally pinball machine. An early train to Dranesville must have brought in that baby. He hummed *Pinball Wizard*. That machine was a beauty. He looked at the band. He'd wait until the last set ended then go over and introduce himself to Carson Handle.

"This is our final song; you guys have been great. See you on Friday night. Happy Thanksgiving," said Carson, his body shifting from side to side even though there was no music playing yet. Seemed he was always shifting, fidgeting. Maybe all his muscles needed to be flexed often. Sometimes his chin seemed to get lost into the upper part of his protruding chest. But when the song started, "Chest Fever," --another Band song, what's that deal, Fran wondered – Carson let go with a punch that showed a voice able to wander at will over a range of octaves. If you weren't looking at him, you'd never know that voice was coming from a little person on a step stool.

Fran watched the band pack its equipment. He looked at dancers with red cheeks and hair drenched in sweat as they began to leave Pearsall's. Some would be back; that thought might be what got them through the week. This week would be easier than usual; Thursday was a holiday. Fran thought about what that meant for him.

There were two roadies making short work of packing up. The band members helped, and wires were getting rolled, guitars packed, and drums put into trap cases. Carson Handle had a towel draped around his neck. Fran walked over, telling himself not to stare. Bend your neck a little if you have to.

"You guys were good, really good," Fran said trying to be enthusiastic without seeming condescending. He stopped when he thought his eyes were about at the right angle.

"Thanks," Carson said as he reached over to pick up two guitar cases that were almost as big as he. "We had a good night; yeah, things came together, doesn't happen every night. But glad you enjoyed it"

"No, you guys were real good. I liked those two original songs, good harmonies, nice beat," Fran said realizing that he sounded like one of the teenagers on *American Bandstand* rating a record. "Liked The Band songs too. Weren't they from around here?"

"Something a matter with your neck?" Carson asked rocking side to side as the guitar cases picked up momentum.

"No, no, just stretching it a little," Fran answered knowing that he must have looked a little foolish.

"Yeah, we're hoping to record those songs, once we finish a bunch of others we're working on now. The Band; man that's another story. They were from about an hour south of here, *Big Pink* and all of that. William, over there; don't call him Bill, our lead guitar is probably the biggest Band fan ever. I mean I know they were good, backed Dylan, etc. etc., but William saw this picture of them wearing hats like the one he's got on now, and he wanted us all to wear these fedoras. Can you imagine me in a fedora?"

Fran wasn't sure how to respond. He didn't want to get into dwarf territory, but was probably there already; he felt himself staring. "I know you guys probably want to get out of here as soon as you can. Don't want to hold you up. I'll be here Friday; you guys are good!"

"Thanks man," Carson said as he took the guitar cases out to the van.

Fran watched him go. He sounded normal when singing, but in a conversation, there was a noticeably higher pitch. Must be like when you hear a British singer, sometimes can't really detect the accent in the song, but when he starts talking, it's really there. Fran watched as the roadie folded up the step stool and picked up the sandbag that kept it from tipping.

The "No Vacancy" sign was on in front of the Best Western. Fran felt lucky he had a place to stay on that cold night in the middle of nowhere. He lay in bed for a while reading the Best Western brochure listing all the motels they had across the country. It fell from his hands as he drifted off. Snapping to, he reached over and turned off the light. He hadn't asked for a wake-up call.

"So whudya think?" Casey asked the next morning, as Fran walked past the check-in desk.

"You were right, that was the best lasagna."

"Get out of there before that band started?"

Fran paused. "No, actually, I didn't have anything else to do so I stayed around and listened."

Casey looked up. "I never done that. I ate late the first time they had a band, and me and the people I was with didn't like all that noise, told the owner we didn't like it. He's always trying something, not happy with having the world's best lasagna, now he wants to have another Woodstock or something."

"Yeah, I don't know," Fran hedged. "What are you doing for Thanksgiving?"

"Same as every year. Drive down to my sister's and her family. Bout twenty miles away. We got a gal that used to work here, she's got no family, so she usually works Thanksgiving, Christmas, New Year's. And they pay her double time so she's as happy as a clam!" Casey said, smiling.

CHAPTER 18

Fran celebrated Thanksgiving by running. He warmed up doing fifty push-ups on his hotel room floor and fifty sit-ups with his ankles under the bed. He pulled his faded wind pants over his well-worn-running shoes and put on an old gray sweatshirt. The blue knit cap and lightweight gloves he'd purchased at the department store on Main Street still had the tags on them. He pulled them off, tossed them in a trash can and headed outside. As he stretched, he noticed how still it was. The glittering frost on the two-lane road in the middle of nowhere had not been disturbed. He pulled his hat down around his ears and strode toward the end of that road.

He took in everything one might expect to see on a country back road. His mind felt sharp. But then he started replaying the past year. The segment on Becky agreeing with her grandmother that he was the worst. Feeney was noticeably more demonstrative than Becky. Fran saw himself opening an envelope. It was a Christmas card from Becky. Then a tape of Jo Ellen started. She was inconsolable; the target of both EDC and her university. And there was Mr. Driscoll explaining to Fran that he and Mrs. Driscoll were caring for their daughter. He hadn't used the term nervous breakdown, but all that talk of earlier emotional problems. Fran loved her, wanted to see her, but he knew the Driscolls blamed him for what happened to their daughter, and he got their message that it would be best not to contact her. He saw himself opening a Christmas card from Jo Ellen. Then Fran was standing on the House floor giving some speech. He had been a player, a bit player, but he thought he had done some good things. He saw Neil being sworn in when the new Congress convened and Maddy helping out in his office.

Now he was running on a lonely road on Thanksgiving morning in a town with Casey the desk clerk, Carson Handle and Dawg Feat, and Pearsall's world famous lasagna. But running was familiar to him. He would remember throughout the day how good it made him feel. He stayed in the room and watched the Thanksgiving Day Parade, football, and then went to Duke's. He ordered the "Thanksgiving Day Special," but when he saw a hot meat loaf sandwich being served to the man in the next booth, he asked the waitress to change his order. He was glad he did. Different than back home; this had a pronounced touch of oregano, but he liked it right away.

Pearsall's was crowded on Friday. The hostess told him he'd have to wait a half-hour for a table. He decided he'd walk up to the sub shop and ate on the bench out front. He arrived back at Pearsall's before the band crowd arrived, and took one of the few small tables in the room. His waitress from the other night saw him and waved.

The side door opened and William and one of the roadies walked in. The cool air brought a welcome draft to the stuffy room.

"Guys! Heard you had a good show the other evening," said the man, probably in his mid-thirties, with thinning hair whipped back on top by some type of gel.

Heard that voice before, Fran thought.

"John Raintree," the man said as he held out his hand towards William, who shook it. "Where's Carson?"

"That little devil is around somewhere," William said with a sly smile.

Fran watched the two talk for a while and then sat up as John Raintree walked toward him.

"Hi. John Raintree with WCSV, good to see you. Here for the show?"

Fran nodded. "Fran Stewart. I was here earlier in the week."

"Oh, a real Dawgs' fan," Raintree said in that smooth DJ voice.

"Well, that was the first time I saw them. I'm new to the area; but I heard you the other day on the radio."

"Well pardner, you just keep your dial right where it is. Welcome to the valley, Frank," the DJ walked away, looking for other members of his listening audience.

The room was packed. Carson climbed to the top of the stool. The back beat was joined by a building bass riff and an evening of good classic rock was underway. At the end of one song, Carson happened to see Fran and nodded.

The lights dimmed as the second set began. It looked as if someone were removing Carson's stool. The punching chords that opened "I Got a Line on You," by the late 60's band, Spirit, were joined by Carson's vocals that were dead-on Spirit's Randy California.

As they went into the chorus, the lights came on, and one of the roadies pulled up a rope, the other end of which was attached to a yellow life jacket Carson Handle was wearing. He was swinging above the floor and instead of singing "I got a line on you babe," he belted out, "They got a line on me babe." He finished the song above the floor with the keyboard player giving him a little push every once and awhile.

Fran couldn't believe what he was seeing. His mouth hung open. Most on the dance floor hadn't seen this part of the act before, if it had been performed, and they stopped dancing then erupted in cheers and thunderous hand clapping.

"Swing that dwarf over this way," yelled some guy who Fran could just tell was a troublemaker. William looked up disdainfully. It wasn't his idea to have Carson swinging around like some chimpanzee. The drummer and keyboard player were laughing away. Carson seemed to be tolerating it; though a couple of times he looked concerned about falling.

The stool came back out, and the band finished the evening without any more circus acts. The room began to empty and Carson walked towards Fran's table.

"Back again? What did you think?" asked the singer as he angled his butt up the chair and then slid the rest of his body over.

"As I said the other day, you've got a real great voice," Fran said pushing the table closer to Carson.

"Carson Handle," the singer said leaning across the table to shake Fran's hand.

"Fran Stewart."

"Good to have some fans out there, thanks for staying through another of our shows."

"That Flying Wallendas' bit was unexpected. You do that often?" Fran asked.

Carson shook his head. "Not my idea. William and I didn't want to do it. We kind of got strong-armed by the other guys. They said we needed some hook, something to start some buzz about the band."

"Get you a beer?" Fran asked.

"Sure, I've got time for a quick one, then got to get to loading up the stuff," Carson said as he rubbed his hair with the towel.

Fran got the waitress' attention, pointed to his bottle, then pointed to Carson and to himself. "You guys from around here?"

"Ray the drummer and Kevin our keyboard guy are. Can't you tell?" Carson asked as he rolled his eyes. "William and I lived in the city, now we just float from gig to gig. We're up here now, staying at some apartments Ray found. We had a couple of gigs in the city; didn't really go anywhere. I even cut a CD single on my own. Still got a box of them if you want one. Then we, well, Ray and Kevin, wanted to go back upstate. I wasn't sure how the dwarf thing was going to play here, but it seems to be okay, piques some people's interest I guess. These folks get pretty drunk, and get a kick out of it. Sometimes people try to lift me up, but that hasn't happened in a while. I have a thick skin most times. Ray and Kevin were laying this story on me about some singer with no arms and no legs, and they used to tie a rope or something around him and hang him from a hook on the wall while the band played. Ray said sometimes these drunks would swing the guy back and forth then they got into a fight with the band. I've heard that story a few times, kind of like one of those urban myths. Maybe just been Ray and Kevin telling their friends to say that stuff to me. But I've got a pretty thick skin most times."

Fran took a sip of beer. He wondered if he were in the middle of a Fellini movie. "Guess this music business is pretty interesting," was the best he could come up with.

"You bet it is," Carson said. "What about you, you from around here?"

"Just passing through. I lived down south for a while."

"Never been down there," Carson said as if the south were one big continent.

Carson finished his beer and hopped off his chair. "Thanks, I got to go help out. We had one of our roadies go home for Thanksgiving, then he called and said he'd quit, wasn't coming back. Believe that? Hey, hope to see you around, we got this gig for another three weeks."

"Need some help?" Fran asked surprising himself. His bottle had volunteered him; thought he might want to see what it was like being one of Dawg Feat's roadies.

"Yeah, sure," Carson said, lifting his little arm and waving Fran over.

Carson introduced Fran to Kevin and Ray, both maybe mid-thirties, bone-thin, long hair, and mischievous eyes which maybe they thought was what rock stars had to have.

"Thanks, man. Nice to meet you," they said.

William just nodded. The remaining roadie, Jimmy, shook Fran's hand.

As the loading finished, Carson motioned Fran back over to the table. "I don't know if you're interested and I'd have to talk with the other guys, but if you're looking for some part-time work you could help with the equipment; it's pretty easy."

Fran's mind raced to its congressional department and wrote a headline for some newspaper: *"Former Congressman Fran Stewart now Roadie for Dawg Feat—I like the change of pace, Stewart says."* "Geez, I don't know about that. I'm a little old, don't you think?"

"No way. What, maybe you're a little older than us, but you're in great shape. And you must like our music, else why would you be here? Look, you don't have to let me know now," Carson said as he started rocking more intensely. "Where are you staying? I'll call you tomorrow."

"Best Western, but I don't know the number," Fran said

"No pressure. No pressure. I'll call you tomorrow." Carson ran to the door and closed it behind him.

Fran was out early the next morning running on a road busy with cars and trucks bringing the valley to life. Snow flurries contrasted with the bright eye of dawn. He hadn't read a newspaper since he left Washington, but there wasn't anything to prepare for any more. He thought he liked it that way. He still had about a month left on his oath, but he was free on that road. If he had frozen snot hanging from his nose, he didn't have to care. That job took more from him than any oath could ever know.

CHAPTER 19

Feb. 4, 1995

Dear Maddy,

This is my first unofficial letter as a former member of congress. Good talking with you over the holidays. I meant to write sooner. I know you and Neil must have been going a little crazy preparing for his swearing-in and first few weeks of the new congress. He sounded happy and excited when I spoke to him, I mean as happy and excited as Neil gets. It's hard even for him to stay low key at a time like this. I remember how much Carter and I relied on you to help us get organized. Seems like lifetimes ago.

Thought I would get something from Becky by now, a card for Christmas, but must have hurt her more than I imagine. I've tried to understand how she sees this whole thing, but I'm not doing a very good job. Don't know what's going on with Jo Ellen. Know you will let me know if anything comes in for me. I've enclosed a card with my new address (I'm subletting a small apartment) and phone number where you can get an emergency message to me.

Thanks for depositing my last paycheck. As I mentioned, think I'm going to stay in this area for a while. I've met some "interesting" people – one's become a pretty good friend, he helped me get a job, actually two jobs. He's the lead singer in a local band and I help them carry their equipment around. I'm what they call a "roadie," Maddy! Remember how I told you that if I weren't in congress, I would want to be a rock star? And how you looked at me? Yeah, I know probably one of the goofier things I said during a long, distinguished (?) congressional career.

I also have a full-time job –needed to make some money and I got bored real fast. My new friend, Carson Handle, (more about him some other time) had a friend at Daley's Department Store in town and well, now, I'm assistant manager of the women's shoe department. I've been there about three weeks. I fibbed a little bit on the application, but they hired me on the spot, guess they needed to fill the position quickly. Would have looked pretty silly putting the Speaker or one of my committee chairmen down as a reference. Sell a lot of these little zip-up boots with fur around the top to the seniors. Snows quite a bit up here. Maybe that's why there are so many bars in town.

What have you decided to do about your retirement? How long are you going to stay with Neil? He must have given his first speech on the floor by now. He's going to do well, just give him a shove in the right direction every once and awhile as you did his predecessor.

Take care of yourself Maddy,

Love,

Fran

Fran got off work at six on Fridays. He usually got a hamburger and fries at the cafeteria in Daley's basement and then drove out to get the van. Dawg Feat had purchased an old van, rusted-out in the back, with about 90,000 miles. But it was cheap and with the new battery it usually started with no problem.

The band stored its equipment in the van parked for most of the week in front of a faded yellow house. Now divided into three apartments and in serious disrepair, the house nonetheless hinted that at one time it could have been one of the town's more desirable residences. Kevin and Ray shared the bottom apartment, and Carson and Fran each had one of the smaller apartments upstairs. Fran didn't see much of Kevin and Ray and that suited him fine. Carson was usually home when Fran returned from work and the two often went to Duke's for dinner. Fran usually got Carson's mail from the black mail box hanging just to the side of the front door. Carson used a stick with a spring-operated claw to reach up, grab the metal ring, and pull the bottom down so the mail would fall out. But if there were a lot, some would fall on the stoop and could get wet. He preferred to let Fran get the mail.

The remaining roadie had left several weeks earlier, leaving band members to work with Fran to move and set up the equipment. Fran also drove the van and kept the schedule. More and more the others saw him as a kind of big brother. He didn't appear to have much in common with them, but he fit in. He was closest to Carson, who was now becoming more and more frustrated with where the group was going. He had a lot of brochures on his kitchen table about his dwarf group – the one Fran had seen in Washington -- and he read them when he was frustrated and down.

"You know, I overheard this agent once tell Kevin and Ray that he didn't care how good my voice was, the group would never get anywhere with a dwarf as a front man. What do you think of that?" Carson asked as he climbed into the passenger seat.

Fran looked at him as the van's engine warmed up. He never felt he had the right words when Carson started talking about these kinds of problems. "Don't listen to that baloney, you know what a great voice you have."

"Well, you tell me how many dwarfs you can name that made it big in rock and roll."

"Carson. I'm no expert, I don't know, but if there aren't any, that doesn't mean you can't be the break-through guy," Fran said as they drove down the street.

"Yeah, yeah. Maybe I should make that announcement tonight. Let them know that one day they'll be reading about me and how I got my start right here in Dranesville."

Friday night the band played at Pearsall's. A steady gig, one Friday wasn't much different from another. But on Saturday nights, the group looked for higher-paying jobs out of town. Tomorrow night they were playing about three hours away at a renovated warehouse, one in a new chain of clubs. The local radio station was to be there doing bits of live feed. Carson had written a new song the group had rehearsed over the past couple of weeks. They would play it tonight, see what kind of response it got.

At the beginning of the third set, with the crowd nice and mellow, Carson picked up the mike. "We have a new one for you tonight; one of our own, that we hope you like." Carson was fidgeting; he took a last drag on his cigarette.

"Hey, put that cigarette out, you want to stunt your growth?" some guy with bulging veins in his neck yelled at Carson.

"The name of the song is 'You're Too Wonderful,'" Carson said, gritting his teeth.

"Thank you, you little shirmp," said the obnoxious guy.

Some in the crowd started laughing at the band. An inauspicious start, Fran thought, breaks the whole mood. Why did that guy have to say that?

How can you ever plan for having a guy like that around when you're trying to do something important?

The intro clicked, the harmonies blended, and the bridge got everyone clapping their hands; even the obnoxious guy was pumping his arm. Kevin and Ray started smiling as William, continuing the lead, looked up briefly at Carson who hit every note as if he were shooting one birdie after another on the back nine.

"You guys recovered well," Fran said to Carson the next afternoon as the two waited outside the van for the rest of the band.

"Got shook at first, that guy was such an asshole, but I think we probably shouldn't change anything with that new song."

Kevin and Ray, their girlfriends flopping behind, walked toward the van.

"All right man, we're still gonna caravan to this gig, right?" Kevin asked.

"Yeah," Fran said. "We have you guys, William, and two other cars of people to help with the equipment. Should be about three hours, that gives us plenty of time."

"Dude, sounds good; sounds like a good gig."

Kevin's goofy look soon ignited one in Ray.

The other cars arrived and the caravan was off as the faded charcoal sky began to break enough for a trace of winter sun to bounce off the snow.

Fran was leading the way in the van with Carson reading some new brochures. "You sounded good last night, everything was right on. You know the Pearsall's crowd can be rough, but they were really into the new song."

"Think so?" Carson asked.

"I know so. I was there. It worked, could be the break-through."

Carson looked at Fran, then down at his brochures with their dwarf-action alerts, all the issues and whom in government to contact. "You know, I wish there were some big shot out there who really understood what it was like. You go to state capitals, you go to Washington, get a lot of talk, a lot of sure we'll help you. I know what people in my office say behind my back."

"Think break-through, man." Fran the big brother found himself getting hip. He was driving the lead vehicle, he had the map, he had the contacts and the phone numbers for tonight, because no one else wanted to be the lead car. He was de facto chairman of this committee and nobody knew who he was.

Carson picked up the cell phone to call Ray's car and then William's car. He told them they were about an hour away and that he'd look for some place to get a quick dinner. "Holy shit," he said as he turned up the radio. "That's us, that must be that WRVO station that's gonna do some of our show." He tried to get the other cars, but lost the signal. "Damn, we sounded good."

"You did sound good. Seems to be some kind of lodge or inn up ahead on the right. Might be a good place to get something to eat."

The cars pulled into the gravel lot in front of a log cabin building. The concrete logs were much in need of a fresh coat of brown paint. The aluminum awning was covered with bird droppings and every window had a neon beer sign. "Latch's Tavern," read the sign swinging in the breeze.

Spring was only a couple of weeks off, but winter fought it off every night until then. And, in these parts, the warmer season was often kept waiting regardless of what the calendar said. It was a cold walk from the cars, and Fran was glad to be inside. The group walked toward the back and the waitress pointed to several tables they could pull together if they liked. Promotional materials with celebrities probably now in nursing homes hung on the rough-hewn, pine paneling.

"Damn, damn, damn," said Carson as he stood in front of the cigarette machine.

"What's wrong?" Fran asked.

"What's wrong? I'll tell you what's wrong. This stupid machine is out of Marlboro Lights. Damn, what the hell am I going to do?" Carson started to rock back and forth in front of the machine. I knew I should have stopped before we left. I can't smoke Winston Lights, not tonight."

"Honey, don't get yourself all worked up. Would a couple of mine hold you over till you get wherever you're going?" the waitress asked as she started fumbling in her apron pocket.

"Bel Airs?! I can't smoke Bel Airs!"

"Well for crying out loud, I'm just trying to help. If you need your Marlboro Lights so darn bad, maybe they have them at Booker's across the road."

Carson pumped hard for the front door and was soon crossing the street.

"Little shit," the waitress said under her breath.

Fran and the others looked at their menus as the waitress took drink orders.

"Carson's uptight, man," William said, his fedora still tilted over his eyes. "He's got to calm down. Man, this is an important gig tonight."

For the first time since he arrived in the valley, Fran wondered who represented this district. There was no place in the United States without them; some congressman claimed as his wherever you were. He thought it might be Marty Sawyer, but he wasn't sure. He looked around the table and realized that probably no one had the foggiest idea that Marty Sawyer was their congressman, and probably could give a rat's ass if, indeed, it were Marty that represented this area. Fran looked at the door, pictured Marty walking in and recognizing Fran, asking "What the heck is this, is that you Fran, Fran Stewart?"

But Fran was done with the gorilla mask. He couldn't pretend to be interested in this or that topic; couldn't go to any more embassy dinners. Then he thought about the New Zealand embassy and the night he met Jo Ellen. He didn't even know where she was. Probably staying with her parents. He thought about her often and wondered if they would ever get back together. His love for Carter was still strong. Maybe he should forget about Jo Ellen. Maybe it had all crumbled because he didn't fulfill his pledge to honor and cherish Carter forever. What would Carter think about his being at Latch's tonight? Would she forgive him for hurting their daughter? Could he forgive himself?

"Anybody seen Carson, man?" William asked. There was no response. "Hey anybody seen Carson?"

This time somebody answered. "Maybe some mama bear saw him in the dark and mistook him for one of her cubs and took him back to her cave," Ray said with that dark look.

"Damn, he has been gone for a long time," Fran said plucking himself from the other world he had entered. He walked outside and headed across the road into the blackness. Booker's looked even more primitive than Latch's. He passed through a row of sagging pick-ups and by rusted muscle cars from a time when gas cost seventy-five cents a gallon.

"I never seen nothing like that," laughed some tall, husky guy with a front tooth missing. He looked at Fran, and, scowling, made no effort to keep the front door from closing.

"Got a problem?" the guy asked Fran.

"No problem," Fran said as he opened the door.

"You're damn right you don't have a problem, cause if you did, I'd have a problem. You hear me boy?"

"I hear you."

"Damn right you hear me and don't you damn forget it."

Fran stepped inside, then froze as he saw what was going on in the middle of the room between the bar and the pool table. Four chrome bar stools with tattered red, Naugahyde seats stood in a square, almost like some cage at the circus. Carson, inside the square, was in a paroxysm of fidgeting and rocking. Around the cage were about a dozen men. It looked to Fran like the family reunion of the banjo player from *Deliverance*.

"Fran," Carson cried as he looked toward the door. "Fran!"

Fran walked slowly toward the bar.

"Fran, come on in, you a friend of the little feller?" asked the man whose dark matted hair spoke of impeccable back-woods credentials.

"Happen to be," said Fran, "just like the other thirty people across the road. What the hell do you characters think you're doing?"

"Well now, Fran," Mr. Backwoods said, "that there is a fair question. Guess you didn't see those packs of beer nuts on the floor. See we got 'em set up as markers, they go on two feet apart till you get to the door. Willie here said he thought the little feller could fly and we all thought we'd take a turn seeing how far we could make him fly. You can play if you like Fran, throw five dollars in the pot, farthest throw takes it all."

"Are you some kind of mental patient?" Fran asked as he pulled out his cell phone.

"Now Fran, that wasn't a particularly nice thing to say. I got a hunch that before you get to the second number on that phone of yours, some of the boys here might make sure you don't do no more dialing. Hell, we might add a second part to our dwarf throwing, see how far we can toss your ass," Backwoods said as he twirled Carson's blue calico neckerchief.

Fran knew the old bartender was as frightened as Carson. "Look, I know you guys probably don't have any place to go, but my friend and I and everyone else across the road have to be someplace in about thirty minutes. They're going to come looking for us any minute."

"You keep sayin that Fran. I assure you that our competition is gonna start no matter whose ass walks through that door. I hope you understand me and the boys here aren't gonna be happy with anyone that tries to interrupt our contest. And I want to get this thing goin before that little feller gets worked up and starts pissin himself."

Everyone in the room turned as the old door started to creak open. A state trooper, his wide-brimmed campaign hat in hand, walked into the bar.

"All right," Backwoods said, "I found my ring. We can put those stools back under the bar. He tucked the kerchief into Carson's back pocket.

"How's it goin boys? Guess you won me tonight, place across the street is too crowded," the trooper said as he walked over, sat down at one of the tables, and pulled the single-sheet menu from between the sugar jar and ketchup bottle.

Carson hurried over to Fran and they both headed toward the door.

"Shit, shit, I thought those guys were going to kill me. I don't think I have ever been so frightened or humiliated. I read about some of that stuff in my brochures. What are we going to do?"

"Carson, I am so sorry this happened. I can only imagine how scared you must have been. We can do whatever you want. Only problem, I don't think that trooper is going to be inclined to do much. And 'the boys' in there will say it's all a misunderstanding. And the bartender will say he was busy and didn't see anything. And we'll be there talking, trying to explain what happened and know what? We'll be late for the gig. But we'll do whatever you want. Maybe we can figure something out in the car."

Carson didn't say anything. He even stopped fidgeting as they walked back to Latch's Tavern.

"Nice of you folks to come back," William said. "I mean we've only been waiting here forever so you could get your damn Marlboro Lights."

So much for the rescue party, Fran thought. The caravan was soon on its way, Booker's disappearing in the rearview mirror.

They played in an old department store with a high ceiling and columns. The local radio station DJ introduced them, and the crowd of several hundred, from teens to baby boomers, cheered as the first song ended. Because the group was up on a stage some four or five feet off the floor, Carson didn't need his stool. The spotlights made it impossible for him to see the laughing faces as the band tuned up. Carson soon captured the crowd, however, with vocals more solid than Fran had ever heard.

Carson waved to Ray who was crammed into a small platform above the main stage. "Time for the new one," he yelled. Ray waved one of his sticks. The bass line hit in, followed by colliding key boards and guitar. Carson delivered pitch perfect each note in the final crescendo. The song hit on all cylinders. The words to the chorus were simple and the crowd sang along as if they were part of the band.

The euphoria didn't last long. Carson turned and saw Ray waving his drum sticks and pointing. Carson smiled and pointed back at his drummer. Ray started yelling something, and Carson finally saw what he was gesturing towards. A thin stream of smoke was trailing from one of the amplifiers. Ray was starting to miss the back beat as he waved more furiously toward the amp. Carson tried to find Fran and walked over to William, who shooed him away with an angry look. Carson continued looking for Fran, but by then it was too late. The mike began to crackle and Ray jumped down from his aluminum foil platform much like a Thanksgiving turkey come to life and jumping out of the oven roaster. One amp blew, then the whole system with one final sputter, died. Ray had gotten to the back of the amp and with a towel had swatted out the sparks that had created the smoke. Everyone had stopped playing except William.

"It's over, dude," Ray said to Fran who climbed up on to the stage. "You want to tell Jimi Hendrix over there that nobody can hear him anymore."

The house lights came on and the undulating bodies stopped. Squinting from the brightness, the crowd soon figured out that the show that night was over.

"Shit, shit. Shit. Why do these things happen to me?" Carson asked. Fran put his hand on Carson's shoulder.

"Carson, stop walking around in circles, you're going to get dizzy and fall off the stage."

Several club technicians surveyed the damage and each one of them shook his head as they looked at the wiring, amps, and other equipment.

"What did you guys do to my equipment?" the club manager asked as he reached to grab Fran's hand and get a boost on to the stage.

"What did we do?" asked an enraged Kevin. "You almost cooked us alive with all your tin-foil decorations and crappy equipment. You're lucky we weren't all electrocuted. Wait till we tell our lawyer about this." Dawg Feat's lawyer existed only in Kevin's mind.

"We had two other groups in here since we opened and they didn't have any damn problems. Look at this, look at this," the club manager said as he stared at the silent stage and then at the hundreds of impatient customers. He turned to an assistant, "I got to get hold of that DJ fast, he's got his own sound system and should be able to hold the crowd. I'll tell the crowd we're gonna take a short intermission and I'll give them a free drink." The club owner started smiling, obviously pleased with his plan. William sat on one of the amps and continued playing his guitar.

"Boys, look, I know the contract says I got to pay you for tonight, but you only played a few songs. Suppose you stay around and help us clean up when we close down?"

William broke out of his trance. "That contract is a standard musician's union contract. I've read a lot of them and never saw anything about musicians picking up trash."

"Listen, you boys better get your stuff out of here right quick. I got a mind to tell the crowd you guys broke our system."

With the extra volunteers that had accompanied the band, the equipment was packed and loaded up fast. As the group headed with the last boxes toward the door, they saw the DJ rolling in his sound system. "Don't you folks worry, I'll have the music going again, won't take me long to get set up. Everything is gonna be fine. Don't worry," he said in his DJ voice. They didn't.

Fran walked toward the door. Carson, William, Kevin, and Ray saw he had a check in hand. They had forgotten about their song; the song that in their minds was going to break them through that night. Instead, the song lay in the shambles of a fried sound system. In the end they had just played for the check. Maybe that's as far as they would ever get.

CHAPTER 20

Fran opened up on Monday mornings. As assistant manager of the women's shoe department at Dayley's Department Store, he was low man on the totem pole in the two-man department. He wore one of the two sport jackets he bought at the discount store just outside of town. More and more stores were opening out there, and more and more vacant stores surrounded Dayley's. Sometimes as he picked through the ties he brought with him he would think about his last year in Washington and those days slinking around hole-in the wall restaurants until that Somali meal nailed him good.

He hadn't heard yet from Becky or Jo Ellen. Maddy no longer worked for Neil, but she checked on any mail that might be important to Fran. Maddy and Neil had spoken to him several times since the first of the year. Fran delighted in hearing about how well Neil seemed to be doing. But they couldn't believe what was happening to their former boss. Roadie? Assistant manager of a women's shoe department? He had traded voting for billion-dollar programs affecting hundreds of millions of people to measuring feet and carrying amplifiers.

Fran liked the quiet of the morning in his department. He got organized, made sure all the displays were perfect. He had a special cleaner that removed dust and left that extra sparkle customers expected to see on new shoes.

Fran lived frugally. With what he earned at Dayley's –salary and a tiny commission – he was able to pay the rent and a have a little left over for food. He drew from his savings for the rest, including Becky's support payments. She didn't return his phone calls. He believed that was Feeney's doing. He dreamed of having his daughter tell him she wanted to be with him. He'd be there in a second. Maybe he'd drive to Tennessee, just show up. But he didn't know what was best for his daughter.

The women's shoe department was across from the candy department. Pre-wrapped boxes and bins behind glass held chocolates, nuts and assorted sweets. Fran's favorite were the Turtles. During a slow time in the shoe department he might take a quick trip to the candy counter. Margaret, an attractive, dark-haired woman, maybe a few years older than Fran, always seemed to have a bag of the chocolate-covered caramel and pecan candies waiting for him. He would say hello, lay his money on the counter and take the bag. One time there was a note inside: "Hope you enjoy these. When's your break? Want to grab some lunch?" He never answered her. She didn't seem to take offense, though Fran caught her staring at him sometimes around the store.

"Pardon me, do you have these in a seven?" asked the woman waving the open-backed black shoe in the air.

"Let me check for you ma'am," Fran responded as he walked into the storeroom. Returning, he told the woman he had only a six and a half in stock.

"Let me look at that please, these styles all fit differently." The shoe was snug on the left but fit well on the right. "Can you stretch this one a little?"

"Let me see what I can do," Fran said as he picked up the shoe and returned to the storeroom. He smiled as he thought about the number of times he had been asked if he could "stretch this a little." It was as if they thought he had wizard tools in his storeroom. He had what looked like an old wooden shoe tree with a screw mechanism that once inside the shoe could be turned to "stretch." Truth be told, it didn't work that well, as most of the newer styles had leather not tightly anchored to the sole. Turn the mechanism too much, and the side of the shoe began to separate. His boss had taught Fran to twist the stretcher an eighth of a turn, and then slap at the shoe with his hand. Fran began the black magic, knowing that when he brought the shoe out it most likely would be no bigger than when he brought it in.

"This feels much better," the woman said. "I'll take them."

The summer styles had been out for a while, in defiance of the chill that could hang in Dranesville even as spring ordered trees and flowers to break out their colors. Customers asked Fran few questions. Many of them were long-time shoppers and they seemed to know what they wanted. Some would get upset if they couldn't find a certain style. They looked at Fran as if it were his fault. Sometimes they could be coaxed into accepting something else. Other times, they walked away indignantly. Fran wondered if being told that your favorite shoes had been discontinued really constituted a life crisis.

He wondered what they'd say if they saw arms and feet sticking out of hastily dug mass graves in Bosnia. What would they say if they saw photos of rape camps? Did they think their inability to obtain a certain shoe style ranked with an African mother's inability to get food and fresh water for her sickly children? He remembered the many late nights, when he and several colleagues tried to strengthen human rights protection under international conventions.

Fran felt a tap on the shoulder that brought him back to Dranesville. He turned and saw Francine, his waitress from the first night at Pearsall's. He looked for her yellow waitress dress, but found the blonde woman in her mid-thirties wearing jeans and a pale green sweater. Fran wouldn't call her a friend, but she was always pleasant when they spoke at Pearsall's. As he thought about it, she had been even more pleasant over the past few weeks.

"They told me you worked here. Thought I'd see if you could help me find a nice casual tie shoe; something good for walking, but not necessarily in the woods."

Fran smiled. "You've come to the right spot. Let me show you our "not necessarily in the woods" collection. He walked over to a display of a half-dozen shoes and watched as Francine picked each one up for inspection.

"Let me try these two."

"And the size?"

"I'm usually a 6, but maybe we should double check."

Fran sat down on the stool in front of her and reached for the clunky shoe measurer. She slid off her shoe and placed her stocking foot on the device.

"You were right, 6 it is. Let's see what we have in back. Fran had learned quickly how the stock was arranged. He prided himself on that. With workman-like efficiency, he wasted no time.

"We have all three," he announced proudly as he sat back down on the stool. He noticed now what he hadn't earlier. Her toenails were perfect, lacquered in a pale red polish that must have been applied recently. He held the bottom of her shoe as his other hand guided the shoe horn along the back of her heel. The foot slipped in perfectly. She got up and walked toward the shoe mirror. Fran had never seen her from this angle, her jeans were very flattering.

"These feel good, very comfortable; just what I had in mind. I think I'll take that color as well."

"Did you want to try them on, make sure they fit?" he asked.

She looked at him as he held the same shoe, just a different color. "Yeah, probably, just to make sure."

Francine put her wallet away and picked up her two packages. "Pleasure doing business with you, Fran. See you later this week." She started to leave then turned around. "Heard you're living out with the guys in that big yellow house."

"Right, it's worked out pretty well. It's a nice place."

She smiled, raised her hand and waved her fingers. "See ya."

"I told you what I heard. She's been asking about you. I think she's got the hots for you," Carson said as one arm stabbed repeatedly into the air. The other hand was moving back and forth across the back of his dog, Otis, who was standing in front of him. Part Dalmatian, Black Lab, Great Dane mix, Otis weighed at least 140 pounds. He had the look of a small pony; something an Indian, a dwarf Indian, might ride. Carson got him at the shelter for twenty-five dollars. He was the only dog that barked and waved his tail furiously as Carson walked down the aisle past the caged dogs. He was a friendly dog and was usually asleep in the corner on his old bath mat.

"Well, I don't know about that," Fran said. "She's a nice girl, cute, let's leave it at that."

"Otis!" Carson yelled.

Fran rolled his eyes after hearing the three short bursts. He knew what was coming. Otis had one problem: a bad case of flatulence. At times he gave no warning, there was only silence. Fran found this out walking up the stairs behind him. Carson would always shout out and scrunch-up his face. Otis never changed expression. Fran didn't know much about dogs. He wasn't sure if Otis thought Carson was praising him.

Everyone except William had gotten over last Saturday's fiasco. They felt the song was good and planned to play it a couple of more times at Pearsall's. If it went well, they'd try to get some studio time to cut a quick CD. Fran could see the dreaming in their eyes. That small piece of plastic would carry all into the big-time world of rock and roll. They would leave Dranesville and never return. Their song had to be good. Rub that CD three times and hope the genie appeared.

Fran had gone to the movies, as he often did on Thursday when the new films came out. He read for a while when he returned home then turned on the TV to catch the eleven o'clock news. He had gotten used to the local newscasters. It was soothing to no longer have to worry about dealing with those issues the next day.

There was a slight knock at the door. He never knew when to expect Carson. Most times Fran enjoyed listening to his friend. Carson was so full of dreams. While Fran's were behind him, he sometimes thought about resurrecting them when he listened to Carson.

Fran opened the door and found a woman in a yellow waitress dress holding a small paper container. Her purse was big enough to be an overnight bag.

"I hope I didn't stop by too late," Francine said. "I saw your light on and from what you described, I thought you lived upstairs."

"You guessed right, but if you had knocked on that door you would have gotten Carson."

"Oh, thank goodness."

Fran knew that for some reason, Carson made Francine nervous. Fran saw it the first day. She was always polite but seemed worried about saying something that might offend him.

"Come in before Otis hears us."

"Otis?"

Fran told her about Carson's dog and she gave him a confused look as she walked into Fran's apartment. "Can I get you something?" Fran asked. Her perfume was fresh.

"I can't stay. I'm a tired working girl you know. But I brought you something. I eat them all the time and hate to see them go to waste." She pulled two doggie boxes from Pearsall's and opened one. "Isn't this beautiful steak? We get some customers, mostly women, I must admit, that just eat a little and end up leaving most of the steak. Do you believe that? They pay for the whole thing and then eat only a little bit. I'm very careful to trim around the part they've eaten from, but the rest is fine. I'm usually able to save one every night. If I don't eat it when I get home, I'll save it for the next day, have a sliced steak sandwich or even make a little stew concoction. Some nights, like tonight, I'll be able to save two steaks. I thought you might like one."

Fran looked at her. His mouth had slipped open several times as she spoke. He had only ordered the steak once at Pearsall's. It was the most expensive item on the menu, a delicious piece of meat with a slight dusting of garlic. He felt it a bit too extravagant given his present circumstances. But taking the remains of someone else's dinner? "That looks good," was all Fran could get out.

"I hoped you would like it. You don't have to eat it right now. You can make a steak sandwich in the morning and bring it to work with you. Slice it on a nice angle. That'll give you the best taste; learned that from the other waitresses."

Fran tried to think about all the lavish meals he had eaten as a representative of the people. How many of his leftovers found their way to someone else's house? "Francine, please sit down, let me get you something," was the best he could think of to stop himself from staring.

"Well, okay, but only for a minute, don't want to keep you from going to bed," she said as she sat down and took off her jacket.

"Coffee?"

"Well, okay, but only if you're having some too."

Fran walked into the small kitchen and Francine looked around the room, illuminated only by the TV screen. She saw a hinged frame that contained two photos. Carter and Becky Stewart looked out at her. Fran had said virtually nothing to anyone in Dranesville about his past. Carson knew about Carter, and about Becky, Fran told him simply that his daughter was staying with her grandmother until he got work after losing a sales job. Carson fired off question after question initially until he saw that Fran was not responding. His questions stopped. Fran hid Jo Ellen's photo from everyone, but it was in his mind every day.

"Coffee will be done in a bit, sorry this is about all I have to offer," he said, as he put a plate before her with a half-dozen Pecan Sandies.

"My favorite," she said, making a big fuss as she took one of the cookies. "I couldn't help noticing those photos, they're gorgeous."

"That's my wife and my daughter."

There was silence and she studied him to see if there would be more. Impatient, she started a question, but he walked into the kitchen.

She looked at the photos again. She hadn't anticipated sharing him this evening. He returned with two mugs of coffee, a half-gallon container of milk and some sugar packets he had taken from somewhere. "They're beautiful."

"My wife was killed in an auto accident and my daughter lives with her grandmother." He felt no obligation to provide further information. He drank his coffee quickly. "Thank you for the steak. I am going to make a sandwich for tomorrow."

She crossed and uncrossed her legs. He looked at them and remembered holding her feet in the store. His eyes wandered toward hers. She brought the mug to her lips then smiled at him.

"What time do you start at the store tomorrow?"

"Got to be there at eight-thirty," he said as his voice trailed off in a yawn.

He knew he was tired, the coffee had no effect. But it had on Francine. She took another sip, never taking her focus off him. She put her mug down and stood right in front of him. He started to rise from his seat in the limited room she had allowed him.

"Thank you for the coffee and cookies. I hope you enjoy your steak. I didn't bother you did I?" She was only a few inches from his face.

"No, that was very thoughtful."

"See how you like it. If you want, I can bring you more."

"Great, that would be great," his mouth said without checking with his brain.

"Good." She placed her hand on his shoulder and twirled her thumb. She reached for her jacket and Fran helped her as she slipped her arms into the sleeves. He opened the door for her and she brushed against him. "I'll call before I come next time."

Otis heard the door and voices this time and started to bark, make loud sniffing sounds, then bark again. Francine was down the stairs before Carson opened the door, but he looked down the stairs and saw her leaving. He looked over at Fran and raised his eyebrows.

"Good night, Carson," Fran said as he closed the door.

CHAPTER 21

Fran began reading the papers again. *The Dranesville Advertiser* was his main source of news. During his break, he worked on the crossword puzzle, usually with a pen. Sometimes the squares filled quickly, other times the page was a mess of crossed-out words. The AP stories gave him a few paragraphs about what was going on in Washington and internationally. He didn't want to know more. Then they put a *U.S.A. Today* box by the bus stop outside of Dayley's. He'd always been captured by the screaming graphics that promised more of a story than there was. But on the several occasions he had been included in the paper -- minus the incident – they were fair and accurate. He started buying the paper on the way home. If it were sold out, he didn't have to read anything that day. He enjoyed that freedom.

He read about his former colleagues engaged in budget battles as each party accused the other of gimmickry designed to fool the American people. If the numbers and names were changed, they could have been the same stories that ran last year, or the year before that, or ten years before that. Those people were on a carousel; some liked the ride and could look at the same scenery forever. Others didn't know how to get off. The international news was as bad as always. U.S troops were now in the Balkans and conflicting reports assessed their prospects in that troubled region. Ethnic fighting there had been brutal and civilian survivors told of unspeakable horrors. Maybe those accounts were supposed to keep showing up until the reader did something about it. It wasn't Fran's job anymore; at least that's what he told himself. Probably no one in Dranesville thought it was their job either.

Fran still tried to understand the stories about the hazy world of international economics with its challenges to the dollar, trade balances, and IMF plans. Every time he thought he understood why something was happening or how some proposal would work, he would find yet some other analysis or new factor that at least to him, threw all the earlier equations on their heads. If there were good news or some encouraging statistics, they usually just appeared and were hard to explain using the experts' conventional theories.

He had been drawn to a series of articles about a summer of burning churches; black churches in the South. Fran was ten when his Dad brought him to a gospel concert back in Tennessee at the invitation of a man his family had gotten to know. Several windows at the church had been blown out and fresh paint covered ugly phrases. Fran remembered holding his Dad's hand tightly as they approached their seats. In the days following the concert, Fran's parents heard many disparaging comments from their friends. It didn't bother his parents; it was the right thing to do. But they became concerned about their son's safety, recognizing that he was their weak link in any effort to speak out more. Fran remembered the names his friend since first grade had called him. What must that boy's parents have told him?

Fran had grown up at a time when the South was still wrestling with the dictates of major civil rights laws. His family fully supported these changes and he absorbed his parents' views. His young age at times tricked him into believing that once the law was changed, things would change.

Many of the old ways escaped the new laws, but he was encouraged as he got older because the new laws seemed to be winning.

Burning churches; any kind of churches, but black churches? The old ways seemed to have returned to throw sand into the eyes of the laws that were now over thirty years old. These churches, as Fran remembered from his younger days and from when he visited them during his days as their representative, were the beating hearts of the black community. So many activities, services, support groups, and community centers were tied to these churches. Those setting the fires knew that the flames would be consuming more than buildings of worship. The flames were meant to burn a faith that congregants had molded to protect them from savagery; savagery that at times wore a badge, and that God alone could understand. Fran read about the groups being organized to go south and help rebuild these churches.

Fran heard Carson at the door. He knew Otis was there as well. Fran opened the door and Otis jumped up on the couch and heaved a sigh that made the pages of the newspaper flutter. Fran and Carson had tried to keep Otis off the couch but it was no use.

"All right, from the beginning," Carson said as he got up into the chair with more effort than it had taken Otis to sit down. "What was Francine doing up here? What's going on between you two?"

"What do you think about this?" Fran asked as he showed Carson the story about the burning churches. Carson rocked and read for about ten seconds.

"I'll tell you what I think. I'd be in deep shit if I were a black dwarf." Fran took the paper back. "Are you going to tell me or not?"

"There's not much to tell. She brought me over some leftover steak in a doggie bag. Said she took it home all the time, didn't think it was right to just throw it away. It was good. I had a nice steak sandwich for lunch today."

"What?'

"You asked me what happened. I told you."

"I told you she had the hots for you, everybody's been telling me that. Did you smell all that perfume? Anything happen?" Carson asked lowering his voice.

"Nothing happened. We had some coffee and Pecan Sandies and she left."

"Nothing happened? Are you crazy?"

"Maybe so, but nothing happened."

"Are you going to see her again?"

"Of course I'll see her again; she works at Pearsall's."

"That's not what I mean."

It was at this point that Otis forced them to change the conversation. It was impossible for them not to. Fran had never encountered a dog or anyone for that matter with flatulence that could, announced or unannounced turn good breathable air into the foulest septic gas. "Geez, Otis!" Carson said.

Fran shook his head and fanned his hands around him. The treatment hung stubbornly in the air. Carson stood up and began to wave as well, reaching up as if trying to find a level of air that had not been soured. He looked like a small plane starting to taxi. Otis stood there calmly, breathing as if in a pine forest.

"You know, I can find out, you know I have a lot of sources," Carson said after determining it was safe to take a regular breath.

"Carson, you've got to stop this, I told you nothing happened."

"But, she . . ."

"I know, she has the hots for me. Nothing happened."

"Okay, be that way. I'll see you tomorrow. Come on Otis."

William knocked on Carson's door. No answer except an abbreviated bark and some heavy sniffing. William turned as Fran opened his door and noticed the lead guitarist.

"Hey William."

"Know where Carson is?"

"No."

"Well, I wanted to tell him personally, but if you see him before I do, tell him that Kevin and Ray are quitting the band.

"What? Why?"

"Kevin knows some guy in Vermont, told Kevin that he just met this agent that convinced him he has an in with this new record label that supposedly has some money and is looking for new groups. This guy's band broke up and they need Kevin and Ray to come up right away. I wanted to tell Carson in person because I know how upset he's going to be, but if you see him first, tell him. I guess tomorrow night is Dawg Feat's final performance."

"Just like that, it's over?"

William grinned. It was the first time Fran had seen him smile. "Just like that. This is the music business, dude. Otis, lay down," he said as he started rapping a rhythm on Carson's door. He knew how agitated that would get Otis whose bark had elevated to a steady howl.

Fran wondered just how much he would miss William and for that matter Kevin and Ray. But he didn't know how he would tell Carson. The band made Carson feel special, like he belonged. His voice was his ante and he knew it could get him into most games. But it wasn't just the voice trying to get through the door, it was the rest of Carson as well. Kevin and Ray's fantasy was that they could make it through that door, that they were good enough, just needed all the stars to be in proper alignment. But they'd never make it through with Carson. If they weren't leaving now, they'd leave some time. Fran thought William felt the same way, though William was kinder. Fran left a note on Carson's door.

When Fran returned, the note was still there. He wondered if William or maybe Kevin or Ray had found Carson first. Had they told him? He knew they would be careless. Fran pictured Carson walking in a daze down by the river. Or was he in some bar getting drunk, it only took two beers and people got some free entertainment by watching a very short man ramble, repeat himself, and flail his arms. Several hours passed before Fran heard a knock at his door.

"I've been looking for you."

"You won't believe the new book the library got in." Carson waved some book, the only word in the title of which Fran could make out was dwarf. "This has everything: history, special studies and research, it shows that we're able to do some really neat things. It also has all this stuff on what we're doing to organize and get things we shouldn't even have to ask for. I saw the note. So you're ready to tell me what happened last night?"

"Want something to drink? Eat?"

"Yeah, Diet Pepsi if you have any left. And I'll have some Pecan Sandies if you didn't eat them all last night."

Carson climbed up into the chair and took his soda and cookies. "Okay, fire away. I knew you'd be telling me sooner or later."

"This isn't about last night. And I'm going to tell you as best I can. Kevin and Ray got an offer to play with a band in Vermont. I'm not sure what William is going to do." Fran spoke very slowly, searching for better words. Carson's face fell.

"Are you shitting me? Vermont? Just like that? What about the band? What about me? Who's going to find a place for me? I should have expected this, but, I thought things were finally coming together with our new song."

Fran said nothing. Carson threw his book on the floor.

"Carson you still have your song. It's yours, you wrote it. You get the royalties. We'll find some way."

"I'm going to have to get a second job. I needed that money. Do you know what that's like, having to go to interviews and having people look at you? Some hide their smirks better than others, but you know they're all smirking on the inside."

"I can check at Dayley's, maybe they have something."

"Oh yeah, I'd make a great salesman. Want to put me in the men's department or the boy's department? Or maybe sporting goods?"

"Carson, don't you think you're going too far?"

"Fran, look, you've become a very good friend. Everyone says you're very kind. But until you've seen things through my eyes, you'll never know how far far is. And you know what? My lease is up next week. Ray, Kevin and I all signed at the same time. I won't be able to afford my apartment any more. Your sublet is up too. Did you sign a new lease yet?"

"Not yet."

"Well, what are you waiting for?"

"I just haven't gotten around to it yet. I have it, I just haven't signed it yet."

"Why not? Are you leaving too?"

"I didn't say I was leaving," Fran said.

"Well are you?"

"I guess I've been wondering whether I wanted to commit for another year."

Carson's hand folded around the Pecan Sandy then began to crush the cookie. "Yeah, sure, leave. William will probably leave too with that dopey girlfriend of his. Maybe Otis and I can go live with my sister or maybe we can get a tent and live in the woods where we belong."

"Carson." Fran saw the vacant look in Carson's eyes.

"Are you leaving?"

"I didn't say I was leaving."

"Well are you?"

"I might be," Fran responded. "Look, I never figured on staying around here this long. Things just fell into place, I enjoyed working with the band, got the job at Dayley's, got the apartment. I've been here almost seven months, not much for me to do up here other than sell women's shoes and I don't know if I can take that for another year."

Carson let the crumbs fall on the napkin and took a deep breath. "Where do you think you'll go?"

"Long term, I don't know. Remember the story I read about the black churches burning in the South? Well, the other day, this customer was in and somehow we got talking about the churches. She told me a group from her church was going down to Alabama in two weeks to help build a new church replacing one that was burned. There's some church organization coordinating the volunteers and logistics and everything down there. I think she said Greene County, wherever that is. They will be there for a week, then another group comes in. I guess they keep rotating in new groups till they get the church built. She said to let her know if I knew anyone who was interested; they were looking for a few more people. I just nodded. Didn't get her name, although I could get it from her receipt." Fran's mind was already packing.

"So you're moving to Greene County, Alabama?"

"No, I didn't say I was moving. But if they still have room, I think I might like to go down to help on the church. Gonna cost $150 per person to help cover the cost of housing and food while you're there." Fran looked directly at Carson. "Want to come?"

"Oh sure. I just got finished telling you how I wasn't going to be able to afford my apartment and you want me to come up with $150 so I can go down South in the middle of the summer and build a church. I've never built a church before. I've never built anything. And what am I supposed to do with my stuff and with Otis? You're just asking me to go, so you can say 'Well, I asked him to go. Not my fault he didn't come.' I know that trick."

"Carson, I'd like you to come. Let me take care of your $150, I've got a little extra. Come on, we can be partners on this. Your sister's got that big, old garage. She can store your stuff for a while, and you told me she gets along well with Otis. He'll have plenty of room at her place. Come on. I'd like you to come. You know I don't know anything about building churches either."

"This is crazy. How long does it take to get to this place?"

"Two days probably."

"Two days?! So that's even more money for a hotel and gas."

"I'll take care of it. Anyway, I still have to get in touch with this woman. Think about it, and I'll let you know what she says."

Carson walked towards his apartment. "This always happens to me. This always happens to me," he muttered. "Just when I think . . . aw what's the use?"

Shelly Strong, the woman with the church group, told Fran they would be delighted to have him and Carson go with them to Alabama. She was light-skinned, probably mid-fifties, with a peaceful expression. Fran met her in front of Dayley's and she gave him all the forms and hand-outs he needed for the trip. They would be staying at a county extension conference center not far from the new church site. Everyone in the group would take turns with daily chores: cooking, cleaning, etc.

"Says here it's air-conditioned," Fran said.

"My word, I hope so," Shelly said, a definite trace of concern in her laugh. "You just fill out these forms, and I'm afraid they need your checks as soon as possible."

Carson was in. He had arranged everything with his sister after he read all about the church burnings. He became so wrapped up in planning one would have thought the whole thing had been his idea. The news clips and reports from volunteers down South quickly convinced him there was a conspiracy: people running around after dark throwing gas on black churches; people like the ones who tormented him that night in Booker's Bar, and others that tormented him on other nights. He thought about the South and what it might do to him. But he wanted to help and he wanted to go with Fran.

Fran had given his one week notice at Dayley's. He was glad the Father's Day Sale signs were finally down. It had been as bad as Mother's Day last year. But then at least, he and Becky comforted each other. She always gave him the best cards. She drew little flowers and underlined all the words she thought important. Sometimes she made her own cards. And she would give him cologne, or a book. When she was real young, she gave him a five-dollar coupon for McDonald's with money she had saved. It was hard not getting a card this year. He wanted to hold his daughter in his arms, give her a big hug, and tell her how much he loved her.

He knew it was time to leave Dranesville. He had escaped Washington, matching it whack for whack just before he left. He knew it had gotten in the last hit, but he didn't care; it existed now only in the papers and TV. But he felt the vacation ending; its diversions could no longer sustain him. It was time to go home. But Fran didn't know where home was. Maybe he would find the answer in Alabama. It would at least keep him occupied for now. He could figure out the big picture later.

"It sucked, you know it sucked," Carson said about their last night at Pearsall's.

"We've got packing to do. You almost done? You know we've got to meet Shelly and the others at seven in the morning. I know it sucked, but it's over, done with, got to move on my friend. I thought we were done with this conversation."

Dawg Feat's last night playing at Pearsall's haunted Carson. William hadn't shown up, so they had to jury-rig most of the songs. Ray and Kevin went through the motions and even made some mocking gestures at Carson behind his back as he sang. They never mentioned this was their last night together. Everyone except Carson just wanted the night to be over. Francine avoided Fran until the music stopped. She told him she had saved more steak she could bring over after work. Fran thanked her, but holding his stomach, and crossing his fingers, told her he'd been suffering from a stomach ache all day and was going to sleep as soon as he got home. Looking like she sensed a brush off, she smiled and left the door open for a future delivery. Fran never saw her again.

CHAPTER 22

"Says here, forty churches been burned since the beginning of the year. Three down where we're going," Carson said. He had read that article at least four times since they left the hotel that morning, each time reading out different quotes to Fran.

"Shouldn't be much longer now," Fran remarked as he looked at the sign on the interstate showing they were only some twenty miles from their exit.

Carson pulled out some more news clips Shelly Strong had included in the packet she gave to each member of her group. "Everyone's involved in this; you got your Congress, the President, your church groups, FBI, Justice Department, unions, local law enforcement, some kind of task force. One guy says here, he can't believe this is happening in this day and age. Some black group knows this is one big conspiracy and then they got this Ku Klux Klan guy who says there's been a real increase in the demand for Klan paraphernalia." There was a pause as he shuffled for something you could tell he was looking for. "And remember this, this hand-out we got about where we're staying says they don't want us to go off the premises after dark and that a full discussion of the security situation will be provided upon our arrival. What's the story with that?"

Fran adjusted his sunglasses and wondered if Carson anticipated the same answer he had gotten the first two times he asked that question. "I'm sure we'll be fine. I think this is us, yeah, one mile till our exit. I think the cooperative center is only about five miles once we get off the interstate. Get a little dinner, talk to the Quaker folks running this show, walk around a bit, then get a good night's sleep. You'll be able to work that hammer real good in the morning."

Carson realized they were almost there. He had the look of a boy who had prepared all week to take his swim test, but now, as he stood at the edge of the pool, wondered what had made him think he could reach the other side. "Are we still in the twentieth century?" he asked as he passed a slew of ramshackle huts.

Worm-eaten fence posts stood only to prop up rangy weeds. Twisted vines grew through broken windows of rusted cars that surely had carried folks who didn't want any trouble from those negro-loving troublemakers up North.

"Shelly and them still behind us, right?" Carson asked as he looked into his side mirror.

"Yeah, the same three other cars we started out with yesterday morning. You're not in Dranesville anymore."

"Stop jokin' around. Imagine if we broke down on this road. You don't know who would ride up in a pick-up and then we'd be in for it."

"There we are," Fran said as he motioned to the small white sign announcing in faded black letters the cooperative center where they would be staying for the next week. Their caravan turned on to the unpaved road with huge potholes from rainstorms of long ago. The tires churned up a fine dust left by what had been a month of long, scorching, rainless days.

A brown cloud advanced like falling dominoes as the cars approached the clearing near a pond where a one-story, cinder block building stood. Several well-aged air conditioners propped in windows struggled against the pressing wall of Alabama heat. Hot like Tennessee, Fran thought. His family was one of the first in his neighborhood to have one of those AC window units. That at a time when the only AC available for most folks was in the movie theater.

"They said there would be air conditioning and there is. Maybe we'll be okay." The car doors opened in front of the building. The travelers stretched and looked around as two men approached.

"Shelly? Shelly?" the man with a slow voice said. His gray hair was combed back in a 1950s' sweep, and his shiny black pants, white shirt and blue suspenders looked to be from that era as well. "Ah, you must be Shelly."

"Yes, and are you Gordon?

"That's me. Thank you for coming Shelly, thank you all for coming. We're blessed that you're here to help us in our mission. The church is coming along, it's coming along. Still a lot to do, but it's coming along. Come in. Let's go inside, get something to drink, I'll explain a few things to you. Then I want to take you down the road, it's just a few miles, and show you the remains of the church they burned down earlier this year."

All of a sudden, Gordon seemed very tired, deep furrows in his face mimicking those in the road his visitors just traveled. His smile and his eyes still welcomed, but it was clear that the old man was preoccupied.

They walked into a large room with a concrete floor. Stacked chairs and several school cafeteria tables stood in front of a kitchen visible through a serving window. A card table held a pitcher of what looked like orange Kool Aid, plastic cups, and a small basket piled high with Oreos.

"Help yourself. Have some refreshments. I have a few brief remarks before we go to the former site of the First Zion Baptist Church," Gordon said, repeating a speech he had given before and surely would give again in the future as new groups rotated in. "Hand-outs, always have hand-outs. Talk about our rules, schedule, meals – we get breakfast and dinner here – ladies from the church will be bringing you lunch at the work site. We've assigned you all to teams so we can take turns with the chores. Look over the rules, no drinking or cussing, and no one is to go beyond the compound area after dark. We have a security guard come in at night and he parks his truck between here and the road. We've learned the hard way, I'm afraid, that some of the town's folk -- and it's a small group compared to all those who've opened their hearts to us -- aren't real pleased we're here. But you'll be okay. Careful near the pond, and for goodness sake don't go into the water; full of water moccasin. We put a sign up just in case you forget. The dorm and bathroom are in that door and to the right. We got your names on the door and a small closet for each of you. You choose who goes where on the bunk beds. Please help yourself to more Kool Aid and Oreos; there's plenty for everyone. Any questions?"

"I'd just like to say on behalf of our group, how fortunate we are to have you and your dedicated staff running this operation. We're here to work hard and help however we can. I'd like to ask that we bow our heads. The Lord be with you," said Shelly.

"And with you," came the group's response.

"Lord, we thank you for Gordon and his staff and the work you would have them do. Help us who are here this week to be strengthened by the knowledge that we are helping our brothers and sisters in their time of need. Let us be enriched by our experience at this place here to which you have guided us. In Your name we pray. Amen."

"Amen."

Gordon kept his head down. In the Quaker tradition, he asked that they pause for a moment of silence and then share any thoughts they might have. He told the group how thankful he was to have them there and spoke about the good progress they had made building the new church. A few statements thereafter broke the silence and after what he determined to be an appropriate interval, Gordon announced that it was time to go to the cars.

Fran looked at Carson whose eyes opened wide. "A pond full of water moccasin right behind the building, security guards, town's folk. Who do you think these town's folk are going to come after first?"

"Come on, you're letting that imagination of yours run away with you again. You heard what Gordon said, it's only a few bad apples and besides, we have a security guard watching the road."

"Who's watching that big field of tall grass and trees between here and the road?"

"You think something is going to happen with all the press, and the president, and the FBI and everybody else involved?"

Gordon led them down twisting back roads until they reached a clearing covered by a leafy canopy punctured by shafts of sunlight. At a gravel drive, the group got out of the cars and approached the ruins. Fran soon stood near a twisted water tank riddled with holes. On top of a charred foundation and pile of burnt wood and shingles, lay once colorful glass shards of a window through which God announced the power of His light. The horror of that night hung heavy in the air and seemed to imply a victory for darkness.

"Oh my," Shelly said.

"God forgive them," George Charles said as he placed his arms around the shoulders of his two teenage sons, Ben and Bill.

"We're right where those bastards were," Carson whispered to Fran. "I wonder how many there were? And they're still on the loose. The bastards that did this are still on the loose."

Fran looked at Carson, but said nothing. No one spoke, although some seemed to be deep in prayer.

"Nothing was saved," Gordon said. "Well, almost nothing. Most of it was wood and tar paper, went up just like that. They did find what was left of a melted cross; they're going to put it in a special place in the new church."

Gordon turned and walked back to the road. The others followed. Fran picked up a piece of blackened brick and took it with him.

CHAPTER 23

George Charles was a friendly man with precise comb lines in his thinning black hair. His weight made him sweat profusely and Fran wondered how the father of Ben, seventeen, and Bill, fifteen, would be able to work at the church. The sons had athletic builds and facial geometry that seemed as angular as George's was round. Both boys were bright and shared George's warm manner.

Christian and Paula Crenshaw were in their early sixties. During one of the lunch stops on the way down, they spoke about the missions they'd been on over the years to support causes, many of which Fran and Carson never heard of. The Crenshaws were big Peter, Paul, and Mary fans and it wasn't long before Christian took out a picture of him and Paula with the famous folk trio. We've been to over thirty of their concerts, he told them. Fran mentioned that Carson was a singer. They both gripped their forks as weapons when Carson carelessly asked if Peter, Paul, and Mary were still alive.

The last two in the group were Roland Wells and Sammie Wayne. Both were in their late twenties and had driven down together. They seemed like just good friends. Sammie was more outgoing than Roland, though both were dressed in hip clothes.

Gordon began to erase the dinner menu from the blackboard and started to write in the breakfast menu.

"Just like summer camp mess hall," Fran said as they walked to their rooms.

"I never went to summer camp," Carson said.

"You didn't miss much. I was shipped there five years straight; my parents thought I loved it."

"Were your rooms anything like these?" he asked after opening the door to a 10'x 10' area with a small bulb on the ceiling. A small air conditioner groaned as it propelled a moldy smell through the room. "We're goners if that thing dies," Carson said.

"It'll be okay. Remember we have breakfast prep tomorrow. Have to be in the kitchen at 5:30, so I'm setting my alarm for 5:15," Fran said as he climbed to the top bunk.

"That's a good idea. I hope Roland doesn't come in too late and make a lot of noise," Carson said as he looked at the bunk across the room.

The door creaked open, letting in light from the hall. Carson's watch read 11:05. Ten minutes later Fran climbed down to shut the door. By then the snoring had begun; fitful spasms of breathing, like a woodpecker with a bad cold. They both begged for sleep that for the rest of the night came to them only in a series of short naps.

Fran's watch alarm spit out a series of short beeps and he struggled to his feet. He woke up Carson and thought of strangling Roland, but gently nudged him several times instead. One by one, the three washed up and headed for the kitchen. Sammie was there, already making pancake batter. Gordon appeared in stocking feet; there was no doubt he had slept in his clothes.

"I'll get the coffee started," Gordon said sleepily. "I'll get the coffee started, you'll see."

After breakfast and clean up, Gordon herded everyone over to the circle of folding chairs for the morning period of silence and reflection. Fran, peeking out of the corner of his eye, saw Carson fidgeting.

"Okay, let's go out back and I'll give you each a tool belt and hard hat." At the shed, Gordon handed each person a belt with a hammer and a utility knife. "Please, don't let anything happen to your tool belts, they've got to last through the summer. There are more tools and everything else we need over at the site. Everyone take a hard hat, one size fits all. And when you come back, leave your equipment in the shed, so I can lock them up. All right, everyone have a ride? Lots to do, don't want to waste any more of the day."

The site of the new church was only ten minutes from the co-op building. It was another clearing, closer to the main road and town. The church was framed and the roof shingled. As they got out of their cars, Gordon explained they would be putting insulation in the rafters and working sheet rock.

"Everyone, I'd like you to meet, John Ridgewood. The church contracted with Mr. Ridgewood to oversee this job. Contract really isn't the right word. This gentleman is volunteering just about everything he's doing. Has a couple of helpers, but he's counting on our labor, the hard work of all the brothers and sisters who will be here this summer, to get this church built. I'm proud to know John Ridgewood, there's no finer man around. Believes in this church, and so does his mother and brothers and sisters. They got right to organizing everything after the other building burned down."

Gordon paused as John Ridgewood adjusted his sweat-stained white baseball cap which together with his faded yellow shirt made his dark complexion look even more so. He had a slow-moving way about him and a weathered look that spoke of countless hours at the mercy of Alabama's punishing heat. He started to speak then moved his hands to either side of his nose. As if clasped in prayer, they could have been a black version of Durer's *Praying Hands*. He was as tall as Fran and as lanky.

"I dreamed of this," Mr. Ridgewood said. "I woke up one night with a scream stuck in my throat as I saw the church caught up in flames. I couldn't get my body out of bed to go there and try to put the fire out. Then I realized it was a dream. But early next morning, my sister called. The church was gone, burned to the ground. I should never have gone back to sleep. That's why I'm building this church. And the hate that burned the old church is no match for the love that has sent you and so many others to help us. God works that way. My dear old mama always told me about God's mysterious ways. There can be no doubt."

Gordon put his hand on Mr. Ridgewood's shoulder. "John is the rock of this new church. We're getting closer every day. Let's get these folks to work, John."

Fran, Carson, and Sammie got their orders and headed outside to bring in the sheet rock. Carson and Sammie struggled with one end and got out of step with Fran. The sagging panel snapped and they looked at Mr. Ridgewood. "It's okay," he said. "It's okay, I've done that myself." He showed them how to carry the cumbersome panels and they brought the rest in with no problem and stacked them against the wall. One of Mr. Ridgewood's assistants took another group and put them through Hanging Sheetrock 101. Fran and Carson waited for their next assignment and saw Mr. Ridgewood waving them over to ladders that reached up to the ceiling joists.

"Is he serious? I'm not going up there," Carson said.

"C'mon, you can do it, you've got those cat-like movements. That's why he picked you; knew you were the most qualified to roll that insulation over those beams. We'll be like trapeze artists up there."

"You're going to need these," Mr. Ridgewood said as he handed them white paper breathing masks. He took a bandana from his pocket and tied it over his nose. He climbed up the ladder and motioned for Carson to follow and for Fran to use the other ladder about ten feet away to get up on the joists.

"I'm going to get you started then it's your baby. Just roll the insulation over the beams so he can get in and pull it tight. Just keep going till you get these rolls done then I'll get more up here for you. We only work on this in the morning, too hot up here after lunch." Mr. Ridgewood watched as Fran and Carson fumbled with the first roll then eventually got it into place. "Good, you guys, got it, real good," the supervisor said as he headed toward the next group of trainees.

"At least trapeze artists have a net. I can't believe you've got me hanging on for dear life to these ceiling beams breathing in this dust and insulation," Carson said.

"Remember what Gordon and Mr. Ridgewood said about God and love and how he brought us down here to help."

"Yeah, I'll remember that when I'm bouncing off that concrete floor."

"We'll get these two rows done and take a break. Toughest job here, but we'll do it, we'll get it done."

"We're losing serious water here," Carson said. "I mean, there's not a dry spot on me, everything's soaked. I have never been this hot in my whole life."

Fran took off the mask that by now was nothing more than a limp piece of paper attached to a rubber band. "Just got to make it to lunch," he told

Carson. "There's got to be a song in here somewhere for you. Just think of it as material."

"Yeah, maybe. Let's see. When I dream of you, I see us rolling insulation in the attic of our hot love nest. Yeah, something like that, something Frank Zappa."

They took two breaks before lunch, drinking from a large orange cooler of Gatorade in the back of Mr. Ridgewood's truck. Back at work, Fran could think of nothing in the world he wanted more.

"Time for lunch," Gordon called out.

John Ridgewood approached Fran and Carson. "You boys did a good job up there, real good. That's enough for today; it gets too hot in the afternoon."

Both Carson and Fran wondered how it could get any hotter. But they had made it to lunch. One of the women of the church called them all over to a piece of plywood resting on two saw horses. Lunch was as divine as the sanctuary they were building: fried chicken, bean salad, coleslaw, biscuits, pie, and two huge pitchers of iced tea and ice water.

"The ladies from Ebenezer Baptist made this delicious lunch for you," the woman said as the ladies standing by the table smiled. "We are so fortunate that the Lord has provided us with such friends in our time of need." After she offered a short grace, the hungry workers began filling their plates.

Fran and Carson sat down with George Charles and his sons. George, Bill, and Ben had been cutting and nailing sheet rock. George was pale and had tied a wet handkerchief around his neck. His wet Finger Lakes T-shirt hugged his beer belly like a second skin.

"Hotter than I thought it was going to be," George said.

Fran had looked down from the beams several times that morning and saw that it was the boys doing most of the lifting, cutting, and hammering.

George looked like he was just doing a little measuring here and there. He wondered how George would have liked hanging on the ceiling beams. As he bit into his chicken, Fran scolded himself. Why be so hard on George? Think of what it cost him to come down here. George probably had a modest income and limited vacation time. How many millions of people read about the burning churches and said, gee that's terrible, before moving on to the next story? George suddenly stood taller in Fran's eyes.

The group had a three-hour afternoon shift. They'd finish at four. Mr. Ridgewood assigned Fran and Carson to an area near the baptismal pool and laid out his plans for sheet rock. Carson caught on quickly, taking meticulous measurements and wielding the razor knife with skill. Fran became his assistant.

"You sure you never did this before?" Fran asked.

"No, just some talent waiting to be discovered. Do you believe this pool?" Carson asked as he nodded in the direction of the 4'x12' framed opening to the back of the altar area. "You get baptized down here and there's no fooling around."

They made several more trips to Mr. Ridgewood's Gatorade cooler before quitting time. Each trip was a religious experience.

"I must have lost five pounds today; my socks are like sponges. You know I'm just realizing, I haven't taken a piss since this morning, and there's nothing there now. I've never seen heat like this, it just sweats the piss out of you," said Carson.

"Made it through day one. We were a good team in there."

"Yeah, we were."

They put their tool belts and hard hats in the back of the car. "I need to stop at that store on our way back to make a quick phone call," Fran said.

"Who?"

"Just someone from home, I said I'd call if I left Dranesville."

Fran finished punching in his credit card numbers. After the fourth ring, he realized he might be talking to an answering machine and he wasn't sure what he wanted to say. Then someone picked up.

"Hello."

"Maddy?"

"Well, it's nice you're finally calling. Neil and I have been quite worried. Where in blazes are you?"

"Blazes is a good word to describe where I am. Alabama."

"What are you doing in Alabama?"

Fran explained.

"Another cause. I've read about the church burnings. Doesn't surprise me you're down there. For how long and where are you going after that?"

"Just a week, probably head back north, to take a friend of mine home and then, I don't know. I thought if you were going to be around maybe I'd stop off in Washington on the way back. Maybe we can all get together."

"I'll be here, but that's still July Fourth recess. House is still out of session. Neil will be back in the district. Remember?"

"Yeah, lost track for a minute of congressional schedules."

"Well, let me know. But, more important, I have what looks like a card addressed to you. It's from Becky."

"Becky?"

"There's no name on the return address but it's her writing, I know her writing, no matter how grown up she tries to make it. She sent it to Neil's office and I guess it was floating over there for a while before someone sent it to me."

He smiled. This moment was more precious than the light green liquid from Mr. Ridgewood's cooler on the hottest Alabama day. "It's a card you say?"

"Yes."

"Open it for me, Maddy."

"Are you sure?"

"Yes, please open it." Fran heard a letter opener rip through the envelope.

"It's a Father's day card. 'To someone I will always look up to.' Inside says,

'. . . you taught me to reach for the stars and have faith that I would get them.' It's signed: love, Becky. There's a handwritten note. 'Daddy, I'm sorry for the things I said. I want to talk, please call me before I leave for the summer. I'm going to Madrid for this program and will be staying with some of Grandma's friends.'"

"What's the postmark?"

"About three weeks ago. I'm sorry that they didn't get it to me sooner."

"Not your fault. I'm going to try her now and hope Feeney doesn't answer, though I couldn't care less. I'll call you before we leave."

"Do you have a cell phone or is there a number where I can reach you?"

"I don't. I promise I'll call. Thanks, Maddy."

Fran looked over at his car. Carson's hand gestured to ask if he was ready.

I'll be right there, just give me a second, he gestured back before entering in the credit card numbers. As the phone rang, he still wasn't sure what he would say to his daughter if she answered. But he needn't have worried; he got the answering machine. "Becky, this is Dad. I don't have a number right now for you to call back, but I'll try again to reach you. I love you so much and miss you."

Fran hung up and walked over to the car.

"Everything okay?" Carson asked curiously. "I got you a water."

"Thanks. Yeah, everything's okay."

After they showered and changed, Fran and Carson walked toward the kitchen. Gordon was supervising the team that had dinner prep.

"Let's see, spaghetti with meat sauce, salad, green beans, corn bread, and apricot halves. And, we have breakfast prep again tomorrow," Carson said as he read from the chalkboard. "I don't get it. I thought we rotated these jobs. I thought we could get a little extra sleep."

"Good job today boys," Fran said as he watched Ben and Bill shovel in their dinner. Their dad looked over and smiled proudly, reaching for more spaghetti. Paula and Chris Crenshaw, Shelly, Roland and Sammie, Gordon, the woman and two boys that were working the summer at the co-op, and everyone else in the room seemed focused on moving their forks' cargo quickly to their mouths.

"Before we start clearing the tables, I have several announcements." Gordon said, as he got up and looked down at a piece of paper. "First I want to compliment you all for a great first day. It was a hot one and you all really worked hard. Mr. Ridgewood told me this is one of the hardest-working groups he's had all summer."

"All right," said Chris Crenshaw as he pumped his hand into the air as though he were at a Peter, Paul, and Mary concert. Gordon frowned.

"Also, please check the board to see what your chores are for tomorrow. I'll be back at the shed at 7:30 to hand out hard hats and tool belts. Final announcement: CNN is doing a special on the church burnings and has a film crew down here. They want to get some shots at the new church with everyone working, and then tomorrow night here at the co-op. The local church council is going to prepare a picnic buffet for dinner and afterwards, one of the choirs will be singing. I'm sure it will be very enjoyable. Try to get to bed early tonight, gonna be another hot one tomorrow."

Fran was not thrilled with the prospect of media coverage. He'd have to be on guard, staying away as much as possible from cameras and reporters. He couldn't think of anyone who needed to know where he was.

CHAPTER 24

Fran and Carson were up early the next morning.

"I am so damn stiff, I can hardly walk," Carson said grimacing as he moved like a miniature Frankenstein to the rest room. Fran said nothing but felt a bow-string tightness in his shoulders and legs. Roland, half-stepping, followed his roommates to the kitchen. Sammie was already at work lining up boxes of cereal and milk containers together with a bowl of fruit on the counter.

"Gordon said he would be in to fire up the griddle and get the coffee started," she said.

"I don't know why we have to wait for him, we can figure it out," said Roland.

At that moment, the other door to the kitchen opened. Gordon moved his lips to say good morning, but there was no volume. The warming griddle and the perking coffee were his starter's gun. He walked, still not fully awake, out of the kitchen. Fran wondered why Gordon felt compelled to go through this routine every morning.

After breakfast, Fran walked to his room and pulled a small yellow note pad from his duffel bag. He had bought the pad at one of the convenience stores on the trip down as the idea seized him that he would keep a diary in Alabama. He had forgotten about it the first two days, but now had some time to jot down a few things. He spoke about the razed church they had seen the night they got there, how the camp was organized, the Spartan living conditions. *For one-hundred fifty bucks, you get to work your butt off at the construction site, and then come back to the co-op building to do your chores. What a deal! But everyone seems happy to be here and do whatever it takes. Everyone is here for a purpose. A little, no make that a lot sore from our first day on the job yesterday. Everyone else worked on sheet rock. Carson and I rolled insulation in the attic. Never been so hot in my life –like faucets with no handles to turn off the sweat -- then Mr. Ridgewood's Gatorade jug saved us. Don't know if I need twenty minutes worth of Quaker meditation before we leave for work, but we'll see. Yesterday had one of the best picnic lunches ever.*

"What's that? Carson asked, looking over.

"Oh, I thought I might jot down some reflections, diary, something."

"Don't forget to write how good I am with the sheet rock. A diary, that's a good idea. I can use that to write a Bob Dylan kind of song about being here."

"Maybe you could collaborate with the Crenshaws and have them get Peter, Paul, and Mary to sing your song."

"That's funny. Maybe I should talk to Gordon about having a comedy night so you can entertain us."

Mr. Ridgewood and one of his assistants were already at the church unloading more sheet rock from his truck. There was more to carry than yesterday. But inside there was a huge fan, had to be four feet high. "Yesterday was just too hot. Supposed to be over a hundred today. At least we'll get a little breeze in here. Hardware store gave me a good price for it," said Mr. Ridgewood.

Fran and Carson climbed up the ladders to what had become their stations of valor. Carson had almost fallen from his perch the day before. Only Fran knew how scared Carson was.

Gordon walked in later in the morning and was followed by a woman with a note pad, a cameraman, and a man with a microphone on a long pole. It was hard, with the fan blowing, to hear what they were saying. Fran saw the CNN logo on the camera. Gordon led them over to a small group wrestling with a large piece of sheet rock and the reporter started asking questions. Next, they walked over to speak with Mr. Ridgewood, then to one of the women from the church. The cameraman took some shots of the interior then followed Gordon outside.

"Do you believe that, they didn't even look up here. Didn't point that camera up once. We're up here sweating our butts off more than anyone else and we don't even get in the picture."

"You know why you're here and I know why you're here, and more important, the Big Man upstairs knows why you're here. Should be enough," Fran said.

"Yeah, but they're going to be on CNN."

They made at least three trips that morning to the back of Mr. Ridgewood's truck. The chilled, green liquid tasted even better today. As they started to head back in, another camera crew and reporter walked up from the road.

"Good morning boys," said the reporter, "Who's head of this outfit?"

The cameraman was focusing more on Fran than Carson.

"He's inside . . .," Fran stopped, realizing he didn't want to get involved with the media. Maybe he was overreacting but the thought of Fairchild's articles was sobering. Did he care if Jo Ellen saw him in Alabama? Maybe she'd try to contact him. He wanted to be with her; maybe that wasn't best for her. "Thanks," the reporter said, and motioned for his crew to follow him.

"See, are you happy? You're going to be on TV."

"Carson, the camera wasn't on. They didn't want to talk with us."

"Yeah, but they didn't even get us on mike, didn't even want to talk with us. And besides, that's MSNBC."

Climbing back up to their perch, they saw the TV crew focusing on Mr. Ridgewood as he cranked up a huge piece of sheet rock towards the ceiling, resting it flat on a frame of yellow metal arms. Once it was tight against an area that Fran and Carson had insulated, several volunteers on ladders began to nail it to the joists. Mr. Ridgewood darted from corner to corner to assure the piece was secure.

Had another picnic lunch from Heaven. Two women from a white church in Tuscaloosa drove sixty miles to bring it here. Their efforts add a lot to what we're doing. Lunch seems to be a very comfortable time of sharing, and of refreshment for the body and the soul. Carson and I finished laying the attic insulation and did sheet rock again this afternoon. He really is a sheetrock master, just picked it up faster than I did. Camera crews visited the church, more about that later.

"I've got to make a quick phone call, but I can take you back to the co-op first if you want."

"I'll go with you. Going to that same store?"

"Yeah."

"Good, they have a frozen custard machine in the back. I almost got a cone yesterday, but there was a bunch of kids waiting. But I definitely need one today. It's that chocolate, vanilla swirl. I used to get those things all the time, then just stopped. Don't know why. Want one?"

"No thanks."

Fran entered the number and when he finished, he realized he again still hadn't prepared exactly what he would say to Becky. His mind had been focused on the number of rings and whether Feeney might answer. But then it came to him. It was easy, he would tell his daughter he loved her and would do whatever she wanted. He was satisfied and confident. The answering machine came on.

"Did you get her?"

"No, not having much luck."

"You'll get her, don't worry. Here, when I saw these things, I knew I had to get one for you. As William used to say, this stuff is so good, your brains fall out." Carson handed Fran a sculpted cone of vanilla, chocolate swirl. It had started to go into ice-cream cone arrest in the hundred-degree temperature and Fran and Carson, tongues out, worked the soft, melting edges above the cone.

"Carson, you're a good man. Got the highlight of the day right here," Fran said as his teeth chomped the last piece of cone bottom soaked in frozen custard.

"I knew you'd like it. That might be the best swirl I ever had. I could eat another one. You know, it's an old machine they have in there and they let you make your own cone. But I don't care how good you are, there's only so much you can get on top. Boy, I'd pay a lot of money for that machine. And on a day like today, it's enough to make you think about moving down here just to be near that baby."

"All, right we'll stop here tomorrow after work. Maybe during our period of reflection in the morning you can give thanks for the frozen custard machine you found at Christie's Grab'n Go Convenience Store."

"Maybe I'll just do that wise aleck."

"C'mon bud, I'm not making fun of you, I told you how nice it was you bought me one."

There were a half-dozen cars in the parking lot at the co-op when Fran and Carson pulled in. There was also a big, white CNN satellite truck. Someone thought something news worthy was happening in the co-op building.

"Hello boys," Gordon called over to Carson and Fran as they walked in. "These are some of our boys, just coming back from the new church," Gordon said to the reporters. "Make some good progress out there? Hot enough for you?"

The reporter and camera crew were checking their equipment. Maybe Gordon didn't know his remarks probably weren't being recorded.

Fran stopped. "Yeah, I think we got a good amount done. Hot as Hades, but it's a good crew out there."

Gordon nodded enthusiastically.

"What really hit the spot, was the vanilla, chocolate swirl cone we got at Christie's Grab'n Go Convenience Store right down the road," said Carson, maybe hoping the plug might get him in good with Christie. The camera-man had a bead on Carson.

Ladies from the church council were busily setting tables covered in red, plastic tablecloths upon which sat heaping bowls of salad, warming plates with piles of fried chicken and biscuits, and mounds of fruit includ-ing four huge watermelon halves. As he and Carson walked to their room, Fran overheard one woman say they expected about a hundred people.

"Gordon wants us to wear these name tags and help greet the guests as they come in. Just go over, say hello, thanks for coming, that sort of thing," Shelly said to her freshly-showered crew.

They walked toward the door and set up their receiving line just as the first group of women, some with husbands and children arrived. The room grew warmer as more people streamed in. "Seems like more than one hun-dred already," Sammie told Roland.

Carson felt the stares launched his way, but he told himself they were harmless -- these were church people.

The camera was focusing on him now, but how much of the final tape would he be in? Would the editors think he was an integral part of the story, or would highlighting a dwarf distract from the feel of the piece? Carson often obsessed on such questions.

"Ladies and gentlemen, may I have your attention please," Gordon said. The chit chat stopped and people turned toward him. "We are honored to have you with us tonight and grateful for the feast you have prepared. Ours has been an army of peace, with many good volunteers from far away, and you, our neighbors. We are working together, guided by the Lord to raise up again the sanctuary built in His name. Your presence here demonstrates your commitment to that sacred purpose. I don't want to keep you any more from the bounty that awaits us. We'll talk more after dinner and hear also from the Mount Olive Baptist Church Choir."

Chris and Paula were the first to start clapping before the room erupted in applause and alleluias. People started linking hands and awkwardly arranged themselves into a circle. The cameramen sensed a photographic feast and darted forward. A member of the Mount Olive Baptist Church Choir exalted the crusaders as she led them in "Onward Christian Soldiers." Her powerful voice revved the congregants into steady crescendos.

Gordon seemed to enjoy the initial minutes of flight, but now determined it was the appropriate time to land. "Thank you sister, thank you everyone who is helping us succeed in our mission. But now it's time to nourish our bodies. Please join us," he said as he started walking toward the buffet table. The singing faded and Gordon offered a short grace. Upon the amen, the buzz of many conversations returned to the room as queues formed by the food.

The camera crew got some footage of them eating before joining in at the end of the buffet line. As dinner ended, the choir, in white shirts and blouses and black pants, organized itself behind the microphone. Gordon followed, removing with his tongue the last remnants of dinner from his teeth.

"We have a real treat for everybody tonight. You got a little taste of it before dinner. And now we have the main course. Recognized throughout the South, this group of fine men and women is known for its inspirational music and fine harmonies. We're honored to have them with us tonight: The Mount Olive Baptist Choir."

Fran felt a bolt of power as the choir unleashed music in command of body and soul. Fran looked at Carson, who stood as one witnessing a revelation designed for him personally. His small arms and legs stood at rest, bathing in the vibrations of the choir's heavenly voices.

"Thank you, thank you," the choir's soprano said as the first song ended. "Gordon had some mighty fine words and we thank him so much. But we're the ones who are honored tonight, being here with our brothers and sisters who have traveled great distances to help us in our time of need. You are proof that the Good Lord is determined to reveal our neighbors' love for us. Bless you. Now, we have a few more songs, but we aren't going to sing them by ourselves. Pick up the sheets on the tables; we want you to sing with us. Lift our joyful noise right out of this building and across the whole county. The power of God has wings and will take our message places you couldn't imagine. No holding back now."

Those at the tables fell in behind the front line troops of the choir. It was uneven at first, some belting out the songs in tune, some not. Most voices stayed at half volume.

"I can't hear you. We got a powerful message, let's get some power into it and send it for miles."

The chastised crowd turned up the power. But of the voices responding to the choir's urging, one stood out. Fran had never heard Carson sing with such majesty and determination. His small friend had pulled Excalibur from the stone.

"My, my, my, don't happen often. You get somebody in the crowd, you say, that voice has got to be in my choir. God brought that voice to me," said the woman. "Now which one of you has that voice?"

Fran pointed to Carson.

"There he is. You come up here." Carson walked up front, his hands fidgeting as he tried to suppress a smile. "What's your name?"

"Carson Handle."

"Well, Carson Handle, welcome to my choir. Where did you learn to sing like that, Carson?"

"Oh, I guess it just came natural," said Carson stretching to reach the microphone that the woman didn't realize she was holding too high.

"That there is a gift, know that Carson?"

"I guess I never thought of it that way."

CNN crew at the church today came to record the large crowd from throughout the area that came to have dinner with us tonight at the co-op. Lot of good feelings in the air that reinforce the sense that while it's only one small church we're working on, we're doing important work in these people's eyes. Haven't had this sense of personal accomplishment in a long time. Carson was singled out by the choir leader. He was singing with a throat of gold. Never heard him like that before. That woman built him up, just like we're trying to build them a new church; stronger than before and out of love they never anticipated. She was very kind to Carson, you could see how impressed she was. She meant it. She saw God in Carson in a way I never have. If the music of God is in Carson what else of God is in my friend that I've never taken the time to find?

Roland's snoring has made it hard for us to sleep. We've tried not to say too much as he was embarrassed the first time we did, then a little defensive. But we've got to talk with him again tonight.

The Charles boys played soccer-volleyball again using that beat up badminton net. They play with Miujizu, the teenager that one of the churches in Rwanda was able to send to the U.S. He's a very pleasant boy. His family was killed in the genocide. He's been assigned to work at the co-op this summer and help Gordon.

"Want another cone?" Carson asked as he got out of the car.

"My treat today," Fran said as he gave him a five-dollar bill. "Small swirl please, I won't be long on this call."

Fran punched in the numbers.

"Hello."

"Maddy, Fran."

"I was wondering when you were going to call communications central."

"What? Did you hear from Becky?"

"I didn't hear from Becky, but I heard from Candice. She was very upset. Becky already left for her trip; she's in Madrid, won't be back till the end of August. Guess she was pretty disappointed she didn't hear from you after she sent the card. But Candice wanted you to know that Feeney exploded both times she heard your messages. She really has it out for you now. Candice also told me that Mrs. Craighill is always talking bad about you in front of Becky."

"Damn."

"I wish I had better news for you . . ."

"Damn it. Well, at least I know why I haven't heard from Becky. Probably no way I can get in touch with her. Hope her disappointment, or whatever she feels toward me now, doesn't fester while she's away. I have to go see her when she gets back. Have to figure some way so there's no big confrontation with Feeney. Maybe I can get word through Candice. I don't know. You okay Maddy?"

"I'm okay. What about you?"

"Yeah, fine. Some experience down here.

"Fran, one more message. You got a letter from Jo Ellen. She sent it to my house. There's no name or return address, but I know her writing. The letter's from Jo Ellen. It was sent five days ago and the postmark says Merrifield."

"Where's Merrifield?"

"It's a big mail center in Virginia, about fifteen miles outside of Washington."

Carson was walking towards the phone, trying to make his delivery before the frozen custard melted through his fingers.

Fran hurried to finish the conversation as his stomach fluttered. "That's interesting." She had finally written! "Look, I'll pick it up when I see you. Talk to you soon, Maddy."

"Bye."

"Timing, talk about timing. I got it to you with a couple of seconds to spare," Carson said as the custard swelled at the ridge of the cone.

"You really know your frozen custard," said Fran, not even focusing on the cones.

"Everything okay? Did you find anything about Becky?"

"Yeah, might not be able to get in touch with her until end of August. I'll get it worked out." He had no idea how.

Went to the local high school tonight after dinner. The Civil Rights Commission was holding a hearing on the church-burnings. They had several panels with all kinds of politicians: local, county, state, and civil rights advocates from all over. They all condemned the church-burners and called for a forceful government response. It was strange watching these proceedings as a "civilian" and not being up on the stage asking questions. Saw the congressman from this district, Edwin Crouthers. Always got along well with Edwin, he has a sly smile, but always laughed at my jokes. Edwin didn't recognize me at first. Fran Stewart, is that you? What are you doing here? Where have you been since you left the House? I told Edwin I'd been traveling, heard about the churches and got with a group going to Alabama. He was very kind, thanking me for helping. You got a bum deal, he said. I was sad to see you go; thought you were a straight shooter. Maybe it's time for a comeback. I smiled as someone reminded him he was needed inside.

Lucky that Carson was still outside or I would have had my cover blown. Maybe I should tell Carson, be up front about what I used to do and tell him I wasn't a salesman before I came to Dranesville. I'm still not sure how he would react and as long as he wasn't there when I was talking with Edwin, maybe I'll just let it go for now.

Loved the table set up by the Socialist Workers Party in front of the school. The banner read "Send Federal Troops to Protect Black Churches." From down here, you can get a little afraid and wonder if that's what it might take. Heard that two other churches burned, one of which was half-way rebuilt. What will it take to secure the ones being rebuilt? The thought of ours being destroyed is overpowering.

I thought we were turning the corner, but the tragedy in the South seems to continue.

Tomorrow's the last day working at the church. Drywall and insulation are done, and we even started on the siding, which the group after us is going to finish. We were all pretty excited to see the CNN story air before dinner. There we were at the church hammering away and at the co-op singing and eating. Some great footage of Carson singing. Maybe someone will discover him at least that's what I told him. Some film of me also. We'll see what happens. Gordon re-emphasized the need to stay in after dark. The security guard's brother heard some ugly things being said about our group and now the piece on CNN. He said it reminded him of the hateful things said when the civil rights people came down in the 1960s. Of course this shook Carson considerably,

"Disgraceful. I am so glad Becky isn't here to see such repulsive, mindless drivel," her grandmother said to a very still Creighton Tillman. "Appalling, look at those left-wingers holding hands and singing for that liberal media scum. It's like some cult and next he'll try to get her into it, try to brainwash her," the elderly woman said as she stood alone in front of the TV and put on her white gloves. Feeney Craighill hadn't noticed that Candice had entered the room. "And, and he's holding hands with a midget. Embarrassing his daughter like that. Wait till her friends tell her what they saw on the television. That man has to be taught a lesson," Feeney snarled, betraying a rasp from a two-pack–a-day cigarette habit she quit ten years ago.

Candice left the room before she was noticed. She had never seen the woman so angry.

CHAPTER 25

"These just came in. They tell me one size fits all," Mr. Ridgewood said to his exhausted and drenched workers. He held out white T-shirts with the words: "Alabama, Fire." Underneath, in script, was a quote from Isaiah 6:4,8: *They shall raise up the former devastations . . . for I the Lord love justice.* "It has been an honor to work with you this week. Thank you for helping our church. I hope when you wear these shirts, you remember all the good you did here this summer. Maybe when people ask you what these shirts mean, you can take some time to tell them about what happened to us down here."

Shelly stood up. "Oh behalf of our group, I want to say how proud we were to work with you, Mr. Ridgewood. Everybody has told me, at one time or another, just how inspired they are by your peaceful determination to right a wrong so that the glory of God can be praised again at this church."

Everyone clapped for their leader that week; a leader in the ways of more than sheet rock and insulation. He urged them all to come back when the church was finished and consecrated. They all made heartfelt promises, but none in the group would return.

"Should get out of here by eight tomorrow morning, maybe sooner," Fran said as he began to pack. "I didn't figure on having to clean this whole place before the new crew comes in; one of Gordon's little surprises. It's kind of hard to believe we're done here already."

"I think it's time to go. Good experience, but definitely time to go. My sister says she loves Otis, but he's starting to wear out his welcome. He crapped on her hall carpet twice. He's never done anything like that before. He must really miss me. Told my sister we'd probably be in late Sunday. Guess Otis is going to have to stay in the garage till then. He'll be all right don't you think?"

"He'll be fine, it's only two days. Geez, ten o'clock already. Pretty dead out there. I think most people have called it a night. Everybody but our own sleep-deprivation machine, Roland. Probably still in the kitchen talking to Sammie. I'm sure we'll hear him when he comes walking in later. I'm going down to the kitchen for some juice. Want some?"

"Yeah, thanks. I'm just gonna read in bed for a while."

"Damn, the hall light is out again. I thought they fixed it. Have to keep our door open so I can see where the heck I'm going."

The putty knife slipped between the jamb and the door, and the credit card met no protest as it pushed the latch aside. The old door at the end of the hall was good for keeping out mosquitoes and snakes, not the likes of this determined lot. They'd take care of others if they'd have to, but they were there for one person. The first piece of duct tape went over the mouth. The other over the eyes as a frenzy of hands pulled the now-struggling person to the floor. The ax handles began to do their work. A flurry of thuds and cracks reported by the wooden shafts was muffled by the white noise whine of the struggling ACs. It was over soon. As commandos on a stealth mission, the men vanished back into the night.

CHAPTER 26

I *refer to it as the Incident. It helps to remember that time before anyone else came into the room. He was the recipient of every imaginable slight, taunt, even threat. Carson had a fist in his mind, but he looked for every opportunity to uncoil that hand. He always made sure that they were indeed prejudices that approached him. It was the only way he could survive. He would hold his hand out in the hope that there was something about him that could be accepted. The slightest positive response, and he had such long experience in recognizing these gradients, was the small boost he needed. He would try so very hard to make that person believe that he hadn't made the wrong decision. No, he would benefit from knowing Carson Handle.*

He must have seen somewhere in me an inviting light that I didn't even know existed. He was a teacher whether he knew it or not, and I began to see things as he saw them. It was important to give everyone another chance and maybe more beyond that. Although maybe it could be a dangerous delusion in a world where the Incident spoke with such a loud, clear voice.

I couldn't see his eyes. They always seemed to jump when he hadn't seen me in a while. I stopped pulling on the tape. We weren't alone long; people started crowding into the room making calls for an ambulance and the police.

I was still holding him. The deep blues and reds of fresh cuts and deep bruises, the swelling; it seemed to be everywhere. I knew his arm was broken. It's okay, Carson. You're going to be all right, I whispered into his ear. Someone told me once that hearing is the last sense to go.

When Chris and Paula came in, they kept yelling at me to let him go. They finally got my arms loose. Paula pulled the tape from his mouth and started to give him CPR. She really was a doer.

I thought my diary would give me a record of things we did to help people this summer. Instead, as I look at it for the last time (I can't make sense of the things that happened), I see rambling thoughts about Carson's funeral, the messy proceedings and hearings involved with the evil men they caught, and Carson's sister, who I know blames me for his death. For bringing him here. She cried at the funeral. I needed to know about Otis, but she won't talk to me. Carson loved that dog.

Fran put his glass down on the woven coaster. He'd been at Maddy's house for about an hour, telling her everything. There was no mention of Becky or Jo Ellen.

"God, Fran, I'm so sorry," Maddy said as she placed her hand on his. His hand was stiff, clammy.

"I wish you had known him. He was funny at times and asked me questions I would never think of asking. He had so much to offer, if people would have let him. He had a great voice, this choir came to sing for us one night, and they knew right away he had a great voice. They didn't care what he looked like. I guess a choir's probably different than regular show business."

Maddy looked at Fran who appeared to be talking to the tops of the draperies. "Sounds like he meant a lot to you."

"He did. You just had to take the time to stop and get to know him."

"What are you going to do now?"

"Don't know, but doesn't take being back in Washington long to make me realize I don't belong here anymore. Sometimes, I wonder if I ever belonged. This place doesn't care who runs it, but not many people around here know that. So many slick people in Washington making high-dollar deals, and there's so much money to be made if all those U.S. budget dollars end up where clients want them. The K Street lobby boys are convinced they're an important part of the system, that they're helping their country. And if they make a little money along the way, well, I guess they feel no one can begrudge them, you know, because they're helping their country and all."

"Do you really believe all that?"

"Some days, I guess. Look, this just isn't the place for me. It's nothing against you Maddy."

"Okay, again, what are you planning to do? She lifted the cut-glass dish toward him.

"Walnuts. I haven't had these since the last time I raided that plastic bag of yours in the office," Fran confessed. She smiled. As he chewed, it was as if he were back in the office, the nuts unlocking years of memories. "I'm not sure, who the heck could have imagined months ago the world I'd be living in today?"

She handed him the letter from Jo Ellen. Fran's fingers squeezed the envelope and determined there were probably several sheets inside. He wondered what she had told him.

"Going to try to get in touch with her?"

"I don't know. I really don't know about anything right now," Fran said as he put the letter in his back pocket. "Thanks, Maddy. For everything. I'll call you tomorrow; maybe we'll try to reach the Honorable Neil Glider."

"Where are you going to stay? You could stay . . ."

"I'll call in the morning. I'm not sure yet."

CHAPTER 27

He turned the climate control knob to hi-cool. The must and starch smells swirled together as if in a blender. It was clear the desk and chair were designed for someone smaller. He pushed aside the motel's water-stained welcome sheet so that the unopened envelope was the only thing on the desk. He had wondered over and over about what the letter said. But he wasn't sure. He wasn't sure about anything.

What had happened to her after she left? Where was she? Was he denounced or yearned for? Would she again be parachuting into his life? He was prepared for anything in that envelope. With his tiny pocket knife, he slit open the envelope.

There was one sheet inside, with writing on one side and some sort of bulletin. He squinted at the letter and focused.

Dear Fran,

It's been a long time. I wasn't sure if I would ever hear from you. It was rough for me. My PARENTS finally got the message that I'm a "big girl" now. They told me that you tried to reach me. I'm okay now, ex-Congressman Fran, wherever you are. I hope you're okay too. My mind trawls through the things we did that summer. You are an amazing man. Found out a lot about myself and you helped me through some choppy waters, although I think many times you didn't even know that. Don't know if this will ever reach you. Working in Virginia, a group called "Saving the Giants" (see bulletin)—you know me, but no pretense now.

xoxo,

Jo Ellen

Fran laid the letter down like a crime-scene detective moving from one piece of evidence to the next. He'd be back to the letter, cracking any codes he imagined were there. He picked up the bulletin. It was a professionally-done piece. SVG was dedicated to saving trees and rallied around "champion trees" sentenced to yield their centuries-old locations to interchanges, new subdivisions, or town centers. Developers said that while they regretted the loss of these trees, the communities were to benefit from everything that new developments had to offer. SVG was a new group that relied on a variety of tactics employed in the court room, legislatures, town hall meetings, press releases or in the field through demonstrations and "tree-sitting." One photo in the bulletin showed several SVG members tethered in defiance to a six-story champion with a hundred-foot wide canopy. It seemed SVG members were determined, dedicated, but it seemed they had more losses than wins in the field. They were forced to joust with teams of corporate and development company lawyers with a deep tap root of their own into limitless funds and resources.

The office was about thirty miles outside of Washington, a place called Manassas Park. On the back page of the brochure, sitting on the porch of a house which must have been a hundred-years-old itself, were the members of SVG. They had on forest green T- shirts with the words "Saving the Giants" beneath the imperial canopy of a champion oak. He recognized her right away, the second from the left, sitting on the top step of the porch. Her hair was a little shorter and her smile not quite as wide as the night she welcomed him to her reception on Capitol Hill. She was wearing khaki shorts and work boots with white socks that barely showed.

He read the two documents several more times. The letter showed Jo Ellen hadn't changed. It was short, to the point -- after a short detour --and inviting. Just a short letter and that bulletin. She planned it that way. There was her photo, and it was a good photo of her, and the office phone number. It would be pretty easy for him to get in touch with her. He looked at the phone. Still early he thought. He walked downstairs for the free continental breakfast, trying to ease his nerves. His relationship with Jo Ellen had been so long ago. Maybe they wouldn't share the same feelings if the two of them got together. No, he was sure they both wanted to see each other. He placed the Styrofoam cup next to the phone. Once he made the call he was in. Did he just want to remember her or did he want to see her, to hold her as if what happened after that night on the mall never occurred? He took a sip of coffee and reread the letter and stared at the photo. Dranesville, Carson, Alabama, burning churches; where would he go next? When did this all stop being temporary?

He picked up the phone. He was hers if she would have him. He didn't think his heart would feel this way about anyone else, and he didn't care what all the other voices in his mind said. "No pretense," she had said. He looked at his work boots and jeans still carrying traces of the red clay of Alabama and hardened splotches of sheet rock mud. The ringing stopped.

"SVG, may I help you?"

"Yes, my name is Fran Stewart. Can Jo Ellen Driscoll be reached at this number?"

"Yes, but I'm afraid she's not here right now. I expect her late morning, early afternoon."

"Can I leave my number for her?"

"Fire away."

Fran turned on the TV and started to read his complimentary *USA TODAY*. He finished it and started to flip through channels. He passed a few hours that way, just surfing through programs.

The phone rang before he could get to another channel. Fran waited until the fourth ring so he could clear himself of the disparate cultural arcana that had dripped as if from an IV bag into his mind.

"Hello," he garbled as he lifted his head quickly from the pillow.

"Is that you Fran?"

"Jo Ellen?"

"Oh Fran, I can't believe it's you, I can't believe I'm talking to you again," she said. He felt suddenly important, wanted, like he would soon be part of her life again. "I have missed you so much. There is so much I want to tell you. Where are you? When can I see you?"

"I'm just passing through, don't know how long I'll be around here. A lot's happened since I saw you last."

"I can imagine, I can imagine. You don't know how glad I am you got my letter and called me. You don't know how much you've been on my mind. But I can tell you one thing, Fran Stewart, you'll be around long enough for us to get together."

She had him roped in, and he smiled.

"Okay, all right, this is what we'll do. I've got a couple of things I'm working on today and a meeting tonight that I can't get out of. But they have a commuter train from here into D.C.; why don't I meet you late morning at Union Station, say about 11:30, main lobby. I'll take a long lunch, and maybe I can get someone to give me a ride back."

"I have a car."

"You have a car? Well that's an interesting development. We may never have met if you had a car back then."

CHAPTER 28

Fran arrived at Union Station at 10:30, parked his car and rode the escalators down to the gate area. "Where would I wait for a train coming in from Manassas Park?" he asked a man whose gaze never left his computer monitor.

"VRE, Gate G."

Fran walked towards an arrivals board. Not only wasn't there a train arriving from Manassas Park around 11:30, there wasn't any listing of a train coming from Manassas Park. He walked towards Gate G. The arrival board by the gate was blank. The only person in the waiting area was a homeless man asleep with one hand on his collapsible grocery cart. His possessions in that cart were worn by weather and time, and stacked like sedimentary rock formations. It seemed sure Jo Ellen was not arriving on that track.

Fran went back to the window. "Any other track that a train coming in from Manassas Park might be coming in on?"

The man sighed. "V-R-E, Gate-G, but you gonna be waiting a long time. No more trains comin in from there today."

How stupid of me not to tell him I would be waiting for a train coming in today Fran thought.

It was eleven o'clock. He started at Gate A and went down the line, seeing if there were a train listed on any of the arrival signs that might be coming from somewhere near Manassas Park. But he wasn't sure that he knew precisely where Manassas Park was, and some of the towns he saw listed, he had never heard of. He had about fifteen minutes before he was to meet Jo Ellen. He wasn't sure how much time she had allotted for lunch. Maybe she had to change her plans. He called the hotel. No messages. He saw passengers arriving at one of the far gates. He power-walked toward the gate sidestepping everyone except an elderly woman whose four-footed cane drifted into his lane. He caught her as she teetered and regained her balance. Her relief at remaining upright seemed to quash any feeling of indignation about being bumped into. Fran waited for all the stragglers to get off a train that had passed through Virginia's suburbs. She wasn't there. He ran towards the main lobby. The old lady hadn't gotten far, but Fran missed her this time by a wide margin.

Eleven thirty-eight. He saw Jo Ellen. She was looking out the front door. He was sweating now and the cool Fran Stewart had disappeared. She started to look around the massive room and they saw each other at the same time. She was wearing a pale-blue and white striped cotton dress. Her hair was shorter, but he could tell it had just been brushed. Her legs were well-tanned and she wore the thinnest leather thong sandals. Her toe nails wore a perfect polish of tomato red.

They walked towards each other then she paused. "Are you all right? Not having seconds thoughts are we?"

"No, no, not at all," he said taking a couple of deep breaths. "Just got here a little late; sorry."

She looked at him then threw her arms around him, stretching up on her toes as far as the tips of those sandals would permit. "Fran, it is so good to see you. You don't know how good it is to see you."

He reflexively held her tighter as she finished speaking. "It's good to see you." She had learned quickly what he was feeling. She knew him, and that meant so much to him at that moment.

"I took the morning off and got here around eight. Had my hair done and then went for coffee and read. It was a very nice morning. You like?" Jo Ellen said as her hand bounced her hair.

"Yes, it's very nice, it looks nice."

"Somewhere I heard you had a beard. I can't picture you with a beard."

"Yeah, I cut it off in the spring as I was coming out of hibernation."

"C'mon," she said as she grabbed his hand. "Nice, very nice, jeans and golf shirt, that's a good look for you. Down around the corner, near where I got my hair cut, looks like a nice lunch spot."

They sat at a small table near the kitchen and spoke amidst the clatter of plates picked up by waiters. Their conversation was at first limited to the menu. Whenever she read an item she liked, he nodded in agreement. Fran sat stiffly, fidgeting with the paper placemat. He would never have made a good opening act; he'd have to wait for Jo Ellen to open the show.

"Brought you something," she said as she pulled a forest green T-shirt from her bag. "This is your color, Fran."

"Thank you, very thoughtful. I saw you and the others in the picture with your shirts; looked very 'woodsy.'" He wondered why it had never crossed his mind to bring her something.

"Fran, this is a serious business, a good group of people. They're getting paid less than Peace Corps volunteers and they're working fourteen and sixteen-hour days. We're the last thing between the champions and the hardened-steel teeth of those diesel behemoths. This isn't some group sitting in some office doing planetary research on the origins of the solar system or working on some legislation that has the gestation period of a great whale. We're on the front lines Fran. We're new, and we've learned from a number of groups before us and there are more groups like us setting up around the country."

"Sounds like they are doing good work." He cleared his throat. "You know I tried to contact you; your dad, well, he didn't think it was the best thing for you. So I didn't call again. I thought about calling or writing, but your father seemed pretty clear about what I should do. I thought about you an awful lot."

Her hand went down his forearm to his fingers. "I thought about you every day. When I sent you the letter and didn't hear back right away, I wasn't sure what I was going to do. In my late teens, I got really overwhelmed; think it was about this guy who broke up with me. Remember the photo in my apartment of me and him? It was between Machu Picchu and the Three Stooges? I told you soon after we met about the rough time I had. I need to tell you everything. Anyway, I was out of it, depression, etc. Really came on fast. My parents had me hospitalized. I was okay for a few years, then the same thing, I don't know what caused it then. They put me on some kind of drugs and I was like a zombie. I got better though, and – do you believe it -- got into grad school and got my doctorate. My parents were against it, thought it would be too much pressure, and I did gain a lot of weight when I was preparing for my dissertation defense. But I did it, did it and a position opened up at the university and it was great. And I always wanted to go to Washington. Again, my parents got frantic, but when I told them I had been accepted for that fellowship, they were resigned to the fact I was going."

She took a deep breath. "But it all happened again after our fiasco. My father came to get me. I was really out of it Fran, for at least five months. I stayed at their house. The university gave me a medical leave, but when I asked them about coming back, I got this mumbo jumbo about cut backs and my position in transition and other administrative jargon I'd never heard before. I've begun an appeal but have no idea how it'll turn out. A friend of mine told me about SVG and I told my parents I was going to Virginia. My father wouldn't talk to me for several days, but he and my mom eventually came round. They recognized it's my life and this is what I want to do. Okay your turn, what were you doing all those months besides telling yourself you couldn't live without me?"

Fran looked at her as if waiting for a translator to finish interpreting her presentation. "Are you okay now?"

"I am, I feel redeemed, refreshed. I was as low as you could get, I never knew who I was supposed to please. But somewhere this last time around, I don't know, it was like getting some super vaccination. I really feel free, I don't know what the right word is, but I think whatever happened, I can fight it off. I don't think it will get me again. I feel good about myself. Thinking about you, talking to you, seeing you today, I think it's you that's been helping me feel good about myself. I just always want to be with you, ex-Congressman Fran."

He smiled. She had gotten her answer. "I don't know if I would have tried any more to reach you. There have just been too many things I've screwed up. As I said before, it's your turn."

He told her about Cooperstown, Dranesville, Dawg Feat, Dayley's Department Store, Carson Handle, Becky's card, burning churches, Alabama, how he lost Carson, and plans that reached no farther than the emblem on the front of his car.

"All right, stop right there!" she said.

He knew she had been taking copious mental notes. She would get that way sometimes, wanting to document each part of his story from different camera angles and then paste together a composite picture so she felt everything as he had.

She rattled off the different parts of his story she wanted to hear again and he elaborated until he was told to move to the next topic. "Look," he said, "we'll be here all afternoon at this rate, which is fine by me, but didn't you say you had to be back to work after lunch?"

She looked at her watch. "You're right. I'll finish taking your deposition in the car."

"I didn't get a chance to clean it much, but I cleared out the front seat, I think there's enough room. You don't look like you've gained much weight."

"What!?"

"Kidding, kidding, kidding – you've lost weight since I've seen you."

"Is this the kind of car an ex-congressman drives?"

"You mean you don't like that little orange, pine tree deodorizer?"

"Let's get back to my questions and then I can tell you what I'd like you to do to this car."

In between reading the directions someone in her office had scribbled out for her, she took Fran back through the story. It was if somehow by asking him questions about the tiniest elements of his story, she could insert herself into those many months they were apart. Fran was surprised about some of the things he remembered.

"How much farther?"

She looked ahead and then at her directions. "I don't know, maybe twenty, thirty minutes."

"I read the bulletin, I have the shirt, and you explained a little, but what specifically does this group you're with do?"

"Want to join? You said you didn't know what you were going to do, and you're right, you already have the shirt."

"Never know, I just might, I like trees you know!"

"This is serious business Fran. From old aerial photos as recent as twenty years ago, you can see the vast swaths of trees that are gone. Developers, politicians, most of them always had this 'there are plenty of trees out there approach' and just let some majestic giants get hacked away. I mean I can understand people need houses and places to shop, but there was no rhyme nor reason. Architects would crank out these captivating visions of idyllic communities and developers would convince local officials that it would be irresponsible not to jump at the opportunity to provide local residents with these amenities. We've lost trees that were hundreds of years old. The tide is starting to turn I think. People, even some of the politicians and developers are realizing these giants can't be replaced. A number of towns are establishing registries to catalog what we refer to as champions; the giants among the various species that must be saved. But some of these developers and their lawyers are trying to come in under the radar. They'll say they support plans and ordinances to save the champions, but these new laws can't be applied to plans in the pipeline, wouldn't be fair, would scare away good projects and, well you'd be amazed what we've seen at some of these open meetings the county's held. These lawyers can argue with such straight faces about their invidious proposals and the need for tax bases. Then and, it's so damn obvious, the developers are paying locals to speak at the open mike at these public meetings with county officials. Some of these characters are pretty shady looking and they wouldn't know a tax base from first base. The developers are even sending out press releases touting their 'new approach to saving trees' and urging others to join them in 'keeping the county green in a responsible way.'"

"So what are you going to do?"

"We're falling back to a combined option. We've filed papers in court, I'm not sure of all the legal ramifications other than we hope to buy time by at least getting an injunction."

"What are you asking they be enjoined from doing?"

"They've already started to clear for this one-hundred fifty house sub-division by the reservoir. It's making us sick to watch it. But because of slope and lay of the land, this company has argued that the approach road to the subdivision has got to come right through where this one-hundred foot white oak stands. This tree has got to be six feet in diameter with branches like some intricate, Victorian ironworks. Trouble is, we're concerned all those behemoth earth-movers rumbling around out there, may have already screwed up the champion's root system. Some of the branches have dead leaves; don't know how bad it might be. Office is not far now, why don't you come in and meet some of the folks?"

Fran ignored the question. "You said you had some combined strategy?"

"In addition to our filings in court, we've had some protestors out there periodically, the builders' people give them a rough time. But, we're going to increase the number of people out there with signs and our office has been in touch with a couple of sitters."

" Sitters?"

"Someone who climbs the tree, rigs a small platform, and stays up there so they can't cut the tree down. We set up a support system for him down below and try to get a lot of press and hope we can buy some time for all our legal and PR stuff to work." She turned to Fran. "You know, I have a room out here. Actually it's almost a room and a half, because there's this big sitting area by the window. There are two other couples with rooms there, and the landlord doesn't seem to mind, as long as he gets his rent on time and you don't make a lot of noise. That is, if you're looking for a place to stay out here?"

"Why would I be looking for a place to stay out here?"

"Aren't you?" she said, straining not to break into the coquettish grin that always got him.

"Guess I am, after all," he said in one of the best straight-man performances since Bud Abbott. She grabbed his arm and kissed him on the cheek, then turned his face and her lips met his. "Okay, you got me out here, wearing a green T-shirt and saving trees. I'll come into the office tomorrow. I've got to get back to the motel and take care of a couple of things if I'm going to be moving. I'll be here tomorrow morning, about nine, reporting for duty. Don't tell anyone, you didn't, did you, about my former place of employment?"

"No, but what's the big deal, if I were to?"

"Just don't do it, okay, I'd really prefer that you not."

"What if someone asks what you do.?"

"Used to be a salesman, now I'm retired and seek out lost causes."

"That's not the least bit funny."

"But you are," he said as he stopped the car and put his arm around her. "It'll be fine, it's no big deal. I'll see you tomorrow morning."

"You can be something else, ex-Congressman Fran."

"Dr. Driscoll you can't say that."

"See you tomorrow, Fran."

Fran tapped on the steering wheel as he headed back into the city. He had some song in his head that played as he and Jo Ellen stood looking out at the trees she was trying to protect. On the big road atlas map of the east coast with all its little markers for the cities and towns and other geographic locales, there was finally one that had his name on it. It was where Jo Ellen was, and he knew he never wanted to leave her again.

Fran heard a lot about it during his time in Washington, yet had been trapped only twice. But there it was; the lumbering chain gang of motorists. He was going sixty while the cars leaving Washington were standing still. These people lived in this traffic every day. They seemed lobotomized. How much time did they lose each year sitting in their cars? How did they get used to these mental death marches? Were the drivers in those cars sustained by the dream of the day when they broke free? Did they even know about freedom?

CHAPTER 29

The red message light on the phone in Fran's room was blinking. He sat in the desk chair and hit the numbers. Two new messages. Message number one: "Fran, this is Neil. Maddy told me you were in town. I'm still on August recess, but plan on getting back to Washington just before Labor Day. I need a few days to get my head together. You know what it's like. I called Maddy also to tell her to get in touch with you if I somehow didn't. It's important that I talk to you as soon as possible. I'll be at the district office till about four. Look forward to hearing from you, boss." Message number two: "Fran, I gave Neil your number at the hotel. He said it was important that he speak with you as soon as possible. He wanted me to call to make sure one of us got through".

"Neil there must be some mistake, I mean this is crazy."

"Do you want me to send it to you?"

"No, I don't want to see it, just read it to me one more time," Fran said.

"Okay, beneath the picture of the two of you holding your hands up and smiling at each other, there's a two-line caption: 'Former Congressman Fran Stewart and friend, Carson Handle whoop it up at Caribbean resort. Sources tell of close relationship between two.'"

"That's a picture from Alabama, when they had the gospel singers at the co-op. But the intent of the story is to imply something sordid: former congressman in a gay relationship with a dwarf."

"Seems pretty clear that's the tone. I know you're thinking the same thing I'm thinking."

"Feeney! But where did she get that photo?"

"Yeah, Feeney. This sleaze-bag reporter fawns over Creighton who gives him all kinds of crap for his column. There's probably more coming. I could get someone to do a letter to the editor or we could wait and see what else comes out."

"No, we should probably wait. We'd be replying to innuendoes at this point and not really helping our case. But I know Feeney will let Becky know about this before I can talk with my daughter. That woman has all the cards."

"Boss, we can think of something; we've got to look at all our options."

"Yeah, okay, maybe she won't try to run anything else."

"Maybe, you all right?" Neil asked.

"I'm good. Been some things never imagined would happen, but I'm good." There was no response from Neil. "I caught up with Jo Ellen today; think I'm going to stay with her for a while. She's working with some tree-saving group. Her heart's always been in the right place trying to save the world and all."

Neil paused, "tree-saving?"

"Yeah, I'll tell you all about it when I see you; we'll catch up on everything. So you coming in next week?"

"That's the plan right now. Couple of things have come up but the plan is still next week, Thursday."

"Maddy says you're doing well. Says you were born to do this. Don't think she ever said that about me. You could always find the angles. I always, until the end, thought the place was on the level. You always had a better eye. They have anyone to run against you yet?"

"Not yet, we've raised a lot of money and I've gotten some good assignments, photo ops from the leadership, etc. So far, so good."

"Feeney?"

"Don't have much to do with her or Creighton. She's been agnostic about me."

"I look forward to seeing you Neil. I'll call you next Thursday."

"Take care, Fran, see you next week."

CHAPTER 30

It was an old house that certainly deserved a paint job inside and out. The main room was a thicket of Xerox paper cartons, make-shift computer stations, and bulletin boards loaded with ragged-edge newspaper articles. A smaller room had a conference table made of two old card tables holding a 4'x8' piece of plywood. Another was a converted storage room not completely converted. There were a few grown-ups, but it looked to Fran that SVG was mostly a bunch of high school and college-age kids.

Jo Ellen approached Fran with a cup of coffee –a touch of milk – just as he liked it.

He listened as she took him through the different rooms where he met people with smiles as sharp and bright as the flaring combustion of a just-struck match head. He couldn't recall when he'd last seen such enthusiasm. Even the two older workers hard at work at the conference table were very pleasant. Jo Ellen told them Fran was a good friend who wanted to help and she suggested he could work with her on some of her assignments. The woman at the table asked Fran what he did and Jo Ellen quickly shot in that he had a background in sales. She saw Fran start to fidget and rattled off several time-sensitive projects she would start him on as she hurried him to her desk. The woman paused then mentioned to her colleagues that Fran looked familiar, but she just couldn't place him. Jo Ellen led Fran to her desk behind several stacks of cartons.

"Afraid, there won't be much time to chit-chat with the folks here today. Everybody's crashing to get things ready for Richard Kipp; he's going to be here day after tomorrow and is going up the next night. I'm really going to be able to use your help today."

Fran looked at her, figuring she would explain. As she started going through a checklist on her desk, he realized there wouldn't be an explanation. "Who is Richard Kipp?"

Jo Ellen's head snapped toward him. "Richard Kipp is a tree-sitter, done a couple on the West Coast. He has this whole thing down to a science. His record is sixty-one days. He bought time, enough to get an injunction stopping plans to take down one of the most beautiful oaks ever created." She pointed to the photo of Kipp in the sweeping branches of the noble tree. "Course there were a couple of places when the cops went up on ropes and a cherry picker and yanked him right off the plank and brought him down. Everyone in the office is scrambling to set up his support system, food, water, waste removal all the stuff. Then there are the hand outs, press coordination, getting some lawyers. We didn't think this was going to happen so soon, but someone in the permit office who has become a friend heard that the developer is going to start moving equipment in tomorrow to start removing the tree early in the morning, two days from now. That's why Kipp is rushing to get here."

"You think these guys won't start whacking away because some guy is sitting in the tree?"

"That's where all the volunteers with signs circling the tree and all the media we will have notified about what's going on come in. The whole production has always bought time to make whatever last ditch efforts there are to save the tree. Media has usually been very supportive, rooting for the underdog, champion versus bulldozers, etc. I'm told that Kipp has really fine-tuned his tactics for giving the guys the slip."

"And there's nothing you can do short of sending Kipp up into the tree?"

"Nope. I told you we haven't been able to stop these guys so far in the courts. Developer is open to move whenever he figures it suits him."

Fran spent the rest of the day as Jo Ellen's assistant: making calls from phone lists trying to get the people out, but also telling them to keep things quiet so word didn't get back to the enemy. The more calls he made, the more animated in support of the cause he became. He helped with filing, moving boxes, running errands. Pizzas came at about seven and the team shared updates on their parts of the project and what remained to be done. Jo Ellen had volunteered Fran to pick up Richard Kipp at the airport next day, early afternoon, and to make sure that all the supplies the sitter requested were on hand. Around ten, lights started going off as people left. Fran sat back in his chair and waved as his new colleagues walked out the door. They were smart, worked hard, and were dedicated. He wondered if they truly understood the system within which they were working. Did they think the system was on the level; that they would prevail because it was the "right thing" to protect some of the most beautiful natural treasures in the country? You had to churn up initially-disinterested people, make these people feel someone was trying to do something untoward to their system. It wasn't easy, but that's how it was done. It wasn't just tree lovers against developers; it was how you brought that extra, fickle force – the public-- into play. Fran knew Jo Ellen hadn't figured this out yet; maybe that's what he liked most about her.

"Time to go home," came the voice that wasn't far from his ear. Jo Ellen's hand moved down the back of his neck, her breast brushed against his shoulder. She hadn't worn perfume earlier in the day, but now it was time to go home. He wondered if she had thought about it as much as he had.

"Quitting time already?"

"You want to stay? That's okay with me, I've got some things I was saving for tomorrow, but we can get going on them tonight if you want."

"Just kidding, boy, where's that great sense of humor you used to have?"

"Used to have?" she said, smiling as she playfully jabbed her finger into his stomach. "Still pretty firm."

"Yeah, I'm in relatively good shape for an old man."

"Don't say that, you're not an old man." She didn't want any hint at all that she might spend part of her life without him. Just because he was older didn't mean that he would be gone first. Her mind had him growing older more slowly so she could catch up with him.

It was a small room in a house whose pleasant smell of cedar reminded him of a house his family rented at the beach one summer when he was a boy. He was feeling that same sense of excitement he felt when he was on vacation and stayed up later than usual. His father never wanted to waste a minute of vacation. He packed the car on Friday night and by three the next morning, Fran and his parents were pulling out of the driveway. Fran would awake to his "we're almost there," as his father pointed to inlets at low tide overflowing with marsh grasses. As they approached the causeway, a whole beach wonderland lay before them.

"I know it's small, but I've been looking around to see what else is available. I just have to know how much we can afford." She pointed toward a small table that had several real estate brochures and a classified section from the local newspaper. Fran picked up the pile and started looking at the ads. "I don't know how much time we'll have to look with everything going on, but maybe they'll give in after Kipp's in the tree for several days."

"Maybe," Fran answered as he continued looking at apartment listings and houses for rent. "How long do you want to stay in this area?"

"Probably forever."

"Forever?"

"Yes, I have everything I want here."

"Forever, that's kind of a long-term lease."

"Forever's forever and that's how long I want to be with you," she said, as comfortable about saying that as she had ever been about anything. "Want some Zinfandel?"

"Sure. How have you been getting around out here?"

"I have a bike downstairs; rented a van when I moved here. And I also get rides from the people in the office. There's a small market several streets over and with my trusty bike basket, I go over there a couple of times a week."

She handed him a glass of wine and sat down on the floor in front of his chair. "We have to get another chair although I'm not sure where we'd put it. Why don't you come down here so I don't get a crick in my neck." He slid down beside her and put his arm around her as she pulled her hair to the side and rested her head on his shoulder. Do you know what it is that most concerns me about you?"

"What?"

"Becky. I wish there was something I could do. I have thought what I will say to her when I see her and nothing sounds right. I want so much for her to like me and see how much I love you and can love her too."

Fran was usually not comfortable talking to Jo Ellen about Becky. But tonight was different. Jo Ellen would be part of him now and he hoped his daughter could recognize that wasn't wrong. We'll get it worked out somehow, he told himself. Then as if an echo, told her, "We'll get it worked out somehow."

She smiled. "I think we can. I want to help her do anything she wants." She took another drink of wine. "And I think if I try hard I can get her grandmother to like me as well."

Fran pictured soldiers getting cut down on D-Day on the beaches of Normandy. "We'll see. Best as I can figure, Becky will be home soon. I want to make sure she's home before I call her."

Jo Ellen finished her wine. "We have so much to do together." Her voiced faded into the whirr of the small window fan struggling to keep the warm air moving. They were both sweating. "Time to go to sleep." Her arms rose as she lifted her forest green shirt up and over her head and then leaned over. His hands reached up as she began to lower herself on top of him. With one hand, she began to unbutton his jeans. The warm air from the fan was soon the only thing covering their bodies.

They were in the office by eight the next morning. Jo Ellen saw the note written in large letters on her desk and rushed into the other room. Fran heard bits of the conversation with Bob, a heavy-set man, probably in his early sixties, with skin cancer scars that formed a blotched pattern on his bald head. Bob was the de facto head of the office and some of the younger volunteers were shocked at the wheezing sound he made when he got worked up. Fran was struck by the amount of wheezing he heard now, and saw the look on Jo Ellen's face when she returned. Their day had run smack into some kind of wall.

"Richard Kipp isn't coming," she said softly.

"What happened?"

"Bob spoke with him on the phone about an hour ago. Kipp was jogging last night. Guess he went out a little later than usual cause he had to get all his stuff together for the flight. Any way, it had gotten dark and he twisted his ankle – bad, had to go to the emergency room. His ankle's all swollen up, he's on crutches. Bottom line, fellow protector of champions, Richard Kipp's not coming."

"Isn't there anyone else?"

"Bob asked him that. There's only two other guys he would recommend, but he said they're both out of the country and there's no way they could get here tomorrow, maybe next week, but not tomorrow."

"What about the dozers moving in tomorrow morning?"

"Bob checked it, they're getting ready. It's going to be a stealth operation tomorrow morning. We're cooked. I'm sure the police will set up barriers keeping all our folks with signs out while the dozers start in. That's what they did out West. That's why we needed someone to sneak in and get up that tree tonight. I don't think any of the guys in the office are up to this. Do you? I mean they're nice kids and all, but . . ."

"You sure you don't think any of the guys in the office could do it?" Fran laid his hand on his chest and tapped his finger several times.

She looked at him with the blankest stare he'd ever seen. "You? Are you nuts? Do you want to kill yourself falling out of some tree?"

"Well, what about Kipp, it's all right for him to fall out?"

"Richard Kipp is a professional."

"Richard Kipp is not going to be here. And if he's not here tomorrow, he's never going to have the chance to climb that tree."

"Would you please be serious?"

"Jo Ellen, I am serious. Look at me, pretty good shape, remember? Heck, growing up in Tennessee, I climbed a lot of trees, spent a lot of time in the woods with my grandfather and he taught me all about ropes and knots and eating Dinty Moore Stew cold if you had to. Those were skinny trees too, not like that big oak with all those big branches and bends and crooks to hold on to."

"What happens to us if you fall out and kill yourself?"

"If I thought I was going to fall out of the tree I wouldn't go up. Now do you want to save that stupid tree or not?"

"It's not a stupid tree."

"I know it's not, that's why I want to help save it. I can do it. Honey, trust me." He didn't know why he called her that, but he knew he'd do it again. "C'mon let's go talk to Bob. If I can get Kipp on the phone, I'm sure he can walk me through this whole thing, at least until one of these other guys gets back into the country."

"You?" Bob asked.

"I'll be able to do it. Besides I don't think we have much choice at this point."

"Maybe we should see if we can get someone else," said Bob.

"Jo Ellen, you know there's no time to get anyone else. I'm telling you I can do this. If we can get Kipp on the line, he can walk us through it."

Jo Ellen and Bob looked at each other.

"Excuse me guys," Fran said. "We're not trying to split the atom here. Either we do this or you can start mourning that beautiful oak tree."

Bob reached for the phone. "I'll try to get Kipp right now." As the phone rang, he looked down at his shirt buttons straining against his runaway paunch. His gaze bounced off Fran's mid-section like a rubber ball hitting a brick wall.

"Haylo. Kipp here."

"Kipp, Bob again. Look, we're still going to try to get into the tree. I'm going to put you on speaker. I've got Jo Ellen Driscoll and Fran Stewart with me. Fran's going up."

"Say, look folks, I'm sorry again for what happened. I mean I got my plane ticket, bags packed, next thing I know, I got an ankle the size of a cantaloupe. Fran you ever climb a tree before?"

"Yeah, a lot of them when I was a kid. Guess I was the kid who always climbed the highest. My friend said it was because I wasn't afraid to look down."

"Good, that's all ya need, man. Climbing trees is like riding a bike; once you learnt it, it always comes back to you. You got your self any good, pliable hiking boots?"

"Got them on."

"Damn, Fran, seems you got what it takes so far. What kind of shape you in?"

"Pretty good shape for an . . ."

"He's in damn good shape, Kipp," Bob called out.

"That's good, that's good too. Need much sleep?"

"As a matter of fact, no."

"Well gang, I think old Fran here may be ready to start moving up in the world. Little tree-sitter joke. Let me start doing a very basic step-by-step guide of what you got to do and some of the things you need to bring up with you. Still pretty warm out there?

"Yeah."

"That's good, that's good. All right let me get going on my list and I'll call you back in about an hour. Hey, I'm still waiting to hear from this one sitter to see how soon he can get back, but the other one is in the slammer in Peru. He was doing a job down there. Guess the police roughed him up quite a bit. But Fran, don't go worrying, cops here don't do that. Hell, they'll even help you down. One way or the other, they bring you down. And it will be on my list, but just remember have two-way radios in case you've got bad cell phone coverage where you are."

CHAPTER 31

Fran could still see the outline of Bob's Jeep just off the main road. Jo Ellen, Bob and one of the boys from the office had spent the last two nights there. Every three hours, one of them would get out and walk over to the tree to make sure Fran was okay.

It was colder tonight than the first two nights and Fran pulled his knit cap down. Kipp was right about bringing a knit cap. His step-by-step guide was perfect. Fran kept that sheet in a baggie and looked at it from time to time to make sure he wasn't forgetting anything. Kipp was really brilliant, Fran remembered thinking the first night, and he thought Kipp would be proud of him. Maybe this was just the type of work for which Fran had been destined. His face rested against the tree. He had started telling it about all the things that had gone on in other parts of the world during its lifetime. He thought its bark was actually responding, trying to make sure he didn't slip. Fran smelled the vitality of the tree and imagined the mustiness that would replace it if it became cord wood. He thanked the champion for sacrificing a piece of one of its tiniest branches for what he was making. Fran thought Jo Ellen would think the gift very special.

His cell phone vibrated. Why wasn't Jo Ellen using the two-way radio?

"Hello," Fran said.

"Daddy," he heard amidst heavy static.

"Becky? Becky, where are you? How did you find me?"

"I've been trying to reach you. I called Maddy who said you had gotten a new number. How are you Daddy?"

"Becky, I am so happy to hear your voice. I have missed you sweetheart. I've just been trying to do my best not to upset you or make matters worse with your grandmother till I come up with a plan to fix all this." Fran strained to hear her response.

"Daddy, I want to come stay with you. Grandma gets nastier every day. I told her to stop, but she won't listen."

"Becky, everything will be okay. You will come live with me. I guarantee it."

"Daddy, I miss you. Do you remember when I was in the Brownies and we built that birdhouse? Do you remember when you, Mommy, and I went out on Halloween dressed as the Three Bears? And all the nights you slept on the floor in my room after Mommy died? Grandma doesn't even think about all the good things you've done. I know you can explain everything that happened these past months. I love you Daddy."

She muffled a sob.

"Becky I just have to see something through, then I'll come get you."

"What are you doing?"

Fran explained as best he could.

"Daddy, the reception is getting worse, but it sounded like you said you were sitting in a tree."

"You heard right sweetheart. But it will all make sense soon.

"Just be careful, please be careful. I love you Daddy."

"I'll call you soon."

Fran stared at the uppermost branches. He tugged at his safety line, a nylon climbing cord secured to the branch above him. Seemed a little loose, maybe just his imagination. He looked up at the broad branch holding an old wooden door he had lashed at all four corners to other branches to keep his supplies. He also perched there to watch the carnival below. Police cruisers with their flashing lights stood just off the main road as officers directed traffic and guarded a perimeter out from the base of the tree. Several TV satellite dish trucks were parked near a coffee wagon. About fifty SVG-organized demonstrators milled around with signs. Some had painted their faces green. Periodically, a car driving by would honk. Men stood near idle bulldozers that had arrived two hours after Fran had settled on to his perch. It was the second day that things started to take an ugly turn. A group of burly counter-protesters roughed up some of the SVG people. Idling police cars across the road sped into action on several occasions. Jo Ellen said the SVG office had been vandalized. Fran implored Jo Ellen to be careful.

Jo Ellen would be the first out of the Jeep in the morning and bring him coffee. She'd pour it into a Thermos tied to a rope he would pull up. The first day he was reluctant to eat or drink much and even now he felt awkward lowering down the large green plastic bag with the "sanitary container." Kipp would have had to do the same thing, he figured, and everyone in the office thought Kipp was a god.

He looked at his watch; another hour till dawn. He was starting to feel more confident. Maybe he could last a week up there, maybe longer. He knew he could wake Jo Ellen if he had to by calling on the two-way radio. He loved to see her first thing in the morning.

He pulled at his safety line again. He hadn't imagined it. The knot on the loop was coming loose. He saw the first flicker of dawn through the leaves; it would be enough light because he knew his resting-place well enough to keep his footing. He unhooked the metal clasp at the end of the rope from the clasp on his belt and started to work the loop down. His feet felt well-braced and soon the loop was in his hand. He heard something. He looked up and saw Jo Ellen walking toward him. He smiled. She was early today.

"Jo Ellen, I've lowered something down in the canvas bag. There's a note also. I would like a reply at your earliest convenience, Dr. Driscoll."

"Fran, tell me what it is. Why do I have to wait?"

"I'd like you to see it first."

Then, in one terrible second, the crack of gunfire echoed without resistance through a morning still barely awake. Her knees bent and her shoulders arched.

She watched as Fran, blood gushing from his shoulder, lost his balance. There was nothing she could do to save him. He lay still at the base of the champion.

CHAPTER 32

The doorman opened the heavy door leading into the visitors' gallery. Maddy guided Becky and Jo Ellen down the stairs in the balcony seating above the House floor. They wore black dresses.

The past month had been a blur. Jo Ellen held Becky's hand and the young girl touched the slender twine and bark ring on Jo Ellen's finger. Maddy pointed to Neil as Fran's protégé walked toward the microphone.

"The gentleman from Tennessee, Mr. Glider, is recognized for one minute."

"Thank you, Mr. Speaker." Neil's mouth tightened and his eyes reddened. He could have lost it right there, but he caught himself. He knew Fran was watching. "Recently, I lost a good friend, Fran Stewart. He taught me a lot, but it wasn't until he was gone that I realized how much. We lost a colleague, one who made significant contributions to his country. He never sought this office in a way that many of us did. But once here, he realized the great responsibility he had accepted.

His last year may have been his greatest. The man who thought the fire had left his belly decided to give it one more shot, one more try with an honesty and spirit of compassion that couldn't be contained. I think he tried to show us why we're here, why we should fight, and not just talk about the things that have made this body worth serving in. He left here knowing he had given this place everything he could. I hope I can say that when I leave this distinguished chamber for the last time. Part of his last weeks were spent in service reaching out to help grieving people robbed of their church. In the end, he gave his life fighting those who would rob us of the irreplaceable beauty of our natural heritage.

I hope you will join me in keeping in our prayers, his daughter, Becky, whom he worshipped, and Jo Ellen, his best friend, whom he loved dearly. Boss, I miss you."

The Speaker of the House walked toward the microphone and looked up at the gallery. "I wanted to take this time to tell Fran's family and friends that I greatly admired his determination to do what was right regardless of what others thought. He helped the homeless, he immersed himself in the campaign to rebuild black churches, and he sacrificed his life for a towering giant of a tree so that its majesty will endure for his daughter, Becky, and others of her generation. Of him, this House can be proud."

Becky gripped Jo Ellen's hand.